J. T. Trowbridge, John Townsend Trowbridge

Neighbor's Wives

J. T. Trowbridge, John Townsend Trowbridge

Neighbor's Wives

ISBN/EAN: 9783743427518

Manufactured in Europe, USA, Canada, Australia, Japa

Cover: Foto ©Andreas Hilbeck / pixelio.de

Manufactured and distributed by brebook publishing software (www.brebook.com)

J. T. Trowbridge, John Townsend Trowbridge

Neighbor's Wives

NEIGHBORS' WIVES.

BY

J. T. TROWBRIDGE,

AUTHOR OF "NEIGHBOR JACKWOOD," "FATHER BRIGHTHOPES," ETC.

BOSTON:

LEE AND SHEPARD.

1867.

CONTENTS.

IV   *Contents.*

Neighbors' Wives.

———oo❦oo———

I.

THE ADOPTED SISTER.

T was three years since old Abel Dane laid down the compass and the chisel on his work-bench in the old shop, and himself on his bed in the new house which he had so lately built for his comfort, and which he never left again until he was carried out by his neighbors.

"To be sure!" moralized one of the pall-bearers, on that occasion,—a pale, meagre, bald little man, John Apjohn by name, and a cooper by trade,—"it's with houses as 'tis with every other airthly blessin'. We're no sooner ready to enjoy 'em than either they go or we go. Here's neighbor Dane, been so busy building houses for other people all his life that he never had·time till now to build one for himself; and to think on 't!" said the cooper, with mournful, wondering eyes, "there the house is, and here he is a-goin' to his final home, and leavin' everything to his heir! To be sure, to be sure!" and he shook his head solemnly at the decrees of fate.

The heir mentioned was Abel Dane the younger, who inherited his father's trade, the old shop, the new house, and a faithful foster-sister.

It was three years since that dark day in autumn ; and now just such another dark day in the fall of the year was drawing to a close ; and Abel's foster-sister, having set the supper-table, took her favorite place at the window to watch for his coming. And there, sitting in the cheerful room, which would soon be made more cheerful by his presence ; remembering the sad day of the funeral, so like this day ; thinking of all God's mercies to her, before and since, — to her, a poor orphan, so unworthy such a home and such a brother ; looking across the gloomy common, whose very bleakness enhanced her sense of life-warm comfort in house and heart, she saw, through thick tears of happiness, which magnified him into a glimmering seraph, with irregular, shining wings, her "more than brother," returning.

Across the brown common, under the wild elm-boughs swinging in the wind, he came rapidly walking. He stopped to leave some tools he carried at the shop, and that gave the little housekeeper time to get the tea and toast on the table. Then she drew up the invalid's chair, beat the cushion, and helped the invalid to her seat, — for this was another important item of Abel's inheritance which we have neglected to mention, namely, a paralytic mother. She was a cheerful old Christian, with the most benignant of double chins, in the full possession of her mental faculties, but physically shattered.

She had suffered two or three strokes, the last of which had produced a singular effect upon her organs of speech.

"Thank you, Gridiron," said she, — for this was the oddity of it, that sometimes she could not speak at all, and sometimes she suddenly shot out the most unexpected and irrelevant speeches quite involuntarily; and sometimes when she meant to say one word, another ludicrously inappropriate would drop out in its place, as much to her own astonishment as. anybody's. The name of her adopted daughter was *Eliza ;* but the nearest she could come to it at that moment was *Gridiron.*

Abel washed his stout carpenter's hands at the sink, kicked off his boots, slipped on his slippers, and the three sat around the little table together, Abel opposite Eliza, — a goodly young man and a strong, brown-cheeked and chestnut-haired, with a countenance not lacking in brightness generally, and particularly radiant on this occasion.

Eliza noticed his gayety, and was glad. They were not lovers, though she loved him. She had never confessed to herself that she hoped in her inmost heart to be nearer and dearer to him some day than she was now. To be to him what she was seemed happiness enough, — his sister, his servant, — his, whom it was so sweet to serve : preparing his meals, which it was her meat and her drink to see him eat with appetite ; making his bed and smoothing his dear pillow, with hands magnetic with affection ; stealing his boots, and blacking them, with the delight which love lends to the meanest occupation ; reading to him evenings and Sundays, or hearing him read from the books that gave her a twofold pleasure because he enjoyed them ; living thus day after day and year after year in the nourishing atmosphere of his out-going and in-coming, and satisfied to live on thus forever.

And now, without questioning what made Abel so joyous, she was joyous too ; for this is the blessedness of love, that it annihilates selfishness, and makes us happy in others' happiness. Filling the cups, she poured her own thankful spirit into them with the fragrant beverage, and sweetened them, not with sugar only, but with her own spiritual sweetness, which both Abel and his mother tasted in the tea she made and gave them, and missed in that which others made and gave them, without comprehending the subtle cause.

"Have another cup, mother ? "

"No, my dear," said the old lady. "But I'll thank you for a piece of the contribution-box."

She meant to ask for cheese. Then she laughed at herself, half-vexed. Abel roared with mirth. And Eliza said, — for Eliza was the wit of the family, —

" I'm sure, old cheese bears a strong resemblance to a contribution-box ; for when it is passed around, you often find a few mites in it."

Upon which Abel flashed his beaming eyes upon his foster-sister. He was going to compliment her wit ; but something better than that, — something glowing in her face, — attracted his attention.

" Why, 'Liza ! how handsome you are to-night ! "

Now Eliza was not handsome, and she knew it. She knew that she was a plain little girl. She did not doubt, however, but that Abel saw something pleasing in her face just then, and the delicious consciousness made her blush like a rose.

" Positively beautiful ! ain't she, mother ? " cried Abel, with fond enthusiasm.

" She is always beautiful to me, she is always so good," the old woman managed to say, without a slip.

" A beautiful soul makes a beautiful face, they say," added Abel. " Consequently a beautiful face indicates a beautiful soul, don't it ? " — with a gay, triumphant smile, which Eliza did not understand till two hours later, — thinking, poor child, that his words referred to her.

But, two hours later, Mrs. Dane having fallen asleep in her chair, and Abel having shut the book he was reading, and taken Eliza's work out of her hand, they two sat together before the fire, which blazed up brightly with shavings from the shop, and Abel looked into her face with ardent eyes.

" 'Liza, I'm going to tell you something."

A sweet tremor rippled all over her, as if she had been a fountain, and his breath the warm south wind. She looked through his eyes into his soul, and saw love there; while he looked — not into her soul.

"It is my heart's secret," he went on ; for she was dumb with fear and gladness. "I have wanted to tell you; I hope it will make you happy. We can't live always in the way we do, you know; and I never can think of parting from you, 'Liza."

How she trembled ! And now she felt a growing terror in her joy ; for, to one whose daily life is blessed, the thought of a great change, whether for good or evil, comes like a portentous shadow.

"So I have concluded it is best to be married. I am going to be married, 'Liza. When we were talking of faces, do you know whose face I was thinking of ? The most beautiful face in all this world ! Her face who wrote this letter which I got to-day, and which has made me the happiest of men. You may read it, 'Liza."

He placed it in her hands. It dropped from them to the floor. She sat rigid, speechless, pallid — a spasm of misery in her face, something like death in her heart.

"Won't you read it ? " He stooped to pick up the letter. "Don't think her coming into the family will make any difference with you. We will all live here together. You will always have a home here with us ; you will love her; you can't help it, Eliza." He regarded her a minute in silence, his brows darkening. "You disappoint me," he added, heavily ; "I didn't expect you would receive the news in this way. Don't you like Faustina ? "

"I think — she is — very pretty," poor Eliza forced her despairing lips to say.

" Why, then, do you object to her ? "

" I ? object ? Oh, I don't ! — if you can make her happy."

" What made you look so, then, when I told you? It made my heart sick. And now that smile is worse yet — such a wretched smile ! I see you don't approve of my choice," turning away resentfully. " I wanted you, of all persons, to love and welcome her. But never mind."

" Oh, Abel ! " she chokingly said, " don't blame me. I can't bear it. I — I *am* glad — I *will* be glad — for your sake."

" You act glad, surely ! " grinned Abel, sarcastic; for he thought her unreasonable, unkind; and so he stabbed her with a look to punish her.

" Mother — I think of her," gasped the miserable girl; " so old, with her infirmity, which every person will not bear with, and cherish her all the more tenderly for, as we do." And covering her face, she shook with a violent, convulsive breath, but did not sob.

Abel frowned at what he considered a mean insinuation against his beautiful Faustina; and, holding the letter in his hand, looked moodily at the fire, utterly ignorant and regardless of the agony in the weak woman's breast at his side. " A girl's caprice; a little trait of envy, — angry, perhaps, because I haven't consulted her before; but she'll be sorry for it; and if she isn't, why, I shall be independent of her " — with such a glorious young creature for his wife ! And the young man self-

ishly calculated the slight loss it would be to him, even
if Eliza should carry her resentment so far as to leave
his house; not, of course, seriously supposing such an
event possible.

Eliza conquered her agony, uncovered her face, and
quietly resumed her work. And there they sat by the
fire, in silence, with such different thoughts! Silence
which rose like a rock in their hitherto united lives, its
·hardness and coldness sundering them, — two separate
streams henceforth, with leagues of misunderstanding
and estrangement broadening between them. Did you
never feel such a rock rise between you and one you
loved ? and see the stream of his future flow toward
flowery embowered vistas of hope, while yours took a
sudden plunge into some chilly, unsunned, melancholy
cave ?

" Well, children," said the old lady, waking, " I guess
I'll — night-cap ! "

" Go to bed ? " said Abel.

" Yes, — I believe I was almost asleep; but I didn't
quite lose myself, did I ? Evenings are growing longer.
Interesting story — where did you leave off ? I'm so "
— touching her forehead — " what do you call it ? —
jewsharp."

" Absent-minded," suggested Abel.

That was the word. And so she went off to bed, trying to recall the story they had been reading ; but catching not even a hint of the drama they had been *acting*
before her face. Such is life; and such are its specta-

tors. Daily and nightly, in street and dwelling, even under the roofs where we abide, and in the very rooms where we meet to laugh and sing away the hours together, tragedies are acting in that little theatre, the heart, and we catch so seldom any hint of them!

Eliza conducted Mrs. Dane to her chamber; nor did she return to sit a little while alone with Abel as usual, but went to her own room, unlighted, and shut herself up there with the dark and cold.

And now once more kneeling, with her throbbing head pressed against the casement, she looked across the bleak common, where the wild elm-boughs were swaying in the wind, and the pallid moonlight fell. The loose leaves rustled along the ground under the window. The gables moaned and thrilled, and the lone crickets sang. And remembering how lately the outdoor desolation had enhanced her idea of life-warm comfort within, she thought her heart would burst.

Leaves of the dying autumn! moonlight spread so white and cold over the face of the night! crickets and whistling wind! who gave you your power over the human soul? and why do you pierce and wring the heart of a poor girl, pierced and wrung enough already with unrequited love? No wonder our forefathers thought the moonlight fairy-haunted, and deemed the waving elder-boughs the beckoning fingers of elves.

The next day, just a little paler than usual, but quite self-possessed, Eliza went about her household-work. She was the same to Abel, in most outward things, as she had ever been; but oh, the hidden mind ! This Abel could not see. He resented her last night's conduct, and waited for her to come to him humbly and ask his forgiveness, when he intended to pardon her magnanimously, after administering a fitting rebuke, and then be again to her the kind brother he had always been, and always meant to be, in spite of her faults. He had even pondered what he ought to say to her on that occasion. And in the mean time he treated her with very proper reserve.

The days passed, the leaves all fell from the trees; it was now November; and Eliza, having worked industriously to prepare the house for the coming bride, when all was done, requested Abel, one Sunday afternoon, to grant her a few minutes' conversation. The generous young man put aside his newspaper, and appeared quite ready to receive her penitent confession.

"Well, Eliza, what is it?" he said, encouragingly, trying to recall his speech.

"I thought you ought to know," she began, in a very low, slightly tremulous voice, "that I — am going away to-morrow."

Abel forgot his speech, — opened his eyes.

"Going! where ?"

"I think — to Lowell."

"To Lowell ! what for ? Not to stay ?"

"Yes," she answered, quietly, "if I can find work in the mills."

"The mills !" ejaculated Abel, frowningly. "What are you talking of work in the mills for ?"

" Because I shall not be needed here any more, and I must get my living."

" Eliza," said Abel, sternly, " you *are* a strange girl ! Can't you understand me ? Haven't I told you that you could always have a home here ? And now what is this absurd notion about getting your living ?"

" Don't be angry. You will do very well without me. You won't miss me, after a few days. I go to-morrow."

Abel looked at her a minute, with fixed teeth. Her subdued, calm, independent way exasperated him.

" You are a stubborn, ungrateful girl ! "

" I hope not," she murmured.

" To leave us at this time ! " he exclaimed; though he did not like to own that he needed her to receive and attend his bride. " I can't understand such perverse-ness ! "

Cut to the heart, Eliza did not answer, and he stalked away.

What gave edge to his reproof was the consciousness that she *was* acting unreasonably. Why not stay till the wedding, and welcome the beautiful Faustina, like a sensible girl ? Simply because she could not. It was not jealousy, but something far deeper than jealousy that set her soul against this marriage. The entire instinct of the woman rose up and prophesied the un-suitableness of Abel's chosen bride. Not solely for her own sake, but for Abel's also, and equally for his mother's, she must regard the wedding-day as an evil

2 *

one to them all; and to join in the festivities of that occasion, to mask her misery with smiles, to kiss and congratulate and witness the joy over an event which was worse than death to her, would have been too terrible a mockery. And so, even at the risk of seeming ungrateful and perverse, she must depart before the bride came.

Did you ever leave a place that had been all that home could be to you, and go forth shivering into the dark future ? Some dreary November afternoon, you take down the pictures from the walls which you may never see again; empty the familiar drawers and shelves which you will use no more, but which somebody else to whom you give place will cheerfully occupy after you; pull out the wretched trunk from its hiding-place, and commence packing. Here are old letters to be destroyed. Here are keepsakes you hardly know whether to take with you or return, Ophelia-like, to the giver who has " proved unkind," they are still so precious to you, while they make your heart so ache and sicken. For relief you turn away and look out upon the bleak sky of November. Small comfort you derive from the drifts of gray clouds that lie like sandbars in the blue, . cold ocean of infinity, type of the sea you are about to sail. It is insupportable ! The very roots of your being seem torn up by this change. How golden are the days that are no more ! How like iron the grim gates of the morrow ! Where will these miserable trifles you are packing up be next unpacked ? Upon the walls of what lonely room will you hang this little Madonna, and this print of the Saviour? Among what unsympathizing strangers will your solitary, toilsome lot be cast? There is One who knows; and what is best for you, he knows far better than you.

II.

MR. TASSO SMITH AND THE APJOHNS.

"To be sure!" said John Apjohn, the cooper, enter-ing his house the next day, and putting his feet on the stove, with a prodigious sigh. "It *is* a sad world, Pru-dy! What would old Abel Dane have said, I wonder? I'm glad we've no children. To be sure, to be sure!"

"There now! let that stove alone!" exclaimed Mrs. Apjohn. "You burn out more wood when you are in the house five minutes, than I do in all day."

The meagre, shivering little man crouched over the fire; and, glancing timidly up at the glowing face, ample proportions, and huge arms of that warm-blooded and superior female, his wife, who stood before him, bread-knife in hand, to see her command enforced, he discreetly laid back in the wood-box a stick he had taken out.

"It's a cold world," he sighed.

"So much the more need to be savin' o' fuel. We should be in the poor-house 'fore spring if 'twan't for me." And Mrs. Prudence trod heavy and strong about her work.

As she disappeared in the pantry, the cold-blooded cooper took occasion to peep under one of the griddles;

and he had his hand on the interdicted stick again, when
her sudden reappearance with some bowls and spoons,
caused him to drop the griddle, the stick, and the following philosophical remark:

"Changes in this world is very wonderful."   He
rubbed his hands over the stove, and proceeded: " Who
knows but what it 'll be our turn next ?   I knowed old
Mis' Dane when she seemed as fur removed from trouble as anybody.   Then she lost her husband.   Then she
was afflicted in her speech.   And now — to be sure, to
be sure ! "

" What now ? " demanded Prudence.   " Has anything
re'ly happened ? or is it only your hypoes ? "

" My hypoes ?   As if I didn't have reason to !   Hain't
I seen 'Lizy take the stage this mornin,' goin' nobody
knows where, to 'arn a livin' amongst strangers ?   She's
growed jest as thin as a stave lately, and she looked like
death when I put out my hand to say good-by."

" Why ! I want to know ! " said Prudence, from the
pantry.   " Has she re'ly gone ?   Wal, I can't blame her,
as I know on, for wantin' to be 'arnin' somethin', — it's
nat'ral. — I hear that stove! "

The cooper softly closed the griddle.

" I see old Mis' Dane as I come by ; thought I'd look
in ; and there she was, a-cryin'.   I tell ye it's too
bad ! "

" I sh'd 'most thought 'Lizy'd staid to the weddin';
most gals would," said Mrs. Apjohn, bringing a pan of
milk from the pantry.   " But probably she felt the ne-

cessity of doin' somethin' for herself; for Abel can't afford to support three women in that house, massy knows! Fustiny 'll have to put them perty hands o' her'n into dish-water. For my part, I don't think she's any more fit to be Abel Dane's wife, than you be to be president, John Apjohn."

"To be sure, to be sure," said John, mournfully acknowledging the force of the comparison. "Or than you be," he added, "to be one of them circus-ridin' women." And at the quaint conceit of those immense feminine proportions, decked out in gauze and tinsel, balanced upon one foot on a galloping saddle, or taking a flying leap through a hoop, the solemn face of the man puckered into a dull, feeble smile. "To be sure!" he cackled.

"Wal, come to dinner," said Prudence, cutting the bread against her bosom.

"Ain't we goin' to have nothin' but bread and milk?" said John, imploringly.

"Bread and milk is good enough. I couldn't afford to cook anything to-day. Here's some o' that corned beef, and beautiful apple-sas."

"Cold day like this, ought to have somethin' warmin'," the cooper mildly remonstrated. "Cup o' tea, — bile an egg; some sich thing."

"Eggs! when we can git thirteen cents a dozen for em!" exclaimed Prudence.

"To be sure!" And Cooper John submissively took his seat at the uninviting board.

" Did you hit the table then ? " with a look of alarm.

"No ! " said Prudence. " Wasn't it you ? " Another knock.

" There's somebody to the front door, Prudy ! " gasped the little man. " What shall we do ? "

" Let 'em in, of course; they ain't robbers this time o' day," and she tramped ponderously through the entry.

It was not robbers the cooper feared, but some dread messenger of fate. He was one of those timorous, doubting souls, to whose morbid imagination life is ever full of terror and difficulty; and even so trifling an incident as a knock at the door has in it sometimes something mysterious and awful. Though the most harmless being in the world, he often thought, and often said to his wife, when a stranger rapped, " What if that should be the sheriff come to tell me I am arrested for a murder or a forgery ! To be sure, to be sure, Prudy ! "

He was slightly relieved on this occasion to hear the soft, simpering voice, and to see the soft, simpering face, of a flashily dressed young fellow, with greased hair, a tender moustache, a thick, unwholesome complexion, pimples, and a very extensive breast-pin.

" Tasso Smith," said Prudence, as with a curious, amused, half-contemptuous lifting of her brow-wrinkles, she ushered the grimacing phenomenon into the kitchen.

" Possible ! Tasso ! Mr. Smith ! " confusedly cried the cooper, springing to his feet, upsetting his chair behind him, and spilling the milk from the pan with the jostle he gave the table. "I shouldn't have knowed ye, you've altered so !"

The young man looked conscious of having altered very much to his own satisfaction; and condescendingly gave the cooper two fingers.

" Seddown, seddown," said John, righting his chair, and placing it for the visitor. "Don't it beat all, Prudy ! — Where did you come from, Tasso — Mr. Smith ?" for he thought he ought to mister such a smart young gentleman, though he had known him from his babyhood.

"From the city," grimaced Tasso.

"To be sure, to be sure !" repeated the cooper ; and regarded him wonderingly.

"Been makin' money, I guess, hain't ye, Tasso ?" said practical Mrs. Apjohn.

She stood with a shrewd sceptical smile, amusedly perusing him ; while before her sat Tasso, perfumed, pomatumed, twirling his rattan, delightfully aware that he was a cynosure.

"Managed to live." He nodded significantly at Prudence. "City 's good place for enterpris'n' young men." He nodded at the cooper. "Thought I'd come out 'n' see what I could do for the ol' folks." Crossing his legs, he thrust his rattan into a button-hole of his blue brass-buttoned coat, hung his hat on the toe of his tight-fitting patent-leather boot, and pompously produced his pocket-book. "I've called to pay — to remunerate — you for them barrels pa had of you some time ago. Can you change a fifty-dollar bill?" Which stunning proposition he uttered as if it was one of the commonplaces of his life.

Cooper John sat right down and stared. Tasso smoothed his moustache, and smiled. Mrs. Apjohn was so well pleased at the prospect of the payment of a debt she had long despaired of, that she began to regard the cynosure with more favorable eyes.

" I declare, Tasso, I never expected you would turn out so well. Re'ly payin' your pa's debts, be you? I remember when you used to be around, the dirtiest, raggedest boy 't ever I see!" She meant this for praise; but it was gall to Mr. Smith. "And now you're payin' your pa's debts! Think o' *that*, John Apjohn!" — in a tone which conveyed a triumphant reproof to the soul of the said J. A.; for the worthy woman had this way of convicting her consort of his short-comings, by citing to him illustrious examples of human conduct. "Think of *that*, John Apjohn!" always meant "Now, why don't *you* go and be a man like the rest of 'em?"

"To be sure, to be sure!" murmured the cooper, feeling very much disparaged, and turning an awe-struck glance upon the shining paragon who was paying "his pa's debts." "Only ten and six, I believe, the account is."

"With interest, it's more'n two dollars by this time," struck in his wife's strong treble.

"Oh, never mind interest, Prudy," said the weak, quavering tenor.

3

"Yes, I will," insisted Prudence. "Call it two dollars, anyhow."

"Sorry I hain't got no smaller bills," said Tasso, glancing over a handful of bank-notes. "But you can prob'ly break a fifty."

John and Prudence looked at each other. Then both looked at the visitor.

"Why, if you can't do no better," said Prudence, hesitatingly, "I don'o' — mabby I can change it."

It was Tasso's turn to be astonished, and he looked, for a moment, very much as if he had no large note to change. He reddened with embarrassment, and fumbled his money, and presently began muttering, as he turned each bill, —

"Hunderd, hunderd, hunderd, — I declare! don't b'lieve got a fifty — hunderd, hunderd, — thought I had — remember, now, paying it out. Can you break a *C.* ?" And he turned on the cooper a foolish smile.

John appealed to Prudence, and Prudence nodded consent. The *C.* was not such cold water to her as Tasso had hoped.

"Yes, I can break a *C.* !" she answered, with just perceptible disdain. "Though you thought it would break *me,* I guess."

Tasso's smile faded; and the effort he made to appear business-like and at ease, sweating over his bills and wiping his red, pimply face, was odd to see. Prudence did not give him time to raise the value of his notes to five hundred; but, taking a key from the clock-case, proceeded to an adjoining room, followed by the cooper. They left the door unlatched, and Tasso could hear busy whisperings behind it. He got up, peeped through the crack, and saw the thrifty couple on their knees by an open chest, counting money. In a little while they came out, and found their guest respectably seated, twirling his rattan, with a serious, honest face, — bank-notes and pocket-book having disappeared.

"I'll look at your bill, if you please," said Prudence, clasping a handful of money.

"Oh," said Tasso, as if he had quite forgotten the subject, "le' me see ! Oh, yes ! After you went out, I found some small bills in my vest-pocket. Save you the trouble." And, fingering the said vest-pocket, he brought to light a little, dirty, rolled-up rag of paper.

" 'He put in his thumb, and pulled out a plum ; and what a brave boy was I !' " laughed Prudence, as she scornfully unrolled the rag. "Two one-dollar bills ! Wal, that's what I call comin' down a little. Great deal of talk for a little bit of cider."

Tasso felt cheap. His game of brag, at which he had been so unexpectedly beaten, had cost him more pride and money than he could afford. He winced and simpered and switched his stick, and said, —

"Might gi'e me back th' change, 'f you're mind to, as pa didn't authorize me to pay no interest."

That was too much for Prudence, already sufficiently provoked ; and she spoke hasty words, which, lodging like evil seed in the breast of the young man Tasso, took

root there, and grew, and in due season brought forth
bitter fruit for the future of more than one actor in our
drama.

"Idee o' your hagglin' 'bout a little interest money,
arter sech a swell with your hunderd-dollar bills !"
(" Come, come, Prudy ! " said her husband, deprecat-
ingly.) " I don't believe you've got a hunderd-dollar
bill in the world. No Smith of your breed ever had ! "
(" There, there, Prudy ! " said the conciliatory John.)
" You'd no more notion o' payin' that debt, when you
come into this house, than I have to fly ; and you
wouldn't, if I hadn't ketched ye in a trap ye didn't suspect." (" Prudy, Prudy ! you're sayin' too much ! "
parenthesized the pale cooper.) " I ain't sayin' anything but the truth ; and he can afford to hear that,
arter all the trouble he has put me to. Here's a ninepence ; I'll divide the interest with ye, and say no more
about it."

Tasso pocketed the ninepence and the affront, and,
white with rage, yet too much afraid of the strong, indignant woman to give vent to it, just showed his
yellow teeth, with a sickly, malicious grin, as he put on
his hat, and went strutting under difficulties through
the entry.

"I wouldn't have had it happen, Prudy ! " began the
wretched cooper.

"I would ! " said Prudence, with gleaming scorn and
triumph. " Sich a heap of pretension ! with that little
bit of a cane, and them nasty soaplocks, and all that

big show of one-dollar bills! I like to come up with sich people!" And she grimly counted her money; while Tasso, who had heard every word she said, as he listened at the door, let himself out, and sneaked away.

3 *

III.

ABSENCE.

IT takes a woman to read a woman. A man, especially a lover, is apt to confide too much in the title-page, namely, the face ; although, like other title-pages, this is often so false that its smiling promise affords scarce a hint, to the unsophisticated, of the actual contents of the volume.

The book of beauty which Abel Dane had chosen, which he took out of the modest covers of maidenhood, and bound in bridal gilt and velvet, and placed in the closet of his affections, to be his inseparable companion and book of life,— was now to be tested. How soon the gilt began to tarnish, the sumptuous velvet to fade, the contents to belie the title, and Abel to learn how much better Eliza had discerned their true character at a glance, than he with all his admiring attention, let us not too closely inquire.

There were at least two individuals that mourned Eliza's departure, and could not be comforted by Faustina's coming. One was old Mrs. Dane ; she felt that one of her roots of life had been severed, when her adopted daughter went, and that she was too old a tree to put forth vigorous young fibres to supply its place.

"Wal, old friend, how do ye git along? to be sure!" said Cooper John, looking in upon her one day.

"Narrowing at the heel," smiled Mrs. Dane; then laughed at herself, for she had meant to say, "Pretty well, I thank you, John." "That's true, though, I suppose. My stocking of life is fast knitting up, and I shall soon be at the toe."

"To be sure, yes!" the cooper snuffled, and produced his red silk handkerchief. "We shall all go soon or late. Dreadful changes. Heard from 'Lizy?"

"I had a wood-box from her — dear me! you know what I mean."

"To be sure, a letter."

"She writes she's gone to work in the mills, and appears to be contented; but, oh, John!"

She wept; and John wept with her; and Turk, the house-dog, laid his great, shaggy head between his paws, and winked sympathetically; for Turk was the other mourner aforesaid: a faithful, grim old dog, that would sometimes lie down before Eliza's vacant chair, and growl at any one who approached it; or, like the old man in the story, go about

> "Wandering as in quest of something,
> Something he could not find, — he knew not what;" —

then suddenly take it into his head to bounce up stairs, and bark furiously at her door, as if he had at last dis-

covered the chest in which his Ginevra was concealed.
What was singular, not all Faustina's attentions, — feeding him and patting him with her fair hand, — could flatter him into forgetting his old mistress and accepting a new one.

Mrs. Dane did not fail to answer Eliza's letter ; and others also wrote to her ; for she had left behind her many friends in the village. And now, in her lonely retreat, she heard again and again how handsome Faustina was, and how much she was admired, and how happy Abel seemed, and what new furniture he had purchased, and what a gay winter they were having, and how almost everybody except the joyous wedded pair often inquired for her, and sent love. And do you suppose that, as Eliza pondered these things all day, and day after day, to the tune of the whirling spindles, her sharp thoughts did not sometimes whirl too, and pierce into her soul ?

So the winter passed, and the summer followed ; and she learned that now Abel had especial reason to be tender of his bride ; that he had bought a new carriage to drive her out in ; that, in his devotion, he spared no time or trouble or expense, if a whim of hers was to be gratified. Then came the intelligence which she had been long prepared to hear, but which, when at last she heard it, smote her with faintness of heart. Abel, far from her, forgetting her entirely, no doubt, in his separate delight, was the father of a beautiful boy.

How the child thrived, and grew to look like his

mother ; how Faustina once more flashed into society, which she dazzled by her beauty and jewels and dresses ; how envious ones reported that she was running Abel into debt by her extravagance ; how careworn he was really beginning to look ; all this, with many dark hints of things going wrong at home, Eliza heard during the two years that followed. But never, directly or indirectly, did she get one word from Abel. Others invited her to return to the village ; he never invited her. His resentment seemed eternal. And though, often and long after, when her life had grown less lonely, her thoughts would fly back to her old home, and her heart, despite of her, would yearn to follow, she saw ever the iron gates, through which she had passed, closed and barred behind her.

But at length, one September evening, as she went home from her work, at the door of her boarding-house a letter was given her.

The well-known hand-writing made her tremble so that she could scarcely break the seal. It was Abel's hand, — changed, agitated, hurried, — but still she knew it well.

This was the letter : —

"Come to me, Eliza. Do not remember my unkindness. Let nothing keep you. I am in great trouble. Come at once.   ABEL."

Terror and dread swept over her. She did not stop

to remember or to forgive. But love, like a strong power, seized upon her, gave her strength, and guided her hands, and sent her, the next day, whirling away upon the train that bore her back to Abel and her home.

IV.

MRS. APJOHN'S ADVENTURE.

AND now, what stress of ill-fortune had hurried Abel
into sending this alarming missive? To answer which
question, we must go back to Tasso Smith and the Apjohns, and to one bright, particular Sunday in this history.

A still, September day, with the peculiar sentiment
of the Sabbath breathing in the air, yellowing in the
sunshine, brooding over field and orchard almost like a
conscious presence, and filling all the silent rooms of the
house with its cool hush. The bells have ceased ringing ; the choirs have ceased singing ; and the naughty
boys, sitting in the wagons under the meeting-house
sheds, can hear far off the monotonous tones of the
minister's discourse.

Abel Dane sits by his brilliant and showily-dressed
wife in their smart pew. His mother has also, by a
strong resolution and effort, got to church this afternoon,
thinking it the last Sunday of the season, and perhaps the
last Sunday of her life that she shall be able to hear the
good old man preach. On one side of this group you
may see the young man, Tasso Smith, occasionally stroking his moustache, with a display of finger-rings, and

casting significant glances at Faustina ; while, on the other, his bald pate shining in the light, sits solemn John Apjohn, choking in black cravat, rolling up his large eyes at the preacher, and now and then drawing down the corners of his mouth with a dismal sigh.

Prudence is not present. In the morning she can usually endure a sermon of reasonable length ; but in the afternoon it is impossible for her to avoid the sin of drowsiness. " The more flesh, the more frailty." And it is so mortifying to the sensitive John to have to keep waking her up, in order to prevent her nodding and snoring, that she has wisely resolved to spend her Sunday afternoons at home.

She reads a little, sleeps a good deal, opens the till of the chest to see that her money is safe, and perhaps counts it over, then thinks of preparing supper. With a basket on her arm, she visits the garden for vegetables. She is sorry the tomatoes are poor and puny. She is fond of tomatoes, and involuntarily looks over the fence into Abel Dane's garden, where there are bushels of nice, ripe ones. Before Eliza went and Faustina came, the Danes used to give her all the vegetables she wanted; for they always had a large garden generously cultivated, while she had but a poor little strip of ground, with only a shiftless husband to look after it.

" Think of that, John Apjohn ! " she says to herself. " If I only had a husband that was wuth a cent ! " — doubtless forgetting that it is not alone John's inefficiency, but her own tight hold of the purse-strings, which prevents his enriching the soil in a manner to insure good crops. "Now, old Mis' Dane, and Abel, too, for that matter, had jest as lives we'd have some of them tomatuses as not. It's a pity to see 'em wasted. They look to me to be a-rottin' on the ground. Anyway, frost'll come and finish 'em 'fore their folks can ever use 'em up. I've a good notion jest to step over and pick a few. They never'd know it ; and John'll think they come off'm our own vines."

Up and down and all around she looks, and sees no eye beholding her.

"They've all gone to meetin' 'cept the baby, and I see Melissy take him and carry him over to her folks's. House is all shet up, I know. Only a few tomatuses. What's the harm, I'd like to know ? I'm sure I'd ruther any one would have *my* tomatuses than leave 'em to rot on the ground. I *will* jest step over and take two or three."

"Stepping over" was a rather light and airy way of expressing it. Did you ever see a fat woman climb a fence, and didn't laugh ? Cautiously feeling the boards till she finds one she has confidence in ; hugging the post affectionately ; tangling her knees in her skirts ; putting her elbows over the topmost board, and finally getting one foot over ; then turning around, as she brings up the other foot ; stopping a minute to arrange skirts, then getting down backwards, very much as she got up, — all this is in the programme. Prudence is not nearly so spry as a cat ; but, give her time, and she is good for any common board-fence, provided nobody is looking. She is particularly anxious, on this occasion, to assure herself that nobody *is* looking. And so the feat is accomplished, and she treads carefully among the tomatoes.

Although purposing to pick only a few, they are so large and so plenty that she fills her basket almost before she knows it. Then, it is "*sich* a pity to see 'em wasted," she thinks she will put two or three in her apron. For this is the subtlety of sin; that a thousand excuses suggest themselves for taking just a little of the forbidden fruit ; then to add a little more to that little cannot really make much difference in the offence ; and so you progress by degrees in the indulgence, till you have not only filled your basket, but your apron also.

Stooping, with broad back to the golden sunshine and blue Sabbath sky; holding up her apron with one hand, and loading it with the other, she is peering among the vines, when suddenly she is startled by a harsh growl. In great fright she looks up and sees Turk bristling before her.

"Massy sakes ! why, Turk ! don't you know me ? "

" Gur-r-r-r ! " answers Turk.

"Dear me ! " gasps Prudence. " You never acted so before, Turk ! You never barked at *me !* Come, doggy ! poor fellow ! poor fellow ! "

She reaches out her hand coaxingly, and the brute snaps at it. Then the soul of the woman grows sick within her, and her knees shake. Right before her stands the red-eyed, snarling monster,—between her and the fence, between her and her basket ; and what shall she do ?

" Turk, it's *me*, Turk ! your old friend, doggy ! " she tells him.

" Can't help it ! " plainly answers doggy, deep in his thundering throat.

But he won't dare to bite her, she thinks. And, if she dies for it, she must get out of the garden before the folks come from meeting. She makes a charge at her basket. Turk meets her with a terrific leap and snarl, and seizes her apron with his teeth. Involuntarily screaming, she retreats. She clings to the apron with her hands, he with his jaws. She pulls one way, he tugs the other. The string breaks. Prudence loses her hold of the apron, and falls in the entangling tomato-vines. Turk goes back upon his haunches, with the captured apron in his teeth.

" I never, never ! Oh, dear, dear ! What *shall* I do ? what *shall* I· do ? " splutters Prudence, as she disengages her feet from the vines, feels the smashed tomatoes under her, gets up, and still sees Turk, with her apron and basket, between her and the fence. And now she thinks she hears the carriages coming from meeting.

The impulse is to run. And leave her basket and apron in possession of the enemy ? No, they must be brought off from the battle-field at all hazards. Prudence is wild, or she would never dare advance again to the contest. Turk waits till she has reached the apron-string, and begun to pull it gently, when, once more considering it time to assume the offensive, he gives a bound, rescues the rag, hurls her backwards to the ground, and seats himself beside her, with his fore paws on her dress, and his red tongue, white teeth, hot breath, and ferocious eyes close to her face. She does not scream ; she does not attempt to rise ; for when she stirs, his growl reverberates in her ear, and she feels his moist muzzle wetting her throat.

A sad predicament for a respectable woman, isn't it ? Oh, what would she give if she had only stayed in her own garden, and never cast covetous eyes at her neighbor's ? If she only had her apron and basket safe and empty the other side of the fence, would she ever, ever do such a thing again ? Never, never !

"Turk, Turk, good doggy !" she pleads, in her desperation, "do let me go ! Only this time, Turk ! I never will agin ! Please do, that's a nice dog, now !" But the inexorable Turk glares over her, looking greedily up the road, and listening, not to her entreaties, but to the sound of the approaching wheels. And there we may as well leave her, for the present, to her interesting reflections.

V.

COOPER JOHN TO THE RESCUE.

THE meetings are indeed out; the wagons have begun to go by, and now the feet of scattered pedestrians clatter along the wooden village sidewalks. A happy throng ! they who ride and they who walk; those in fine silks and broadcloth, and those in cheap prints and homespun; verily all are blessed whom the sun shines upon this day, except one. If you are not lying on your back among your neighbor's vines, with your neighbor's watch-dog growling at your throat, what more felicity can you desire ?

There goes, with the rest, the sweet youth, Tasso Smith, elegantly strutting. If he but knew ! Behind him — curious contrast ! — walks the meek John Apjohn, choking in his Sunday cravat, winking over it, ever and anon, with his melancholy eyes, and screwing his mouth into a serious one-sided twist, as he goes pondering awful things. He passes within a stone's throw of the crushed tomatoes, whose juice is oozing out from under Mrs. Apjohn's unhappy shoulder-blades, but sees not the pleasing sight for the intervening cabbages.

4 *

And now Prudence, where she lies, can hear the familiar sound of her own gate slammed. John has got home.

"To be sure, Prudy!" begins the cooper, as he enters the house, carefully laying off his black hat the first thing, and giving it a final polish with his red silk before putting it away for the week. "Them was two dreadful good sermons to-day. Desperate smart man, old Mr. Hardwell, — as feeling a preacher as ever I sot under. You should have heard him dwell upon the vanities of this world this arternoon! All our pride and selfishness, and what we call the good things of life, where'll they all be in a few years?" he said. "You ought to have heard him, Prudy; to be sure! to be sure!"

Indeed, Prudy would give anything just now if she had heard him; even if she were but present to hear her worthy John! How free-hearted and beatified she would feel if she were at this moment taking off her silk dress after church, instead of spoiling her calico gown down there among the tomatoes!

"Why, where be you, Prudy?" says John, entering the bedroom; for he had surely thought she was there, not finding her in the kitchen. Still not much alarmed, he takes off his Sunday coat and cravat ; and having laid the one away in a drawer, and hung the other up in the closet, he feels more comfortable. "Prudy," he calls, "are you there?" putting his polished little head up the unanswering stair-way.

No Prudence in the house, no Prudence in the garden, where her husband looks next. What can it all mean ? It is one of those little mysteries that appall the imaginative John. He remembers that the back-door of the house was open when he came in. The stove is filled with fuel just ready to kindle. A fresh pail of water has been drawn. The cloth is on the table. But where is Mrs. Apjohn ? Pale, at the wood-pile, the cooper stands and startles the Sabbath stillness by feebly trilling her name.

" Pru-d-u-n-ce ! "

" D-u-n-ce ! " echoes Abel Dane's shop, as if it were laughing at him.

But what is that ? Another voice ! a faint, far-off, stifled scream.

" John ! John ! help ! "

" Where be ye ? " cries the terrified John.

" Here ! " says the voice.

It sounds as if it were in the well. Prudence in the well ! In an instant the cooper's vivid fancy pictures that excellent and large-sized woman fallen, head-foremost and heels upward, into the deep and narrow cavity. How can she ever be got out ? A rope tied round her heels and several men strenuously hoisting, is the image which flashes through his brain. He is at the curb in a second; peering fearfully in, with his eyes shaded by his hands; but making no discovery there, except the silhouette of himself projected black upon the glimmering reflection of the sky in the placid water.

" John ! come quick ! " calls the muffled voice again.

On the roof of the house this time ! How came Pru-

dence on the roof of the house ? To run over to Abel
Dane's and borrow a long carpenter's ladder is John's
first thought. To get a good view of the roof, his next.
To this end he hastens down into the garden, and is
standing on tiptoe to discover Prudence on the ridge-
pole, when once more calls the voice, this time unmistak-
ably behind him, —

"Where be ye ? and what's the matter ? " gasps the
cooper, gazing all around in vain.

"Here I am, and you'll see what's the matter. Don't
make no noise, but come as quick as you can, and git
away this horrid dog ! "

Then John Apjohn, rushing to the fence, sees the
prostrate woman, and sedentary dog, and the guilty tomatoes, — some in the apron and basket, and some on
the ground. He clings to the fence, bareheaded, in his
shirt-sleeves, white as any cheese-curd, by trembling and
ghastliness quite overcome, and uttering not a word.

"Quick, I say ! " cries Prudence on her back. "Take
off this dog, and I'll tell ye all about it by'm'by."

Over the fence tumbles the astonished cooper. But
to take off the dog is not so easy a matter. Turk is
averse to being taken off. He glares and growls and
snaps at the little man, as if he would swallow him.

"I can't, Prudy ! " falters John, retreating.

"Ketch right hold of him ! " commands Prudence.
"Choke him ! pull him ! "

"I da'sn't ! " articulates John.

"If I had a man for a husband!" exclaimed Prudence. "Git a club! Kill the brute!"

"To be sure! to be sure!" and John starts to find a club. There is a pole leaning on an apple-tree near by. He secures it, and hurries back to stir up Turk. The combat begins, with John at one end of the pole and Turk at the other. Turk seizes his end with his teeth; John holds his in his hands; and there they stand. Turk growls to make John let go; John *shooes* and *ste-boys* to make Turk let go.

"Pull it away from him!" exclaims Prudence.

John pulls till he has dragged the dog half across the good woman's waist, when, as it would seem, the sagacious brute, seeing a chance for a fine strategic effect, suddenly releases his grip, and leaves the pole with the cooper, who loses his balance, staggers backward rapidly, and sits down, with his Sunday trousers, in an over-ripe muskmelon.

"Now take the pole," says the commander-in-chief, "and knock him on the head with it, hard!"

"I shall hit you!" utters John.

"Never mind me!" says the resolute Prudy.

Up goes the pole, unsteadily and slow.

"Ready?" says John.

"Yes; strike!"

And down comes the heavy, unwieldy weapon. Turk sees it descending to damage him, and considers it honorable, under the circumstances, to dodge. He is out of the way before the radius has passed through one half the arc; but the momentum of the stroke is such that it is impossible for the cooper to stay his hold; and the blow alights upon Mrs. Apjohn's stomach.

"Ugh!" says Mrs. Apjohn.

"Now I've killed ye!" exclaims John, despairingly, throwing away the weapon.

"Don't ye know no better'n to be murderin' me 'stid of the dog?" cries Prudy.

"I didn't mean to!" murmurs the wretched. man. "Broke any ribs, think?"

"I don't care for my ribs, if I could only —Oh, dear! why *can't* ye beat off this dog? Empty out them tomatuses, and throw the basket over the fence, anyway. And give me my apron. Quick!"

But Turk, also, has something to say about that. Neither apron nor basket shall John touch; they are confiscated.

"How come the tomatuses in the basket? in your apron?" asks the cooper. "O Prudy, Prudy! To be sure! to be sure!"

"Wal! wal! wal!" chafes the impatient woman. "I s'pose I'm to lay here till doomsday, or till Abel's folks come home. There they come now, — don't they?"

"Yes," answers the cooper. "They're late, on the old lady's account. I'll tell Abel to come and call off his dog."

"Don't ye for the world! Squat right down; mabby they wont see us!"

"What! ye don't re'ly mean to say you — you've been — hooking the tomatuses?" For hitherto John has indulged a feeble hope that the affair could be honorably explained.

"Squat down, I say!" And John squats, hugging his knees, with his chin between them, — as ludicrous a picture of dismay and terror as was ever seen. He feels like a thief; he knows he looks like a thief; and the storm of calamity and disgrace, which he has imagined impending above his little bare, bald head so long, he is sure is now going to burst.

And there the three wait, — Turk guarding both his prisoner and the prizes; for the basket and apron are so near that he can protect them without letting Prudence up.

"Prudy!" whispers John.

"What!" mutters Prudy.

"It's dreadful! it's dreadful!" moans John.

"Hold your tongue!" says Prudy.

The cooper sinks his chin still lower between his knees, sighing miserably.

"Prudy!" — after a long pause.

"What do you want now?"

"I wish you'd gone to meetin' this arternoon, Prudy!"

"You can't wish so any more'n I do!"

"If you had only heard that sermon, Prudy!"

"Stop your noise about the sermon!"

Another long pause.

"Prudy!"

"Well! what?"

" I wish I was dead ! — don't you ? "

" I wish this dog was dead ! "

Upon which, to convince them that he is not nor anything like it, Turk begins to bark.

" It's all over now ! " says Prudence.

John feels that there is nothing left him but suicide. He can never confront Abel Dane after this; so he looks about him for something on which to beat out his brains. No convenient and comfortable object for the purpose meets his eye, but a good big squash. And before he has time to consider which may prove the softer of the two, his pate or the vegetable, in case of a collision, he hears a foot in the grass. He twists his neck around on his shoulders, as he crouches, softly turns up his timid glance over the cabbages, and beholds the dreaded visage of Abel Dane.

Abel stops and gazes, too much amazed to speak. Turk wags his tail, and looks wistfully for approbation of his exploit.

" Come here, Turk ! " says the severe voice of Abel.

With ill-concealed misgivings, Turk takes his paws off his captive's calico, drops his head between his fore legs, and his tail between his hind legs, and cringes at his master's feet.

Cooper John, having once turned round his head, softly turns it back again, and sits as still, in his former toad-like posture, as if he had seen the face of a Gorgon, with the old-fashioned result. Only the rear slope of his little, shining bald crown, his broad, striped suspenders crossed behind over the back of his clean Sunday shirt, and a section of the Sunday trousers, bearing the imprint of the aforesaid over-ripe melon, are visible to the wondering eyes of Abel.

As for Prudence, she loses no time, but gathers herself up as soon as Turk permits, and begins hurriedly to shake and brush her gown.

"Wal, Abel Dane, this is a pooty sight for Sunday, I 'spose you think ! And so it is ! " flirting violently, and speaking as if he had done her an injury. "And I want to know, now, 🌳 you think it's neighborly to keep a brûte like that, to tear folks to pieces that jest set a foot on to your premises ? For here he's kep' me groanin' on my back an hour, if he has a minute." Then, turning sharply to her husband: "John Apjohn ! what are ye shirkin' there for ? "

Thus summoned, the petrified man limbers, and rises slowly upon his miserable feet; glancing, with those woe-begone, large eyes of his, first at his wife, then at Abel Dane, and lastly at the filched tomatoes.

"I am sorry," says Abel, "if my dog has put you to any inconvenience. IIe didn't bite you, I hope ! "

"No ! well for him ! " exclaims Prudence, red and embarrassed, but trying still to pass the affair off with a brave air. "The fact is jest this, Abel Dane: if you begrutch me a few tomatuses, it's what your father never done before ye, and I never expected it of you; and I'll cheerfully pay you for 'em, if you'll accept of any pay; and my husband here knows I only jest stepped over

5

the fence to save a few that was bein' wasted, which I thought was sech a pity, and you'd jest as lives we'd have 'em; and I meant all the time to tell ye I took some, when that plaguy dog ! " —

Here, having poured forth these words in a wild and agitated manner, the worthy woman broke down, and wept and sobbed, and continued confusedly to brush her gown. John stood by and groaned.

"Well, well, neighbors," said Abel, "you're quite welcome to the tomatoes. I haven't known what I should do with 'em all, and I'm glad to get rid of 'em. If you had come in through the gate, Turk wouldn't have meddled with you."

As he spoke, kindly and consolingly, Prudence only cried the more, and blindly flirted her skirts; while John, wretchedly bent, with a supplicating countenance, approached his neighbor.

"Abel Dane," said he, in a voice scarcely audible, it was so weak and hoarse, "me and you've knowed each other ever sence you was a child, and I knowed your father 'fore ever you was born; and I believe I've always had an honest name with you till now."

"And so you have now, Mr. Apjohn," said Abel, cheeringly. "Don't let a little thing like this trouble you. I understand you," — and he shook the cooper's helpless, cold hand with genuine cordiality.

"Thank ye, thank ye; to be sure ! " murmured John. I *am* an honest man; and, though things don't look jest right, I own, yet you know, Abel Dane, I'd no more be guilty of takin' anything that didn't belong to me than I would cut my own head off."

Abel, pitying him sincerely, and seeing well enough that this poor, shaking creature was innocent, whoever was guilty, assured him again and again of his confidence and good-will.

"Thank ye, thank ye; to be sure, to be sure!" said John, gratefully, hunting in vain in his pockets and on the ground for his red silk handkerchief to wipe his eyes with. "And, if 'twon't be too much, I've one request to make. 'Twould make talk if it should be known, and we would never hear the last on't, probably; and I'd ruther die at once than be pinted at."

"I promise you," interrupted Abel, "nobody shall ever hear of it from me. Never fear; you won't be pointed at. Now let's say no more about the matter. Here are your tomatoes, Mrs. Apjohn; and, whenever you want any more, you've only to come in through the gate and get them."

"I declare!" gulped the woman; "I've no words, Abel! And, if you *will* be so kind as never to mention it, I'll be so much obleeged!"

"I never will. So that's settled." And Abel hurried them away; for he saw Faustina approaching.

John took the basket of tomatoes, heavily against his will, and Prudence, with a sick heart, gathered up her apron with its original contents; for it would not do to refuse the gift which she was willing to take before it was given. And so, dejected and chagrined, making

sickly attempts to utter their thanks to Abel and to be
civil to Faustina, who came out, splendid in silk, and
stared at them, the cooper and his wife departed through
the gate, and went home to their waiting, vacant house,
every room of which seemed conscious of the shame
that had befallen them, and the very atmosphere to be
heavy and depressed therewith.

VI.

SUNDAY EVENING AT ABEL'S.

"ABEL," said the astonished Faustina, "what has happened to Mrs. Apjohn?"

The cooper and his wife were hardly yet out of hearing, and, as Abel walked slowly toward his own door, with the beautiful face in the beautiful bonnet by his side, he shook his head and was silent.

"Who told them they could have the tomatoes?" Faustina insisted.

"I did," said Abel.

"But what has she been down in the dirt for? And what makes 'em both look so like death? Come, I am dying to know!"

Faustina had one of those restless minds which crave excitement, and which, having no solid food of thought or occupation, keep the appetite of curiosity continually whetted for such slight morsels of village gossip as you, of course, sage reader, hold in disdain. Abel saw at once how difficult it would be to hide the secret from her.

"You didn't give them liberty to take the tomatoes, — did you?" she questioned, suspiciously.

5 *

" Yes," said he, resolving to trust her, and relying upon her discretion. " Mrs. Apjohn had got a little the start of me, however, and helped herself before I came."

" Stealing ! " ejaculated Faustina.

" Absurd ! " answered Abel. " She intended, of course, to tell us what she had done; but, unluckily, Turk interfered, and rather disconcerted the poor woman by keeping her on her back, as she declares, a full hour."

The handsome face grew excited. .

" But it *was* stealing ! What right had she ? Such people ought to be exposed at once, and made an example of."

" On the contrary, my dear, I look upon it as a very unfortunate affair. The less said about it the better, and I pledged my word to them never to speak of it."

" You did, did you ! " said Faustina, indignantly. " The idea of letting a thief off that way ! "

Abel sighed, as he did very often lately; and the weary, care-worn look he gave his wife was nothing new.

" I don't think she meant to steal, I tell you," he said, with some impatience. " And if she did, I wouldn't tell of it. What should I ruin a poor woman's reputation for, when it is probable she never did such a thing before, and would never do it again ? "

" You are mighty easy with such folks, seems to me. For my part, I am not. I say they ought to be punished."

" Let him that is without sin, cast a stone; I will not.

It isn't at all likely," added Abel, "that you or I will ever be tempted to commit so foolish a trespass. But are we never guilty of anything we need to be forgiven for ? In this case, if only for Cooper John's sake, I would hush up the affair. I pity him from the bottom of my heart. His wife might survive an exposure, but it would kill him. So remember that my word is pledged."

Faustina sneered. She was not so very beautiful then. And as Abel looked at her, he saw, as he had seen many times before when he had refused to credit his perceptions, that there was no beauty of soul, no informing loveliness, in that fair shape; and that hers was a shallow, selfish, merely brilliant face at the best.

They entered the house, — a far more showy dwelling now than when Eliza left it, but to Abel a home no longer. The atmosphere of comfort and content was wanting. For houses, like individuals, have their atmosphere, and a sensitive soul entering your abode can discern, before he speaks with its inmates, whether harmony and blessedness dwell there, or whether it is the lodging of discord and mean thoughts.

Proud and stern as he was, Abel could not hide from himself how much he missed his foster-sister. He missed that even and gentle management of his household affairs, which he had never known how to prize until her place was filled by an extravagant wife and wasteful servants. He felt the need of her sympathy and counsel in the worldly troubles that were thickening

upon him; for, somehow, he could never open his heart
on these subjects to Faustina. The holes in his socks,
the wandering shirt-buttons, the heavy bread, the want
of neatness and order from cellar to garret, reminded
him daily of his loss. In his mother's face he saw, under a thin veil of cheerfulness, perpetual sorrow for
Eliza's absence. When he came home to his meals, he
thought of the tender spirit that had welcomed him
once. And in the evening he remembered with regret
the books they used to read together. Faustina did not
like to read, and no book had power to interest her, unless it were one of those high-wrought fictions, romances
of unreal life, which disgusted Abel.

What she liked was company. Every evening, to
please her, they must go out somewhere, or have callers
and cards at home, and the small talk of some such nice
young man as Tasso Smith. Abel hated Tasso Smith.

" *I* like him," Faustina would say, with a little toss of
her head, which added, as plainly as words could do,
" and that settles it."

So Tasso, when he was in town, frequently favored
the Danes with his choice company. Faustina expects
him this Sabbath evening. She is irritable and restless.

" Go to your father, do ! " she says to little Ebby, who
is pulling her dress, and begging to be taken up. Grief
swells the baby face at the repulse; and he hastens for
refuge and comfort to his father's bosom.

And now, suddenly, having had a glimpse of a visitor
from the window, Faustina's discontented brow lights

up. Abel's countenance, a moment since, gentle and tender, darkens as suddenly when the nice young man walks in.

"Goin' by, thought I'd look in, see how you liked the disquisition 's aft'noon," says Tasso, munching his words and grimacing.

"I do wish the minister wouldn't have so much to say about extravagance in dress!" exclaims Faustina.

"If we can't go to heaven in decent clo'es, what's the use?" says Tasso, stroking the moustache, and showing the finger-rings.

"Besides," adds the lady, "I don't think the dresses in our society are much to brag of, anyway. Taken as a set, they are the homeliest women, and the worst dressed women I ever saw."

"One or two 'xceptions, could mention," responds Tasso, with a flattering simper.

"There's Mrs. Grasper's bonnet, — what a fright!"

"That's so! Looks like a last year's bird's nest, feathers left in. Do to go with her shawl, though. Same shawl Grasper used last winter for a hoss-blanket; 'pon my honor; hi, hi, hi!" giggles Mr. Smith, twisting his ear-locks. "How je like the disquisition, t'-day?" patronizingly, to the old lady.

She smiled placidly, and, struggling a moment with her organs of speech, which refused at first to articulate, she observed, —

"'Withdraw thy foot from thy neighbor's house, lest he be weary of thee.'"

The text happened to be in her mind, and when she opened her mouth to give Tasso a civil answer, it leaped out. She tried to catch it, but it was gone. And it seemed such a decided hit at Tasso, that he could do nothing but look confused and silly, while Faustina reddened with resentment, and Abel just lifted his eyebrows with a smile of surly humor.

"Excuse me, Mr. Squash," the kind old lady hastened to say. That did not mend the matter; and she frowned and shook her head at herself with good-natured impatience. "Mr. Smith!— there, now I've got it! I meant to say, I think the minister gave us, this afternoon, one of his very best fricassees — no — what is the word?"

"Sermons, I call them," said Abel. "Tasso calls them disquisitions."

"One of the best sermons I ever heard," added the old lady; "and probably the last I shall ever hear."

"Old Deacon Judd 'peared to like it," said Tasso, rallying. "Je see his mouth stand open? Ye c'd 'a' drove in a good-sized carriage, and turned around. — Fricassees!" he whispered aside to Faustina, and tittered. .

"Mrs. Judd's ribbons took my eye!" said Faustina.

"They look like pine shavings nailed to a well-sweep!" added Tasso. "Ye mind what a long neck she's got? Most extensive curvical appendage, ye und'stand, they is in town. Comes by stretching it up every Sunday so's't she can hear the minister; deaf, I 'spose. It's so long a'ready, she has to get up on to a barrel to tie her bunnit." He whispered again, "Fricassees!" and snickered as before.

Abel, weary of this unworthy Sunday-evening talk, and perceiving that his mother was a subject of ridicule, felt his wrath boiling up within him.

"Jim Locke's bought him a melodeon," was the next theme started by Tasso.

"What for ? He never can learn to play !"

"He ? no ! soft ! Think of Jim Locke with a melodeon, Abel !"

"And why not ?" sternly demanded Abel.

"Pshaw !" said Tasso; "he don't want a melodeon, more'n a dog wants a walking-stick."

"And why shouldn't a dog have a walking-stick, as well as a puppy ?" And Abel glanced contemptuously at Mr. Smith's rattan.

Melissa, the servant, now came to help the old lady to bed; performing, as well as such unsympathizing hands could, the task which always painfully reminded both Abel and his mother of Eliza. And now, Abel, full of ire and spleen, arose and left the room, hugging little Ebby in his arms.

"Crusty t'-night. What's the matter ?" whispered Tasso.

"I don't know. Nothing pleases him," sighed Faustina.

"Don't believe that, now."

"Don't believe it ? why ?"

"'Cause," simpered the eloquent youth, "there ain't a man in the world *you* can't please, though he was as cross as seven bears."

She sighed again, and regarded her visitor gratefully.

"Did you ever see such a tiresome old woman? Don't care if I do say it!" she exclaimed. "And he thinks I ought to be thankful for the privilege of having her in the house."

"Fricassees!" said Tasso.

"He don't like company, and thinks I ought to settle down and be a dull old woman with her, and never see anybody else from one year's end to the other." The pretty face pouted. "In such a stupid place as this!"

"Ought to be thankful for such near neighbors." Tasso never neglected an opportunity to speak disparagingly of the Apjohns. "Interesting! I could tell a story!"

"So could I." Faustina laughed. "Some of our neighbors are extravagantly fond of tomatoes."

"Do tell! How fond?"

"Oh, enough so that they don't mind getting over fences into other folks' gardens, and helping themselves!"

"You don't say!" cried Tasso, eagerly.

"Of course I don't; for I was told not to. And you mustn't let Abel know I've hinted a word about it, nor any one else. What do you suppose we found when we came home from meeting to-day?"

"Something funny, I bet! Give us the story! Come!"

"Will you give me yours? You said you could tell one."

Tasso promised.

"But then," laughed Faustina, "Abel charged me strictly not to mention how we found Mrs. Apjohn on her back among the tomatoes, her apron and basket well filled, and honest Turk holding her down, while John skulked behind the cabbages."

Tasso was so delighted that he jumped up, clapped his hands, and laughed with unbounded glee.

"Oh, that's too good! it kills me! Oh, no! I'll never mention it, if you say so. But wouldn't I have been tickled to have been there?"

"Now, what's your story?"

"I don't dare to tell it now; you won't believe me. You won't believe these poor people, who steal their neighbor's tomatoes, are — misers!" whispered Tasso.

"Nonsense!"

"It's so, I tell ye. Perfect misers! Rich as Jews! Keep a pile of money in the house all the time, and nobody knows how much more in the bank!"

"How do you know that?"

"I'll tell ye. 'Bout the time you was married, — united in the bonds of high menial blessedness, y'understand, with your amiable consort, — hem! — 'bout that time I'd just come out fr'm the city, toler'ble flush, so I thought I'd look into Apjohn's and pay him some money father was owing him, — compensation for work, ye know. Well, so happened I had some large bills; and so I thought I'd bother Cooper John a little, and asked him to change a C., — y'understand, a hunderd.

By George! I never was so surprised 's I was when Mrs. Apjohn took a key from the clock-case, and went into the bedroom, and, after jingling silver and counting bills there for five minutes, brought out change for my hunderd-dollar note! It's so," said Tasso, as Faustina appeared incredulous. "I never told on't before, fear somebody'd rob the old misers. Now, by George, since they've hooked your tomatoes, I don't care whether they get robbed or not! I can tell you just where they keep their treasure," — and Tasso specified the chest-till.

"Yes," said Faustina, "very pleasant weather indeed," as Abel, having tucked Ebby away in his crib, reëntered the room and sat down.

VII.

MR. SMITH'S FRIEND'S JEWELS.

MORE than one cause was operating, that Sunday evening, to make Abel appear, as Tasso expressed it, crusty. The cheerlessness of his home was nothing new. These frivolities of the evening had long since usurped the place of the good old-fashioned readings and social comforts. He had become accustomed to seeing Faustina's features light up with animation at the silly conceits of Mr. Smith, and he was not jealous. But now there was a new burden on his mind; his pecuniary troubles were culminating. Not long after his marriage he had been obliged to mortgage his house. Since then his debts had been constantly increasing. He had many times been sorely pushed to meet his liabilities; but never had he seen a darker week before him than this which was coming.

He slept little that night. Monday dawned. After a light slumber, the gray morning beam stole in upon him, and with it came the thought of the payments which he could devise no means of making. A tide of restlessness tossed him. He looked at the beautiful be-

ing by his side. She was sleeping a heavy, most un-
spiritual sleep.

"Oh! if she would only sympathize with me and help
me," thought Abel, "I could bear anything; but she
doesn't care. I have been too indulgent to her; I could
refuse her nothing, and so I am deep in debt." He
glanced at their sleeping child. "For your sake, little
one, I will be a braver and stronger man in future!"

He arose. His movements in the room awoke Faustina.

"Are you going, Abel?"

"I have a hard week's work before me, and I must
begin it," he answered.

"O Abel! I don't feel very well, and I don't know as
I shall get up to breakfast; but can't you leave me a
little money before you go?"

"How much?"

"Oh, ten, or fifteen, or twenty dollars,—I don't care."

A bitter smile contorted Abel's face. "For what?"
he asked.

"I am going into the village, by-and-by, and I always
see so many things I want; and I haven't had any money
to spend for myself for ever so long. I *must* have me a
dress right away," she said complainingly.

"Don't you know well enough," demanded Abel,
"that I am harassed almost to death with money-mat-
ters already? Haven't I told you that I have no more
idea than a man in his grave how I am to raise half

enough to pay what must be paid this week ? And you talk to me of new dresses ! "

When he was gone, Faustina consoled herself with the reflection that he was the cruelest husband and she the most injured wife in the world; sighed to think she couldn't have a new dress immediately, and went to sleep again.

For three days Abel struggled manfully with the obstacles in his way; and when his utmost was done, he wanted still a hundred dollars to make up the necessary amount. A small sum to you, flush reader, but an immense one at that time to Abel Dane. But on the fourth day he entered the house with tears of joy in his eyes.

" What good news ? " asked his mother.

" A miracle ! " exclaimed Abel. " I will never lose my faith in Providence again. Just as my last resources were exhausted, and I had given up all hope, what should come to me, in a blank envelope from Boston, but a draft for a hundred dollars ! "

Faustina, who had not yet got over the feeling that he was an inhuman husband and she an injured wife, and did not neglect to manifest, by her morose conduct, how much she was aggrieved, was almost surprised out of her sulkiness by this strange announcement.

" Who sent it ? " she inquired.

" I have not the remotest suspicion; but whoever he may be, he has saved me from ruin."

Whilst he was putting the draft away in the drawer

6 *

which contained the money he had raised, and his mother was inwardly offering up a prayer of thankfulness for this favor to her son, Faustina was saying to herself, "Well, I should think he might let me have a new dress *now*, if I have to run in debt for it."

Poor Faustina! let us not blame her too severely. Her beauty was her misfortune. It was that which had spoiled her. From her childhood, flattery and the unwise indulgence of over-careful friends, had instilled into her the pernicious belief that she was the fairest and choicest of God's creatures, and that it was the duty of everybody to administer to her pleasures, while it was her privilege to think only of herself. She had never in her life known what it was to make a sacrifice. The blessed habit of helping others,— of forgetting one's own happiness in caring for the happiness of others, — this unfortunately fortunate beauty had never learned. No doubt she had in her soul germs of noble womanhood, which affliction, and wise kindness on the part of her teachers, might have developed. But, as it was, she had grown up to be a child still, with the proportions of a woman, unreasonable, self-willed, with a mind undisciplined, and impulses uncontrolled.

That forenoon Tasso Smith called. He found Faustina with her hair in curl-papers.

"Got sumthin' t' show ye; sumthin' nice, or I wouldn't have took the trouble. How's tomatoes? and how's fricassees?" he chuckled, as he undid a package. "Friend of mine's got some jewelry he wants to raise

money on, and he sent some of it to me. *You* know
what jewelry is; so, just for curiosity, thought I'd bring
it over."

"Oh–oh–h — splendid !" cries the enraptured Faustina. "That's the most magnificent bracelet I ever
saw. O Tasso ! you must give me that bracelet !"

"Most happy, if 'twas only mine," smiles the sweet
young man. " Just the thing for you, Faustiny !" He
clasped it on her too willing arm. "By George ! ain't
it a stunner ? Didn't know it *was* so splendid, by
George ! Takes a beautiful arm to show off a fine
bracelet like that."

Faustina's cheeks were kindling, and her eyes began
to burn. Jewelry was an intoxication to the poor
child. She passed before the glass with her jewelled
arm gracefully folded beneath her breast. "O Tasso !
I must have this bracelet, some way ! Come, you never
gave me anything in your life. All my friends make me
presents but you," poutingly.

"I'd give ye the set that goes with it, if I could.
By George ! if you was my wife, Faustiny, — 'xcuse me
for saying it, — I'd make ye sparkle till men's eyes
watered ! If Abel was only a man of taste !"

"Don't talk of Abel. Taste !" said Faustina, scornfully; and she sighed and caressed the bracelet.

"What did a plodding fellow like him ever marry
such a lady as you are for ?" said the insinuating Tasso.
" *He* don't want a brilliant wife, no more'n a toad wants
a side-pocket. You ought to be the lady of some man

of taste and enterprise, — see the world, and not live cooped up here."

"Hold your tongue, Tasso Smith!" cried she, with flashing eyes. "You make me wild. Do you think I don't know what I might have been, and that I like to be reminded of it?" Yet it was evident that she was not displeased; and Tasso knew that his flatteries were wine to her ambitious heart.

"Here, put 'em all on," said he. "That's a love of a pin!"

"Oh, it is! And those ear-rings, — what beauties! Tasso, you make me crazy showing me these things. Oh, if I had some money!"

"They can be had dog-cheap," Mr. Smith observed. "It's a rare chance for anybody that wants such a set of jewels. They won't become everybody, you know. Takes a woman of style to wear such things. It's nothing to me, — I've nothing to gain by it, — but I should like to see you in them sparkling gems. I tell ye, that bracelet is a screamer! Why don't ye buy 'em?"

"Buy them?" repeated Faustina, tremblingly. "I wish I could! What do they cost?"

"That bracelet and the set together retails for a hunderd dollars in Boston. The lowest wholesale price is sixty, and they cost my friend about that. He wants me to get sixty for 'em if I can; but, if you like, I'll take the responsibility and let you have 'em for fifty. If he ain't satisfied, why, 'twon't be but a few dollars difference, and I'll make it up to him."

" Fifty dollars ! " sighed Faustina. " Oh, I can't buy 'em, Tasso."

" Sorry," said Tasso. " You never'll have another such a chance. You might go all over Boston, and you couldn't find another such set as that for less 'n ninety dollars, 't the very lowest. I don't care so much about ?commodatin' my friend, as I do to see you wear somethin' that becomes you." He watched her cunningly. " Well, I suppose I must be going; for I must write to town by the next mail, and either send back the jewels or the money."

The thought of giving up those precious ornaments was too much for Faustina.

" I'll keep them," said she, " and pay you as soon as I can get the money of my husband."

" If 'twas my affair, I'd give ye as long a time to pay for 'em as you want," replied the smooth-tongued Smith; " but my friend's only object in disposing of 'em for any such low price is to raise money the quickest possible. I don't happen to have the funds to spare jest now, myself, or I'd 'commodate ye. You may never come acrost another such a set of gems; for there's very little such gold in the market; not to speak of the stones, which are re'l Berzil di'muns."

" What's fifty dollars ? " suddenly burst forth Faustina, in one of her ungovernable impulses. " I'll take them, Tasso ! I may as well have something now and then to make life pleasant, as to live in constant submission to — I hate the grovelling necessities of life, and I won't be a slave to them any longer ! "

What she meant by these wild words, Tasso did not know nor care to know. His mind was fixed on the sale of his fictitious friend's very fictitious gold and " di'muns; " and when he saw her sweep from the room, impetuously, and presently sweep back again with a fifty-dollar bank-note in her hand, he was content, without raising any more questions.

" There, my beauty ! " said he, " though I've no personal interest in the matter, allow me to congratulate you on securing a bargain, which wouldn't happen to you again prob'bly in a lifetime. And now, I must hurry and get this bill into a letter, and mail it to my friend, — enclose it t' my correspondent, y' understand; — bless me, by George ! " looking at his watch, which, by the way, did not go, being pinchbeck, like the rest of his jewelry, " I've scarcely time to get around now ! Good-by ! "

He was gone almost before she knew it. Then, looking once more at the ornaments he had left upon her person, remembering Abel and his payments, and realizing fully, for the first time, what she had done, a guilty fear came over her, and she ran to call Tasso back.

Too late; he was already out of sight.

VIII.

FAUSTINA'S TANGLED WEB.

"A WEIGHT like a mountain has been taken from my mind!" exclaimed Abel, coming in to dinner. "I don't see how I could raise another dollar without putting up my goods at auction. What I should have done but for the draft which came this morning, I don't know, — yes I do, too; I should have been a bankrupt for the want of a hundred dollars. To have been fifty dollars short would have been just as bad. I have seen Mr. Hodge to-day, and he says he must have the money without fail. I am to see him this evening and have a settlement. Faustina," Abel added, with real tenderness, "if you could know what an ordeal I have passed, and the relief it is now, to feel that I have in the drawer there the means to help myself out of the worst place I was ever in, you'd forgive me for refusing you money as harshly as I did, and be glad I did refuse you."

Faustina listened to these words with conscience-smiting fear. The jewels, which she had hastily hidden away at his coming, were no solace now, but only a terror to her soul. What would he do when he found he had been robbed ? What would he say when he learned how she had squandered the missing money, and for what ? Could she hope to pacify him by a display of the baubles which had, in the hour of temptation, seemed to her more precious than his honor and his peace ? They were beginning to appear, in her own eyes, worthless as they were. His scorn and wrath, if he should see them, she could well imagine. More and more, as she looked forward to it, she dreaded the inevitable exposure. Abel perceived her flush and agitation; but, remembering how sullen she had been since he refused her the money she required, he thought her resentment had taken some new form, and was not surprised at it.

"You don't mean to say," she ventured at last to suggest, "that only just fifty dollars would make such a difference in your affairs ?"

"The difference would be," replied Abel, "that in helping myself out of the well, the chain I am to climb up by would lack just so much of reaching down to my hand. And when a man has strained every nerve to grasp an object, it might as well be withdrawn ten yards from his hand, as ten inches."

"But," faltered Faustina, "ain't you afraid — the money will be stolen ?"

"Not with you in the house," replied the confiding Abel. "Guard it as you would my life ! I could about as soon face death as learn that any part of that money had been lost ! Faustina," he said, cheeringly, "don't look so gloomy. Better times are coming. We will live more within our means, think less of the world and its trifles, and be much happier. It don't require silks and gewgaws to make a home comfortable."

He folded her in his arms. He was so thankful and happy that he desired to bless her also with the overflow of his large heart.

She suppressed her feelings as well as she could till after he was gone. He had eaten his dinner, and departed full of joy in his present good fortune and hope for the future. But night would soon come, and with it disclosure and disgrace. She could imagine him unsuspectingly welcoming Mr. Hodge, taking out the money to pay him, and starting suddenly appalled by the discovery of her theft. What should she do? At heart a coward, she felt that she could never meet her husband's just and terrible wrath. It was a characteristic trait of her selfishness, that, all this while, she thought little of his ruin, and of what he would suffer when the disclosure was made, but only of the shock and the shame that would befall herself. And now, the restraint of his presence removed, she gave way to wild and desperate resolves. Without staying to take her hair out of the curl-papers, she threw on her bonnet.

"Melissa," she said, " stop this child's crying. I am going out a little while. Perhaps " — the bitter impulse prompted her, and she muttered the words through her teeth — "perhaps I shall never come back."

For she had thrust the jewels into her bag, and taken the bag upon her arm, with the blind, passionate feeling

7

that she would never return to that house and to her wronged husband without bringing back with her the money of which she had robbed him.

In the slovenly kitchen of a slovenly house, in company with a slovenly woman, two slovenly girls, and a ragged old man, the elegant Tasso Smith was at dinner, in his shirt-sleeves, when a quick rap came at the door.

"It's Faustiny Dane; she wants to see you, Tasso," said Miss Smith, having gone to the stoop with her frizzled hair.

Tasso turned all colors in quick succession during the half-minute that ensued, — either from embarrassment at having the beautiful Faustina find him in such a home, and see his uncombed, slatternly sister open the door, or because he supposed she had discovered the worthless character of the trinkets he had sold her. He wiped his lips hurriedly on the dirty table-cloth, put on his coat, and went palpitating to the door, with the most inane, simpering expression which it is possible for the human countenance to wear.

"Tasso," said Faustina, in quick, decisive tones, " I want to speak with you a minute."

" W-w-will ye walk in ? " stammered the reluctant Tasso, " or sh'll I get m' hat ? "

For he knew that it was not a house fit to show her into.

" Get your hat," said Faustina, with strange eyes and hectic cheeks.

She walked with nervous steps to and fro on the half-rotten plank before the door, until Tasso got his hat and came out.

" Folks ain't very well; m' sister hain't had time to change her dress to-day; I'd invite ye in, but " —

She interrupted the silly apology.

" Tasso, I can't keep the jewels ! "

" Can't ? Why not ? "

Mr. Smith grinned and picked his foolish teeth.

" I took some money my husband had got to pay off a note with and the interest on a mortgage; he don't know it yet, but when he does, I suppose he will kill me; and I must have that money, and take it back. Here are the jewels."

She pulled open her bag, and eagerly handed out the package, which Tasso did not touch.

" Don't speak quite so loud," he said. " Step this way."

For the truth about that interesting young man was, that, when not absent in the city, he was living upon his thriftless relations, without making them any other compensation than that which his elegant manners and the value of his society afforded; and he was unwilling they should know that he had that day received a sum of money which would have gone far toward paying his summer's board.

" Like to keep my business little bit private; sisters 'u'd think might give them some jewels, if they knew I had any in my possession."

"Take them," said Faustina, "and give them to any-body you please. And give me back the money, at once!"

"Sorry to say," replied Tasso, "I've jest sent the money off to my friend. Why didn't you tell me of this before? It was no interest to me to sell you the jewels. I mailed the letter an hour ago," he added, with a smile on his countenance, and the money in his pocket at the moment.

Faustina drew a quick breath, and cast upon him a stony, despairing look; the hand which held the jewels dropping by her side.

"Tasso," she said, "you have been my ruin. I can never go back to that house without the money. What shall I do?"

"Sure, I don't know," palavered the deceiver. "I consider it the most unfortunate circumstance 'n th' world, 't you didn't mention the way you was situated, 'fore I sent off the money. Might stop the letter now, only the mail has been gone as much as an hour. What *will* you do? If I only had the money to lend you now! Most always have as much as that about me," said he sympathetically, with the only fifty-dollar bank-note he had had in his possession for six months peeping then out of his waistcoat pocket.

"You *must* lend me the money!" exclaimed Faustina. "You must *get* it for me! or else"—her heart throbbed up into her throat with the wildness of the thought that dared to enter it—"you will never see me again, Tasso:

I shall go — I don't know where; but I shan't go back to his home, that is settled."

"I have it!" said Tasso. "I know where you can borry the money."

"Where? for mercy's sake!"

"Of those misers so fond of tomatoes, you know."

"The Apjohns!" she exclaimed. "Oh, I don't believe they have got so much as you tell of; and they wouldn't lend it, if they have."

"By George! what I told you, now, it's a fact, by George! — hope to die if 'tain't!" said Tasso. "And they'll lend, I guess," significantly.

"Go and ask them!"

"Not to me, I don't mean; they wouldn't lend to me. But you jest go and mention the tomatoes, and tell the old woman you can't keep the secret no longer without she 'commodates you to a hunderd dollars, — may as well get a hunderd while you're about it" (Tasso remembered he had more pinchbeck to sell), — "and she'll shell out her miserly hoards, I bet ye, now!"

"O Tasso, I don't know! But I'll try. Wait here for me, won't you? Or, no; meet me somewhere, — where?"

"Up by the meeting-house," suggested Tasso.

"Yes! Don't fail me, now! for if they won't lend me the money, I don't know what I can do without you."

She hurried away on her exciting errand; while Tasso looked after her with a pale, sickly, cunning leer, picking his rotten teeth with one hand, and fingering the bank-note in his pocket with the other.

7 *

IX.

FAUSTINA RETURNS MRS. APJOHN'S VISIT.

FAUSTINA walked back toward the cooper's house, with dubious and undecided steps at first, but gradually quickening her pace as her doubts gave place to determination. Why had she not thought of the Apjohns before ? They should help her. Would they dare to refuse what she asked ? And could she not compel them, by threats, to lend her the money ?

She reached the cooper's house. In her impetuous impatience, she did not stop to knock, but would have entered straight, without ceremony, had not the door been locked. She hurried around to the kitchen door,— that was fastened also. A shade of disappointment passed over her; but it fell like the shadow of a cloud on a rushing stream, without checking its course. Her purpose could not be thwarted; though she might have to wait.

Mrs. Apjohn was certainly not at home. Perhaps the cooper was. So much the better; for it would be easier to deal with him than with his wife. She hastened to the shop. That was likewise shut and silent. Here was an unforeseen difficulty.

Should she go and meet Tasso, and then come back after the Apjohns had returned? Or should she go home and wait? She could do nothing, think of nothing, till this exciting business was over. If she could only get into the house!

Then she remembered a circumstance which she had several times observed, looking across from her own house to her neighbor's. When Mrs. Apjohn was going away and leaving John in the shop, it was her custom, after putting on her bonnet and shawl and locking the back door on the outside, to carry him something, which Faustina conjectured was the key. But when John was not there, she used to stoop down and secrete the said something under the door-step; in order, probably, that he could have the means of entering the house in case he should come home before her. Faustina had also observed that the one who returned first, on such occasions, invariably took something from beneath the step before unlocking the door.

What if the key were there now? She was back again at the rear of the house in a moment. There she stood, just long enough to look about her. Nobody was in sight. No unneighborly watch-dog was there to interfere with her operations, as Turk had interfered with those of Mrs. Apjohn in the tomato-patch. Quickly she put down her hand where she had seen Prudence put down hers. She touched something metallic, smooth, and cold. It was the door-key.

" I'll go in and wait anyway. There can't be any

harm in that," was Faustina's excuse, as she unlocked the door.

The next minute she was alone in the closed and silent house.

She sat down and breathed. But she was too nervous to remain long seated. She got up, and walked about, and looked out of the windows, and peeped into the different rooms. She listened to hear her neighbors coming; yet she almost dreaded to have them come. Supposing they should refuse her the money, and laugh at her threats ? Oh, if she was only sure they *had* money !

In the bedroom she saw the chest as Tasso had described it. She entered softly, hesitating with that superstitious feeling which often haunts the visitor in a still and empty house, especially if he has no rightful business there. Perhaps Prudence was hid behind her own petticoats that hung over the bed; or what if the little cooper was tucked away in the corner behind the bureau, on the lookout for burglars ? Faustina just tried the lid of the chest, and, finding it fastened, walked back rather quickly to the kitchen, with starting and creeping sensations in her nerves, which were not agreeable.

" Will they never come ? " she said to herself. " I won't wait much longer ! "

She looked at the clock; but she forgot to notice the time in the perturbation of thinking of the key which Tasso said was kept hidden there. Summoning a bold·

resolution, she stepped to the high mantel-piece, opened the clock, and found, sure enough, a key hung up within the case. She ran with it to the bedroom, and was almost frightened to find that it fitted the chest.

Well, she might as well finish what she had begun. Though the Apjohns should suddenly come in and catch her, she could easily silence them by holding the tomatoes over their heads. So she turned the key, and the chest opened.

But here she met with an unexpected obstacle. The till, in which she now firmly believed that there was cash, was also locked; and Mrs. Apjohn, if she was the prudent female we take her for, no doubt had the key of it in her reticule. What was to be done? Break open the slender till? That Faustina dared not do. Abandon the search? That she would not. Into every corner of the chest she thrust her hand, and overhauled John Apjohn's shirts and Mrs. Apjohn's folded pillowcases and sheets and bedspreads, in pursuit of the missing key. She often thought she heard footsteps, and stopped to listen, then with trepidation renewed her search.

But no key was to be found. She tried the key of the clock-case and the winding-up key; but neither of them would fit. Should she give up so? There was a key in her bag; she would try that. It was too large. Then she bethought her of the key to the case of jewels. She tried it, — it was too small. No, it would enter! she could turn it; and lo, the till was unlocked!

Ah, well was it for Faustina, who had condemned her neighbor's trespass so severely, that there was no big dog to pounce in upon her now, and arrest her in the midst of an act that looked quite as much like larceny as anything Prudence Apjohn ever did ! It would be interesting to know if she thought of the stolen tomatoes then, and the remarks she had made on the occasion. Alas for this poor human nature of ours, which prompts us to pass sentence to-day upon the very sins we may have been guilty of yesterday, or may commit to-morrow ! The more liable we ourselves are to yield to temptation, the sterner our judgment is apt to be of those who have fallen. Whereas the truly wise man, who has known by experience what temptation is, and has conquered it, is he of all others whose cloak of charity is broadest and warmest.

Yet Faustina had never believed herself capable of such an act as she was now committing. She had approached the cooper's house full of virtuous indignation against robbing and pilfering, and had the speech ready by which she intended to humiliate the wrong-doer, and exact indemnity for the wrong. And here she is, self-abandoned to the sin which she had deemed so monstrous and unpardonable in another !

For Tasso had spoken truly once. In the till there was a pocket-book. In the pocket-book there was a roll of bills. These she hastily opened, and folded up again as hastily. With quivering fingers she had extracted the sum she required, — a fifty-dollar note, the sight of which had sent a thrill of terrified joy to her soul. This she thrusts into her bosom. The rest of the money she returns to the pocket-book, places the pocket-book in the till, and locks the till with the key of the jewel-case. Then, having smoothed the rumpled linen in the chest as well as she can, she lets down the heavy lid again,-and locks it with the key, which she returns to the clock-case.

All this has passed almost too quickly for thought. But now, standing in the room, lingering and listening, with tremors of heart, she begins to reflect, —

"Maybe they never'll know who took it. I'll threaten to tell about the tomatoes if they go to make a fuss." But suppose she should meet them as she goes out? This is now her great trouble. "Who cares?" she says to herself. "I'll tell them I came to borrow some money, and have taken it, and mean to repay it; and if they say a word, they shall hear of the tomatoes all over town. I've got the money and they can't help themselves."

So saying, she flirts a curl-paper out of her hair. Without perceiving the insignificant loss, — for has she not a far more precious bit of paper in her bosom? — she quits the house, locks it after her, puts the key under the door-step, and hurries home — unobserved?

Now, breathless, in her own room she stands; takes off her things, and arranges her hair before the glass; incorporates Mrs. Apjohn's note with the sum which Abel had saved, inventing a score of arguments towards self-justification; hides away the miserable jewels; and then, forgetful of her engagement with Tasso, establishes herself at the window to watch, through the curtains, for Mrs. Apjohn's return.

X.

FAUSTINA'S SUSPENSE.

IT is an anxious hour to Faustina. With all her reiterated assurances to herself that she has done only what necessity compelled her to do, and what she had a perfect right to do after Mrs. Apjohn's example, she feels a deep concern to know whether her visit to the house will be discovered, and, in that case, what will be the issue. For a long time she perceives no signs of life about the Apjohn premises. The grocer's boy comes with a bundle, knocks, and, after waiting a few minutes, deposits it on the door-step. Then Cooper John appears, and Faustina holds her breath. But he passes by, just looking at the bundle on the door-step, and enters his shop, where presently he can be heard hammering the old tune on the hoop, — "Cooper Dan, Cooper Dan, Cooper Dan, Dan, Dan !" — sounds which never fell so heavily on Faustina's heart before.

But soon she has more dreadful things to contemplate. Prudence Apjohn has returned, with her arms full of packages from the store. These she lays beside the larger bundle which has already arrived, and inserts a

8

hand beneath the door-step. Then she unlocks the door, and opens it. Then she loads up her apron with the packages, and enters. Then she shuts the door behind her, and all is ominously still, and Faustina waits for the anticipated explosion. Prudence has had plenty of time to go to the chest and discover the burglary; still there is no movement of alarm. But now it is coming! Faustina feels her cheek blanch as the kitchen-door of the Apjohn cottage flies open, and the portly figure of Prudence appears. But apprehension is useless. No scream is heard; the ponderous arms are not flung upward with despair at the loss of half her treasure; Mrs. Apjohn has a tin teakettle in her hand, which she fills at the well, and goes back with it to the house again.

Faustina's fear is relieved. And now she considers within herself the expediency of going over and telling Mrs. Apjohn what she has done. But her evil genius whispers, " You will never be discovered; keep still!"

Faustina kept still accordingly. She entered the kitchen, and finding some work to do, set herself about it with remarkable industry. Faustina was cheerful. Faustina was demure. She spoke pleasantly to Melissa, and did not scold. She actually tolerated little Ebby, and did not say, as usual, "Oh, go away; you spoil my nice collar; take him, Melissa." And what was most extraordinary, she appeared quite amiable toward the old lady.

"Do you feel pretty well to-day, dear mother?" with a smile of filial solicitude.

"Oh, quite well," smiles back the old lady, "with the exception of the pain in my bootjack," — meaning her rheumatic shoulder.

Abel comes home to supper, and is, at first, pleased with the change in his fair young wife. The cloud has passed from her brow. She greets him with a serene aspect. But she is almost too affectionate, too eager to please. He half-suspects that she means to coax money out of him by putting on these fascinations. There is a nervousness in her manner, an ill-concealed excitement in her looks, and often an incoherence and singular abruptness in her words, which do not seem quite natural. Lively as she would fain appear, her replies are frequently mechanical and absent-minded. So that Abel hardly knows whether he ought to feel gratified, or view her behavior with suspicion.

But she lisps no syllable of a wish for money. He therefore concludes that what he said to her at noon has produced a salutary effect. She evidently regrets her late extravagance and unreasonableness; means to be a better wife to him than she has been; and is now trying hard to appear contented with her lot. Regarding in this light the part she is playing, he can well forgive her for overdoing it. And once more he hopes — as he has so often vainly hoped before — that happier days are at hand. Alas, Abel !

Faustina cannot help starting and losing her color, when she hears any noise without. Visions of the affrighted cooper, of Prudence, furious at the loss of her money, rise before her at every slight sound. Turk, knocking at the door with his wishfully-wagging tail, as he waits to be let in, makes her heart sink. And now footsteps actually approaching take her very breath away.

It is Mr. Hodge, come to have his settlement with Abel. She is glad it is not somebody else. Yet his presence disturbs her; for now the money is to be counted, and change hands, and she dreads she knows not what. Her hand shakes so that she puts the candle out when she goes to snuff it. She lights it with a match, and then blows the candle out instead of the match, which burns her fingers. Fortunately, Mr. Hodge and Abel are talking and do not observe her.

The settlement takes place in the sitting-room. There she leaves the candle with Abel and the visitor, and pretends to return to the kitchen, but finds some excuse to linger at the door and listen.

"Well," exclaimed Abel, looking over his money, " I didn't know I had a bill on the Manville Bank! I had a fifty-dollar bill — but — it's curious ! I should think I'd have noticed it."

" One bill is as good as another, if the banks are good and the bills genuine," carelessly observes the merchant.

"Yes; but I don't see how I could have that bill in my possession, and not know it," says the puzzled Abel, while Faustina's heart throbs suffocatingly.

" If you handled as much money as I do," replies Hodge, " you couldn't always think of keeping the run of it." And the conversation turns upon other matters. Faustina is faint.

Hodge soon after took his departure, which now proved as serious a cause of disturbance to Faustina as his coming had been; for he carried away with him the irrevocable bank-note, to which his attention had been drawn in such a manner that he could not fail to re-member and trace it back to Abel, in case any trouble came of it in future. She had fondly imagined that, as soon as the money was out of her husband's hands, her mind would be at rest. But there is no rest for the guilty conscience. Half the night she lay tormenting herself with fears of detection; while Abel, for the first time in weeks, slept tranquilly at her side. Then she also slept, and dreamed that Mrs. Apjohn's apron was a huge bank-bill, and that it contained, in place of toma-toes, several red and bleeding hearts, one of which was hers and one Abel's. She thought that she and Tasso were waiting for Mrs. Apjohn to fall asleep, in order that they might unlock the lid of the apron, and steal her heart out of it, which they had just succeeded in doing, and were running away with it, when she — Faustina, not Mrs. Apjohn — awoke.

There was a loud knocking below; Abel was bestir-ring himself; and presently Melissa screamed at their chamber-door, —

"Mr. Dane! Mr. Dane! here's Mr. Apjohn wants to see you!"

"Well, well; I'm coming," answered Abel. "What

8*

can the cooper want, making such a racket this time of day ? "

It was just daylight. Abel, half-dressed, hastened to the door, where the cooper met him, with a face as white as chalk and eyes starting from his head.

" Good-morning, Mr. Apjohn," said Abel. " What's the news this morning ? "

" I'm a ruined man ! " said the cooper, with grief, despair, and bitter reproach in his tones; " and it's you that has ruined me."

XI.

TASSO'S REVENGE.

WHILST Abel is drawing the poor man into the house and getting from him his story, and whilst Faustina, having overheard the alarming outburst at the door, is quaking with consternation, and trying in vain to harden her heart with indifference and stubbornness, it is necessary to go back a few hours in our narrative, and relate how John Apjohn came to be knocking at Abel Dane's kitchen in the gray morning.

Prudence, on her way home from the village with her purchases the previous afternoon, had encountered Tasso Smith, walking up and down by the meeting-house green. Tasso was waiting for Faustina, and impatient at her failure to keep the engagement. He had some more of his friend's jewelry to show her, in case she had succeeded in borrowing more than fifty dollars of Mrs. Apjohn. At length he had a glimpse of a female figure approaching by the young elms up the street. That was not the direction from which he expected Faustina; but he concluded that she had gone around the square, and come that way to the rendezvous, in order to avoid the appearance of going directly to meet him. He turned and walked back slowly, that she might overtake him; when with mutual surprise they would recognize each other, and walk on together. He had his face made up to the premeditated expression; he lifted his hand to his hat as the footsteps came beside him, and, turning with his genteelest bow and most ravishing smile, saluted — Mrs. Apjohn !

Did you ever, when a child, throw a chip at some proud cock of the walk, just as he was stretching up his neck and beginning to crow ? The jubilant, shrill-swelling note breaks off in the middle, and dies in a miserable choking croak; the loftily curving neck and haughty crimson crest are suddenly abashed; down sink the flapping wings; and chanticleer, dodging the chip, hops from the fence to the ground, humiliated at being put thus to confusion in sight of the admiring pullets and envious young cockerels, before whom he is desirous of showing off.

Such a bird was Tasso; and such a chip the look Prudence Apjohn gave him. It was too ridiculous; it was exasperating: instead of the anticipated smile from Faustina, a sarcastic sneer from that hateful woman ! Instead of the beautiful countenance, that great, round russet face ! Instead of the superb form, about which there was such a grace and style, an immense, waddling female shape, with adipose folds rolling over the tight-drawn apron-string. And he had got up all that elaborate flourish, put on his sweetest expression, and actually touched his hat, to that disgusting creature ! The smile petrified on his lips.　His waving bow broke, withered, bore no fruit.

"'Scuse me !" he muttered.　"Thought 'twas some-b'dy else."

"No doubt you did think it was somebody else !" answered Prudence.　"You wouldn't have took sech pains to bend your back and look sweet to *me*, *I* know ! You han't liked me a bit sence that affair of changin' the hunderd-dollar bill which you never had,— come, now, ain't that the reason ?　You used to come to my house, often enough, and beg a doughnut, or a piece of gingerbread, when you was a little boy.　You remem-ber, don't ye ?　You used to sing them days.　Don't ye remember how you used to sing ?　You'd come in when we was to supper; I can see you now in that ragged little roundabout you wore, all grease and dirt; hair wasn't quite so slick as 'tis now, for if it see a brush or a comb once a month them days, 'twas a wonder; and you'd commence and walk round the table, and sing that little song of your'n, —

> ' I wish I had somethin' to eat,
> I wish I had somethin' to eat.' —

Remember it, don't ye ? "

Tasso remembered it only too well ; and he could have throttled Mrs. Apjohn for remembering it too.

"Many's the doughnut you've had to my house, and welcome," she resumed.　" I never'd refuse even a beg-gar 't I never see before, — much less a neighbor's boy

that never seemed to have enough to eat to hum. I don't
say this 'cause I've anything laid up ag'inst ye; only to
remind you 't I've always been your friend, and never
give you no reason, as I know on, to act so insolent
towards me as you do lately. You think you're a gentleman, Tasso Smith; but you ought to know that
wearin' Sunday-clo'es every day, and them mustawshy
things on your upper lip, and that great, danglin' watch-
chain, and struttin' up and down when you should be
helpin' your pa git a livin', and sayin' to a woman like
me, after bowin' to her by mistake, *Oh, you thought
'twas somebody else !* — so insultin' ! — this kind o' conduct don't make a gentleman, and you ought to know
it. If you was re'ly a gentleman now, you'd offer to
carry some of these bundles, seein' you're goin' the
same way I am."

"Much obliged to you," said Tasso; "I turn off
here." And he took a by-street, returning to the meeting-house, while Prudence trudged along home.

Stung to fury, — burning for revenge, — he parted
from her with a white smile. A generous soul would
either have forgiven her on the spot or have answered
her on the spot. But his was one of your grovelling and
cowardly natures. He preferred a secret and safe revenge, to an open one that might expose him to danger.
Besides, he saw an advantage in postponing his resentment on this occasion. He felt that he held in his hand
a weapon that would have annihilated the strong, plain-
speaking woman. As David slew the Philistine with a

pebble, so he could have brought Prudence low with a tomato. He longed to suggest that she was hardly a fit person to give lessons in good behavior, who furtively filled her apron in her neighbor's garden. But that would take the wind out of Faustina's sails, he reflected; for what would her threats of exposure avail with Prudence, if the latter knew that her fault was already published? "After Faustina has got the money, then!"— and he walked back towards the church, pondering an ingenious revenge;

Home went the unsuspecting Prudence in the mean time, unlocked the house, took off her things, and put on the tea-kettle. She had cheated John and herself out of a dinner that day; and she was going to have supper early. The cooper, cold and starved as usual, came in just as she was blowing ashes and smoke into her face and eyes, trying to kindle a smouldering brand and save a match.

"Now, what do *you* want, I'd like to know?" she cried, naturally cross under the circumstances. "Supper'll git along jest as fast without you, and a little faster." (Blow, blow.) "Musn't bother me now." (Blow, blow, blow.) "Hateful smoke! And I've got my mouth full of ashes. I do declare! why can't the pleggy thing kindle?"

"Shan't I blow?" said the meek cooper.

"You! ther's no more breath in you than there is in my shoe! I wish you'd stay in the shop. How I do hate to have a man nosin' around!"

"To be sure! to be sure!" answered John, more melancholy and submissive than ever since the affair of the tomatoes. "I haven't got a right to come into my own house, I suppose. But I was gitt'n' hungry. Haven't had anything but a crust to eat sence mornin'. But never mind." And he turned up his eyes with a resigned expression.

"Guess you won't starve; it's only a quarter-past two." Blow, blow, — smoke, ashes, blow.

"Prudy!" remonstrated John, in a feeble, dejected way, "it was two o'clock before I come home; and that was an hour ago."

"Jest look at the clock there. If you won't believe your ears, maybe you will your eyes."

"To be sure, to be sure!" said the cooper, in mild astonishment. "But, Prudy! Prudy! that clock has stopped!"

True enough; when Faustina replaced the key of the chest, she had touched the pendulum unwittingly, and the pointers remained fixed at the minute when the larceny was consummated.

"Massy sakes! so it has! and it may have been stopped an hour, fur's I know. You didn't wind it up last night; jest like your carelessness, John Apjohn!"

But John demonstrated to her, by the position of the weights, that the clock had not run down. And he seemed to consider the mysterious circumstance as the forerunner of some dire chance.

"It never done sich a thing afore, Prudy; it never done sich a thing afore."

" Wal ! " — contemptuously — " I wouldn't be so scart by a little trifle like the stoppin' of a clock ! Here's the chist-key all right. And now, while I'm puttin' away my things, and the fire's kindlin', you run over to Abel's and see what time it is."

The cooper only groaned and shook his head. Not even his wife's energetic wishes could induce him to face one of the Dane family, after his last humiliating errand to their garden.

" Wal, now, I wouldn't be so sheepish ! I ain't goin' to let that thing trouble me. I'll hold up my head, while I've got one; and let folks put upon me, if they da's't ! I give that Tasso Smith a piece of my mind, as I was comin' home. He mustn't think he's goin' to have over his impudence to me, and not git as good as he gives. I say for't, John Apjohn ! " opening the chest, to lay her shawl into it, " you shan't come to this chist at all if you've always got to tumble it up so, — now jest look here ! You shall keep your shirts in the ketchall, and never come near my things, if you can't be a little more careful."

In vain the cooper protested that he had not opened the chest. Who had, if he hadn't, she desired to know.

" To be sure ! " he answered, helplessly, the evidence being against him. " I must have done it in my sleep, though."

" I say, in your sleep ! You're never more'n half awake. You han't touched the money, have you ? I ain't goin' to have that touched, till we buy two more

9

railroad shares with it and what Mr. Parker will be payin' us now in a few days. I run in debt for the things
I got to-day, for fear we might fall short, and I'm very
anxious to have the shares, and put the money out of
our hands, and have it bringin' in somethin'."

Then, having unlocked the till, to see that the pocket-
book was there, she locked it again, and returned to the
kitchen. The smoke had by this time got out of her
eyes; the tea-kettle was simmering, and her heart, too,
began to simmer cheerfully. She told John about her
purchases, whilst she was setting the table; the pork
was soon fried and the potatoes warmed up; and they
sat down to supper. They had no tomatoes that
night. Indeed, John had lost his appetite for tomatoes, and Prudence herself was not very fond of them
lately.

The cooper felt lost without the time. He was afraid
they might not go to bed at just eight o'clock, and seemed
to think something dreadful would happen if they failed
in that important particular. And then, how would
they ever know when to get up in the morning? These
doubts so harassed the poor man's mind, that he lay
awake half of the night, and heard robbers around the
house, and was out of bed at four o'clock, with a candle
in his hand, looking for daylight and burglars.

"I guess if there'd been anybody around I should
have heard 'em as soon as you would," said Prudence.
"I don't care half so much about the thieves as I do
about the taller you're burnin' out with your narvous-

ness. Come, either dress ye or come back to bed agin.
I don't think it's much after midnight, anyway."

But John is so sure of the noises he has heard during
the night, that he cannot be easy till he has opened the
door and looked out. It is a still, cold morning. The
earth is hushed and dark; the east is scarcely yet tinged
with the dawn ; overhead the constellations glitter.
Hesperus stands with golden candle in the dim doorway
of the world, and looks down upon John Apjohn standing with tallow dip in the doorway of his humble
kitchen. In the northern sky, Cassiopeia and the Bear
are having their eternal see-saw, balanced on the Pole.
The cooper beholds and wonders, for the vastness and
silence and majesty of the night have a meaning for the
soul of this man also.

Forgetful of the burglars, heedless of the flaring and
dripping candle, he stands in his shirt and trousers,
agaze at the heavens. An astounding circumstance re-
calls him to himself. Something is dangling at the
door. He feels to ascertain what it is, — advances the
candle, — utters one stifled cry of dismay, and retreats
into the house, horrified.

"John Apjohn ! what is the matter ? " demands Prudence, rushing to his side in her night-clothes.

He cannot speak, but he points; he helplessly holds
the candle, to call her attention to an object which he
has partially dragged into the house, and let fall across
the threshold.

"Sakes alive ! what is it ? Where did you find it ?

Vines! What under the sun? Tomatuses!" **And** the terrible significance of the symbol burst upon her, too.

Tasso was revenged.

"To be sure! to be sure! to be sure!" were the only words the miserable cooper could utter, as he stared at the portent.

But Prudence, more resolute, pulled the vines from the outer door-handle to which they were attached, and finding a piece of paper pinned to them, took it off, and held it to the light. It bore the following inscription:

"*For Mrs. Apjohn's apern.*"

She spelled it out, aloud, as she deciphered it. If Cooper John had any strength remaining up to this time, it was now taken from him, and he sat down shivering on the cold stove. Mrs. Apjohn also succumbed to the chirographical thunder-bolt, and went down upon the wood-box, with all her burden of flesh. The light she placed on a chair; the trail of vegetables variegated the floor; in her hand she still held the missive. And there the twain sat, in a long and very awful silence, — a scene for a Dutch painter.

"Wal!" said Prudence, as soon as she could regain her powers of respiration and utterance, "I hope that's mean enough, anyway! That's Abel Dane's work, John!"

"Oh, no! no! Abel Dane wouldn't do sich a thing as that," moaned the cooper.

"So much the wus, then! If he didn't do it, he has

told somebody; and didn't he promise never to tell ?
And which is the wust for us, I'd like to know, — to have
him insult us in this way, or tell all over town, and send
somebody else to do it ? "

" To be sure ! to be sure ! " The stricken man took
the paper from her hand, and held it to the light to study
it. "*A, p, e, r, n, apern !* It is somebody that knows
how to spell, Prudy; it's somebody that knows how to
spell ! " And he turned to his wife with the air of one
who has made an appalling discovery.

Like most ignorant men who have a large element of
wonder in their nature, he stood greatly in awe of learn-
ing; and he naturally thought that if the vicious joke had
been perpetrated by some blockhead, whose orthographi-
cal attainments were not equal to the spelling of *apern*,
it would not be so bad.

"It's Abel Dane, or he's to the bottom on't, take my
word ! " said Prudence, with mingled chagrin and ex-
asperation. "Oh, the smooth-spoken, desaitful wretch !
He never'd have da's't to do it if I'd had a man for a
husband ! Oh, it's too mean ! too mean ! " and the
worthy woman burst into tears of anger and shame.

Suddenly the cooper started to his feet.

" I'll know the truth of it, Prudy ! I'll see Abel, and
know the truth. If it's all over town, we may as well
go and jump into the well fust as last; for what'll be
the use of tryin' to live where everybody'll be pintin'
at us and hootin' ? "

" I'll live to be even with Abel Dane ! " vowed Pru-

dence. " I shan't think of dyin' till I've come up with
him ! Oh-h ! you'll see ! " (through her teeth). " If
he hadn't been so 'ily-tongued and ready to promise, I
wouldn't mind. Goin' right over now ? That's right.
Show your spunk for once, John. But put on your hat,
— put on your hat, and your jacket, too."

" To be sure, to be sure ! " murmured John, confusedly turning round and round, till at last he got hold
of the table-cloth instead of his jacket, and was on the
point of donning the skillet in place of his hat.

" Don't you know what you're about ? " said Prudence, putting her hand on her knee and helping herself
to get upon her feet, which ponderous operation was
performed with considerable more alacrity than usual.
" Here's your hat." She clapped it on his head. Then she
opened his jacket for him to get into. " Here, stick out
your arms ! " And, having thus equipped him as if he
were a knight of old and these coverings his armor and
coat-of-mail, she sent him to meet the foe. " Look out
for that pesky dog ! " she counselled him as he sallied
forth.

The earth, that slept under the night's dark blanket
and spangled coverlet, was now throwing them off and
putting on her glorious morning-gown. Dim in its
socket flickered the candle of the watcher Hesperus, his
feet on a threshold of silver. Immortal youth and
freshness breathed in the atmosphere like a finer air.
Music awoke with beauty, the birds twittered, and the
cock blew his bugle in the misty tent of dawn. But

what was the joy of sight and sound and honeyed taste
of life to Cooper John Apjohn, rushing to his neighbor's
on such desperate business ? What to Faustina, peeping
wildly from the window, were the crimson sleeves and
refulgent, rosy scarf of mother earth at her dewy toilet ?
Alas, for mortal man ! Daily the harmonious doors of
the museum and picture-gallery of God open to invite
us; nor is wanting the mystic key by night, which unlocks them again to the wise; and there, in celestial
livery, with star-torches, attendants wait to guide us
among the white and awful forms of contemplation, as
the pope's servitors show, by the light of flambeaus,
the statuary of the Vatican. But we are hurrying to
market or to mill, chasing pleasure, or pursued by fear,
absorbed in calculations of profit and loss, or preoccupied by shame and heart-ache, — the hat of vulgar habit
slouched over the eyes, — so that glimpses of the shining
vestibule and perfect pageant do not reach and win the
soul.

XII.

THE GUILTY CONSCIENCE.

AFTER the cooper entered, Faustina drew back from her window, and waited, scared and palpitating, for the expected catastrophe. It did not come. The sitting-room door closed upon the voices of Cooper John and her husband; and now all was still. Her guilty and impatient spirit tormented itself with conjectures; and she stood with brows knitted and lips apart, wringing her thoughts for some drop of certainty regarding the object of their neighbor's early visit, when Melissa ran to the door and rapped.

" Mrs. Dane, you're wanted ! "

The summons went to the wretched woman's heart. So the hour had arrived, and she was to be arraigned and accused.

" Melissa ! " she whispered, " come in ! — What is it ? "

" That's more'n I know, ma'am. But Mr. Apjohn 's in a terrible way; and it seems it's something you've done."

" I ? What ? What have I done ? " And poor Faustina catches hold of the girl's arm, as if she meant to hold her till she hears the truth. "What have I done, Melissa?"

"That you know best, ma'am. Mr. Dane says come quick. Shall I help you?" offering to assist in dressing her mistress.

"I don't know — O Melissa! — if I dared to tell you! How do they know it was me?"

"You went into Mr. Apjohn's house yesterday, when they wa'n't to home, and mabby that's it," suggested Melissa, thinking to throw a little light on the subject.

"I did? — How dare you say I did, you wicked girl!" shaking her.

"Why, I seen ye!" says the innocent and amazed Melissa. "But I didn't think there was any harm in it."

"Did you tell any one? Did anybody else see? Tell me the truth, Melissa!"

"No! not as I know on. I hain't mentioned it."

"Don't you, then! not for your life. I'll give you that watered silk — I'll get Abel to raise your wages — you shall have those satin shoes you like so. O Melissa! I'll be the best friend you ever had, if you'll stand by me."

"Why, ma'am!" — the girl opened her honest eyes betwixt delight and incredulity at these extravagant promises, — "I'll stand by ye, and be thankful; but what dreadful thing is't you've been and done?"

"Melissa!" said the unhappy woman, eager to gain the sympathy and counsel of some one, no matter if it was only her servant, "promise me never to lisp the secret so long as you live !"

Melissa, who had suffered enough from the capricious pride and temper of her mistress, was glad of an opportunity to establish more confidential and friendly relations between them. To promise. secrecy is easy; and she promised.

"Swear it !" said Faustina, like the heroine of a melodrama. "Put your hand on this Bible, and swear ! Say, I swear a solemn oath "—

"I swear a solemn oath !" repeated the staring Melissa.

"Never to breathe to any mortal soul " —

"Never to breathe to any mortal soul "—

"What I am going to tell you."

"What I am going to tell you."

"Now kiss the book."

Melissa smacked the leather. Then Faustina poured forth her story.

"But I didn't steal the money; I meant it for borrowing, true as I live, Melissa. But won't it seem like stealing? And now they have found it out, — oh, what shall I do ? What would *you* do, Melissa?"

"La, ma'am!" said Melissa, with unaffected concern, "I don't know ! Seems to me I should go and tell 'em I only borrowed it, and meant to pay it back."

"It's too late !" Faustina shook her head and compressed her lips. "I shouldn't care for the Apjohns, if 'twasn't for my husband. What *will* he say ? Melissa,

I shall deny it. And you must bear me out in it. Oh, dear! there's Abel calling, and I must go. Am I very pale?" And she turned to the glass, and put her knuckle into her fair cheek, which whitened under the pressure.

"No, you look red," said Melissa.

"Do I? I mustn't appear agitated. I won't! There!" with sudden resolution, putting on a haughty and brazen air, "I am not going to be afraid.— Remember, Melissa, — the watered silk and the shoes!"

Little Ebby had been crying unheeded for the last five minutes. Melissa remained to take care of him, while Faustina, trembling and faint-hearted in spite of her effort to seem unconcerned, went to the dreaded interview.

The cooper was sitting with his feet upon the chair-round, brooding dejectedly over his knees; and Abel was endeavoring to soothe and reassure him, when she entered.

"Here she is," said Abel. John lifted his colorless and woe-begone countenance. "Faustina, neighbor Apjohn brings a serious charge against us; and I want you to clear yourself from it, if you are innocent."

He spoke earnestly. He was convinced of her guilt, she thought. She did not answer, but looked down as coldly as she could at the cooper, who looked up aggrieved and disconsolate at her.

"I wouldn't have supposed," said John, with an affecting quaver in his voice, "that a lady like you could do sich a thing. Have I ever done you any harm?"

"No, Mr. Apjohn," replied Faustina. "Who said you had? And what have I done to you?"

"Done! What *have* you done! To be sure! to be sure! O Mrs. Dane, I hope you may never suffer as you have made me. To be robbed of the hard earnings of years, — that would be nothing, but" —

"Robbed!" interrupted Faustina, feigning surprise, "who has robbed you, Mr. Apjohn?"

"Who has, if you have not? And sich a robbery! Not gold or silver!" sobbed the poor man, thinking of his good name gone forever.

"Gold? silver?" cried Faustina. "I haven't touched your gold and silver. Not a dollar of it. Who says I have?"

"It isn't gold or silver I've lost," said John, moaning, as he brooded over his knees. "Gold and silver, — no! no!" And he shook his sorrowful head.

"I haven't touched your paper-money, either!" cried Faustina, assuming an indignant air. "How should I know you had any? You might keep thousands of dollars in your house, and I never should know it; and I never should care. But you mustn't come here accusing me of breaking into your house, and stealing the money you have been hoarding up, while you have passed for poor people with your neighbors. No, John Apjohn! And I shouldn't think it was for *you* to charge *others* with stealing, any way. If you live in glass houses, you mustn't throw stones. I warn you, Mr. Apjohn!"

This vehement speech produced a strange effect upon

her audience. The cooper raised himself gradually upon his elbows, then sat bolt upright in his chair, regarding her with vague and helpless wonder. Abel fixed upon her an expression of severe disapprobation, believing that this vociferous denial of an offence with which she had not been charged, was only a feint to parry the real point at issue.

"These are useless words, Faustina," he said. "What do they mean?"

"Useless words!" she echoed; "what do they mean!" Flushed with passion, and chafing violently, she turned upon him. "You, Abel Dane! my husband! you! would have me stand here and listen tamely to an insult from this man! I, guilty of purloining money from his till! And you credit it! Oh, it is too much!" And she swept across the room, flirting out her folded handkerchief, and stanching with it imaginary tears.

"Faustina!" cried Abel, amazed, and utterly at a loss to comprehend her conduct, "hear me a moment. I said they were useless words, because you have misunderstood the poor man."

"To be sure! to be sure!" broke in the cooper, sympathizing with her passion and distress, "I never thought of laying such a thing to you, Mrs. Dane."

"Oh, didn't you?" she retorted, with bitter scorn. "I wonder what you call it then. You'd better take it back! If you've been robbed, I'm sorry for it. You shouldn't keep so much money locked up in your chest, if you don't want to invite burglars. They broke in last

10

night, I suppose. You must have slept soundly ! I'm
sorry for you," she went on, so rapidly that neither Abel
nor the bewildered cooper could put in a word; "but
you must take care how you accuse innocent people.
When you talk of robbing neighbors, look at home.
What if I should accuse ? What if I should tell about
the tomatoes ? Take care, then ! "

"Now you touch upon the subject," said Abel.
" Haven't you already told about that unfortunate
affair ? "

"I ? No ! " replied Faustina, surprised.

" You have not mentioned or hinted it to any one ? "

"No ! truly ! " A positive denial; though she had
not quite forgotten her confidences with Tasso. But
this was only a white lie, she thought, and necessary to
cover the black one. For, in order to hold the Apjohns
in awe of her power, they must believe that she had not
yet made the exposure which, of course, she would
make, if the charge of robbing them was persisted in.

"There, Mr. Apjohn," said Abel, "I told you she
would clear herself. We have not betrayed you. And
you may be assured that neither of us would stoop to
the pitiful device of insulting you in the way you complain of."

The cooper only groaned, and got down over his knees
again, in an attitude of the deepest despondency.

"So much the wus, then ! as Prudy said. Our disgrace is known; but to who ? and how many ? That's
the misery on't ! " And he buried his face.

Faustina, sobered by surprise, and unable to comprehend the cooper's mysterious trouble, asked an explanation.

"Why," said Abel, "some wretched scamp went last night, — in the night, wasn't it?" he asked, to divert John Apjohn from his gloom.

"Yes; I heerd 'em around the house," said the cooper, to the relief of Faustina, who was afraid he would say, "No, it was in the afternoon, when we were gone from home."

"Went and hung some tomato vines on his outside-door, labelled, '*For Mrs. Apjohn's apern.*' And he thought I had done it," continued Abel. "And when I assured him I had not only not done it, but had not told anybody but you of the little mistake his wife made in getting the wrong side of the fence, the good man thought you must have told somebody else, or have gone yourself and left the tomato vines."

"I? I never dreamed of such a thing! But is that — is that — all?" Faustina eagerly asked.

"All? Ain't it enough?" said the cooper, between his knees.

"Why, I thought — dear me! — indeed!" Faustina fluttered, and grew wonderfully smiling and affable — "you haven't been robbed, then?" I'm so glad of that! How could I have misunderstood?" Her smiles became sicklied o'er with the pale cast of thought. What folly had she given utterance to, betraying her guilt, perhaps, in her very eagerness to deny it! Still she

smiled. " I'm sure, Mr. Apjohn, you don't think I would
go and hang tomatoes on your doors, do you ? "

. "No ! no ! no ! — to be sure ! to be sure ! to be sure !
— well ! well ! well ! " He rose to go, looking about
him like one whose wits are slightly damaged. " Did I
have a hat ? I think I had a hat ! Thank ye, Abel. A
fine morning, a very fine morning, Mrs. Dane," he said,
in accents which foreboded that there were no more fine
mornings for him in all this weary world.

He bowed with feeble politeness, and, after trying to
get into the closet, found his way, with Abel's assistance,
to the outer door. Faustina followed, with the same
forced smiles, and strangely shining eyes.

" Good morning," she said lightly. " A pleasant day
to you, Mr. Apjohn."

" You'll excuse me for troubling you," said the cooper,
from out the dust of his humiliation. " I — I wish you
well. You're both young. There's happiness for you;
but none for me ! none for me ! " and he pulled his rue-
ful hat over his eyes.

" Come, come, man ! " cried Abel, encouragingly;
" don't take it too much to heart. Cheer up, cheer up.
If the matter has got out, never mind ; it will soon
be forgotten; you'll live it down, honest man as you
are. I wouldn't mind the mean insult of a spy and
coward, who plays his tricks in the dark, and dares not
show his face by daylight."

" Ah, yes ! you're right, Abel, you're right, and very
kind. To be sure, to be sure. I hope the old lady is

well this morning ! I hope she is very comfortable. I
hope — yes, sincerely — I " —

He faltered, like one who forgets what he is saying,
stood aimlessly pondering a moment, then, suddenly
catching his breath, as it were with a stitch in the side
of his memory, he blindly waved his hand, and, without
looking up, jogged heavily homewards.

10 *

XIII.

THE SAD CASE OF THE COOPER.

PRUDENCE had all this while been waiting anxiously
for her good-man's return ; wishing a hundred times,
in her impatience, that she had gone herself and settled
the affair with Abel.   The hour of John's absence was
perhaps the longest in that worthy woman's life.   The
morning twilight was never so provokingly cool and
slow.   The mists were in no hurry to lift from the hills ;
the sun took his time to rise, just as if nothing had
happened.   " I shall fly ! " she repeatedly informed the
deliberate universe, as she looked over towards her
neighbor's, and the sluggish wheel of time brought no
sign of the cooper's coming.

The wings were not yet grown, however, with which
that massy female was to perform the threatened aërial
excursion. . She was by no means a volatile animal.   The
consequence was, that when at last John's doleful phys-
iognomy appeared coming through the gate (the very
posts of which looked solemn, in sympathy with him,
and seemed to squint pathetically at each other, from
under their wooden caps, as he passed), the solid housewife still gravitated as near the planet as any unfledged
biped on its surface.

"O John Apjohn!" said she, reproachfully, "I've wanted to git hold of you! What was you gone so long for?"

"To be sure, to be sure!" said meek John, "I might as well have not gone at all. No use, no use, Prudy." And he sat down as if he didn't expect ever to get up again.

"O you dish-rag!" ejaculated Mrs. Apjohn. "There's no more sperit or stiffenin' in you than there is in my apron-string!"

"Don't speak of aprons! don't speak of aprons!" implored the cooper; the subject being so painfully associated with that of tomatoes, that he did not think he could ever see an apron again without qualms.

"Well!"—sharply—"what did you find out? You let Abel soft-soap you to death, I know by your looks!"

"Prudy," answered the cooper, lifting his earnest, melancholy eyes, "Abel Dane's an innocent man. So is his wife. 'Twasn't neither of them that hung them things on our door, and they haven't told nobody. I've their word for 't."

"That for their word!" Prudence snapped her fingers scornfully. "Don't tell me! don't tell me, John Apjohn! They may make you believe that absurd story, but *I* know better. Jest look here!"

She displayed before his eyes an old letter-envelope which had been rolled up, pipe-stem fashion, and which, when unrolled, showed an obstinate tendency to fly together again,—very much after the manner of one of Faustina's curl-papers.

" What is it ? where did you get it ? " John asked, with feeble interest.

" Don't you see what it is ? It's one of the kivers, — what ye call 'ems, — of Abel Dane's letters. Here's his name on't, — don't ye see ? And where do you s'pose I got it ? On this very floor, — see ! " exclaimed Prudence, " when I went to sweep up after them nasty tomatuses."

" Abel Dane ! " pronounced the cooper, with difficulty holding the scroll open with his unsteady fingers, whilst he spelled out the name. "To be sure, Prudy; to be sure ! On the floor ? How come it on the floor ? I don't understand. I don't understand."

" No, you never understand ! " said bitter Prudence. " You can't see through a grin'stun without somebody stands by and shows you the hole. It's jest as plain as day to me now that Abel Dane come here last night and stuck them tomatuses on our door, — jest as plain as if I'd seen him do it. He had his label ready to put on to 'em, but in takin' it out of his pocket, he dropped this. Then when you dragged the vines into the house, you swep' it along in with 'em. Who else should have one of his letters ? Answer me that, John Apjohn ! "

" Wal, wal ! " said the cooper, convinced by this overwhelming circumstantial evidence, " it must be as you say, Prudy. But I wouldn't have thought he'd have done it; I wouldn't have thought he'd have done it ! "

" I swep' the house only ye's'd'y mornin', and there's been nobody in't sence but us two, has there ? Tell me that ! "

" No, not as I know on," said John.

" There ! " she exclaimed, arrogantly, as if he had been opposing her theory. " How, then, I'd like to know, did this paper come here ?   If you know any better'n I do, why don't you say ?   If *you* can explain it, why don't you ?   Come, you know so much ! "

" I don't pretend, I don't pretend," murmured John.

" Wal ! " — triumphantly — " I guess you'll give it up, then, that I'm right for once.   Takes me, after all; as you'll learn after I'm dead and gone, if you don't before, and I never expect you will; but you'll think of me, and miss my advice and judgment in matters when I'm laid in my grave; and I guess you'll wish then you'd heerd to me more, and thought more of my opinions; but I hope your conscience won't trouble you on that account, Mister Apjohn ! "

" Don't, don't, Prudy ! " entreated the cooper, holding his leg on his knee, and bending over it, and rocking it plaintively.   " I can't bear it ! "

For the frail mortal saw nothing absurd in the hypothesis of surviving his robust spouse; and he didn't know but he might feel remorse for his supposed cruel treatment of her.

" I shan't be always spared to you, Mister Apjohn ! " — The *Mister* was peculiarly cutting. — " I hope you don't wish me out of the way before my time comes; though I sometimes half think you do," she continued, giving vent to her feelings in a strain to which she commonly had recourse, when very much in fault, or very much perplexed and depressed. "It's nat'ral, I know; and I don't say I blame you. A woman can't expect to git credit for her vartews now-days; but if she happens for once to be a little unfort'nate in her ca'c'lations, oh, it's a dreadful thing ! and it's laid up ag'inst her as long as she lives." Prudence sighed and snuffed.

"Prudy," said John, "I hain't laid up nothing agin ye; nor I don't blame ye for nothin', nuther;" which powerful array of negatives, seconded by a strong sympathetic snuffling on the part of the cooper, afforded her the solace she sought for her wounded self-respect.

"Wal ! " she exclaimed, wiping her eyes with the corner of her apron, " as I said afore, I ain't a goin' to die till I'm even with Abel Dane, if I have to live to be as old as Methusalem. Come, don't set mopin' there over your knees ! I'm a goin' to have breakfast; and I shan't let this thing spile my appetite, nuther ! "

Prudence was herself again. But John could not so easily extricate himself from the slough of despond; and she felt that she ought to do something to encourage him.

" Come, John," said she, at table, " drink your tea, and eat your flapjacks, and be a man ! Don't let it worry you a mite. We've got our house and home left, and a little property to make us comf'table and respected in our old age, and about money enough a'ready to buy two more shares; and I'll tell ye what, John Apjohn, — don't le's lot on doin' much work to-day. We're gittin' forehanded, so's't we can begin to think of a holiday once in a while. And I've an idee of what we'll do. Soon's I git the dishes cleared away, we'll count over the money and see jest how much there is, though I s'pose I know perty near ; then we'll go and see about gittin' that money of Mr. Parker, and buyin' two more shares. And jest think, John ! that will give us sixteen dollars more dividends every year, which'll be a comfort to think of dull days, now, won't it ! "

John failed to be much enlivened by his wife's schemes. He had not the heart to show himself to the eyes of the world that day; and, sorrowfully shaking his head, he answered, as she urged the subject of going out, —

" No, Prudy, no; you may go and enjoy yourself, but I shall stay to hum."

Accordingly Prudence, craving some stimulus to her dashed spirits, set out, about an hour afterwards, unaccompanied, to see Mr. Parker about the money, — her proposal to compute, in the mean time, the contents of the till, not having been carried into effect, in consequence of John's dismal lack of interest.

" What's money now ? " said the poor man to himself, sighing as he saw her depart, and wondering how she could care for such things any more. " O Prudy, Prudy ! I'd give all we've got in this world if we could hold up our heads as respectable as we did a week ago ! But now ! " —

He was going mechanically to feed the pigs; but at the door his eye fell upon a coil of green vines in a basket, where Prudence had thrown them, and some red tomatoes floating on the swill; and he was so overcome by the sight, that the swine were left to squeal in vain for their breakfast the rest of the morning.

Back into the kitchen crept the cooper, and shut himself up. There was no one to observe him now; and he gave vent to his woe, uttering a groan at every breath, tearing out imaginary handfuls of hair, and scouring with imaginary ashes that smooth, naked scalp of his, until it shone. Then for a long time all was still in that doleful kitchen; and he might have been seen sitting, in a reversed position, astride, upon one of the splint-bottomed chairs, his arms folded upon the back of it, and his head bolstered upon his arms, — a little doubled-up human figure, motionless as an effigy.

John was having a vision, — not of the heavenly kind. He saw innumerable doors festooned with tomato-vines. He saw his neighbors, with sarcastic polite faces, nod coldly at him as he passed on the street, and wink significantly at each other behind his back. He saw the children rush out of the school-house to jeer and hoot, whenever he and his wife appeared. He saw the suspicious clerks keep an unusually sharp watch over the goods on the counters, when they entered a store. He observed the sly glances, and the unnatural hush, — indicative of a sensation, — when they walked down the church-aisle on a Sunday morning. He beheld troops of roguish boys flocking to his house by night to fasten the badge of disgrace to his latch; and he heard the scornful laughter. This part of his vision was so vivid, that he, for a moment, actually believed that there were impish, leering faces at the windows, looking in upon him, and insulting hands holding up red tomatoes to taunt him. He started to his feet. The vision vanished; but the intolerable burden of his shame and distress was with him still.

"Oh, I can't live ! I can't live !" he burst forth. "I never can show myself where I'm known again; and what's the use ? "

He thought of the well. He went and looked into it. It was thirty feet deep,—cold, dark, and uninviting. If Prudy had been there, to fortify his resolution by her sympathy and example, he might have jumped in. But, alone, he had not the heart. He concluded that his razor would open the most expeditious and least disagreeable door of exit from this dreary world, and went back into the house. He examined the tonsorial implement, and honed it. But at every stroke his dread of wounds and his horror of blood increased. He would not like to present a ghastly, mangled appearance *afterwards*, and aggravate Prudy's feelings by staining her clean floor. He cast his eyes upwards. There were hooks in the ceiling, supporting a kitchen pole,—one of those old-fashioned domestic institutions devoted to towels, dishcloths, coils of pumpkins, sliced in rings, drying for winter use, and on the ends of which farmers' hats are hung.

John thought of ropes and straps, clothes-line and bed-cord,—none of which promised to be very comfortable to the neck,—and concluded that his red silk hand-

11

kerchief would best answer his purpose. The red silk
was brought out of the bedroom, folded to the requisite
shape, and a solemnly suggestive noose tied in it. This
he slipped over his neck, and drew reasonably close, to
see how it would seem. Then he ascended a chair, and
passed the loose end of the handkerchief over the middle
of the pole, and fastened it, — only to see how it would
seem, you know; for it was his intention to write Prudy
an affectionate letter of farewell before committing himself to the fatal leap.

Or it may be he had as yet formed no inflexible determination to destroy himself, — wiser men than he having
been known to divert their melancholy by playing at
suicide. Perhaps, in a little while, he would have descended from the improvised scaffold, removed the halter,
wiped his eyes with it, and felt better. Let us hope so.
Unfortunately, however, at a critical juncture, a noise,
real or imaginary, startled him. What if his neighbors were coming once more to insult him? He turned
to look; then turned again hastily to disengage his neck,
and get down. It was an old splint-bottomed chair he
was using, and to avoid injuring the half-worn seat, he
stood on the edges of it. In his agitation, he made a
terrible misstep; the chair was overturned, — it flew
from beneath his feet, — and he was launched.

XIV.

MORE AND MORE ENTANGLED.

WELL might Faustina's heart, meanwhile, be filled with stinging regrets and fears, — a restless swarm, — although she knew not yet half the mischief she had done. She wished she had never seen Tasso Smith; she bitterly repented confiding her secret to Melissa. Of her blind and foolish haste to deny her real guilt, when only a minor fault was charged against her, she could not think without anger at her own stupidity and dread for the result. And the jewels, — she loathed them. And the purloined money, — the remorse and terror it gave her grew momently. She was in such a state of suspense and alarm that, when she saw Mrs. Apjohn going to the village that morning, a wild fancy seized her that the robbery was discovered, that Prudence was in pursuit of a magistrate, and that the safest course now would be to overtake her, confess the borrowing, and offer the jewels as a pawn for the repayment of the money.

Accordingly, this creature of impulse once more threw on her bonnet, thrust the jewels into her bag, and hurried forth. Not often had she ventured to show herself in the street in a calico morning-dress; but this time apprehension conquered pride. Her step was swift, and she came in sight of Prudence as she was passing the meeting-house green. Then well would it have been for all, had Faustina promptly carried out her original intention! But, at the critical moment, her courage failed. She shrank from the humiliation of placing herself, by a confession of her trespass, on a level with her neighbor. And the secret hope revived that her fears were after all groundless, and that her guilt might never be known. So she resolved to delay a little, and watch Mrs. Apjohn's movements.

Prudence passed down the main street of the village, and appeared to enter a shoe-store, — Faustina following, vigilant and anxious, at a safe distance. Waiting for her to transact her business and come out, the young wife proceeded more leisurely, and began to think of her unpresentable attire, and to hope that she might not see anybody that she cared for. Vain wish! A young gentleman was sunning himself on the sidewalk. He had a self-satisfied smirk, a complacent, airy strut, a little moustache, and a little rattan. He bowed rather formally to Faustina, and was passing on.

"O Tasso," she cried, stopping him, "you're doing everything you can to destroy my peace!"

"Be I? Wasn't aware." And Tasso, who not only resented her failure to keep her engagement with him the day before, but also foreboded importunities anent the jewels, treated her with provoking coolness.

" Didn't you promise me you never would tell about
Mrs. Apjohn? But I was a fool," said Faustina, "to
expect you to keep a secret I couldn't keep myself!
Though I *did* rely on your promise, Tasso, and never
suspected you of betraying confidence ! "

" Who said I had betrayed confidence? I haven't
betrayed no confidence, madam ! " said Tasso, stiff and
distant. " I said I wouldn't tell, and no more I hain't."

" Then it was you that hung the tomatoes on her door
last night ! "

" Have I promised not to hang tomatoes on anybody's
door ? " retorted Tasso, with an inward chuckle. "And
what if I did, — though I don't say I did, mind, — what's
the harm to you ? "

" Oh, you don't know, Tasso ! " And Faustina did
not dare to inform him, though she longed to.

" I sh'd think you had time enough to borrow the
money, by the way you kept me walking up and down
yesterday, waiting for you, by George ! " And Smith
tapped his patent leather with the aforesaid rattan. " I
walked in sight of the church there fourteen hours
or more. Never was so disappointed in my life, by
George ! " — Switch. — " I keep *my* engagements."

" Forgive me, Tasso. You know what a trouble I
was in. I couldn't come."

" Well, never mind," said Tasso, softening. " Good
joke, though, about the tomatoes ! Hung on Apjohn's
door ? Hi ! hi ! hi ! How'd you learn ? "

" Oh, there's been such a time about it ! Mr. Apjohn

11 *

was at our house before daylight to know if we had done it."

"Hi! hi!" tittered Mr. Smith. "Capital joke, by George! Wish I'd seen him! I'm waiting now to meet the old woman, when she comes out of the lawyer's office; see how she looks; see if she'll be so deuced independent with me to-day. Look here; I've got something to please her!" Tasso unfolded his handkerchief, and displayed a tomato.

Faustina scarcely heeded the malicious insinuation, a word he had previously dropped distracting her thoughts.

"What lawyer's office?" she asked, excitedly gazing. "She went into the shoe-shop, — if you mean Mrs. Apjohn."

"No, she didn't; though't might have looked so to you. She's in Lawyer Parker's office now; over the shoe-shop; entrance next door."

Taking legal counsel! Then all was lost; and all might have been well, Faustina thought, had she but made haste and carried out her first intention, instead of delaying to reconsider and observe. And yet, perhaps, the faint hope kindled within her, it was not too late to retrieve her error. Why not go straight to the lawyer's room, call out Mrs. Apjohn, and stop legal proceedings?

"What's the matter?" said Tasso. "You look scared! Going? What's your hurry? Didn't you git the money of her yist'day?"

"Yes — no — I must see her now. Wait till I come back, Tasso!"

And she hurried away from him; while he, crossing the street with the smiling air of a gentleman of elegant leisure and happy adventures, ensconced himself in an alley where the warm sunshine fell, and where, screened from general observation, he could mellow his tomato and watch the course of events.

Up the lawyer's stairs rushed Faustina; and her hand was on the latch before she had taken an instant to reflect upon what she was doing. There she paused to regain her breath, still her rapid heart-beats, and think over a speech to Prudence. But already the wind of impulse began to fail her, the sails of her spirit to collapse and shake, and the fogs of doubt to loom before her. And such were this woman's feebleness of conscience and fickleness of heart, that she might have changed her purpose once more, and stolen away without lifting the latch, had not the lawyer, hearing a movement, opened the door, and found her standing there confused and irresolute, and invited her in.

" You — are occupied ? " she faltered.

" I shall soon be at leisure," said the cordial old man; " won't you sit down and wait ? "

His broad and genial manners restored Faustina's confidence. He would not be so civil, she was sure, if he had undertaken a case against her. The proposal to sit down and wait seemed to her almost providential; for, so deep is the natural instinct of faith, that even the wrong-doer will often flatter himself that his course is shaped by some divinity. An opportunity to compose herself, frame excuses, look about her, and then proceed warily, was what she most desired. And she went in.

Near the desk sat a farmer. He had the appearance of doing business with Mr. Parker, who went back to him, after placing a seat for Faustina. In a retired corner was a third visitor,—a female, russet-faced and portly, with stoutest arms, and a form whose adipose folds quite buried her close-drawn apron-strings, as she sat compressed into one of the office-chairs.

We recognize our friend, Mrs. Apjohn. She has the look of a client, awaiting her turn. A most fortunate circumstance for young Mrs. Dane, you think; for of course she will take advantage of it, to do her difficult errand, won't she ? Not at all. She nods a good-morning, takes her position as far from Prudence as possible, and pretends to read a newspaper which she picks up; while the other holds aloft her head with an air of indifference, — not at all natural, — and by sneers and frowns and wry faces and contemptuous snuffs, expresses the opinion she has formed, since yesterday, of her fair neighbor.

Faustina, who nervously turns and rustles the newspaper, and runs her eye over it without understanding a word that is in it, understood very well these demonstrations of resentment on the part of Prudence. But she is at a loss to determine the cause of that resentment. Is it the money of yesterday, or the tomatoes of last night ? In either case, she feels that she ought to be more conciliatory in her manner, and prepare the way for explanations.

" How pleasant it is, this morning, Mrs. Apjohn ! "

" Pleasant ! " mutters Prudence, with a scowl, elevating her chin another degree. And with grim satisfaction she perceives that the cut has told.

Poor, proud Faustina ! At another time such insolence would have angered her forever. But this morning she cannot afford to take offence. She must humble herself even at the feet of that miserable, low-bred woman; and, with her heart guiltily sinking, and her throat rebelliously rising, she must smile serenely, and respond sweetly, —

" Rather cool, however; quite a change in the weather since Sunday."

" Change ! " snarls Mrs. Apjohn, regarding this as an insulting allusion to her Sunday-afternoon adventure. And, giving her head a jerk, her frock a flirt, and her chair a hitch, with a parting look of hatred, she turns upon Faustina a shoulder of the very broadest and coldest description. The latter was smitten dumb; not doubting but it was the complete and certain knowledge of her guilt which made Prudence so insufferably rude to her. Then, to increase her confusion, she perceived that the outrage she dared not resent was observed by the farmer, who had risen to go, and by the lawyer, who was advancing to learn the business of his female visitors. And the time had come for her to act, or at least, to offer some pretext for being there; and she had not yet formed a plan, and her wits were a chaos. She was glad that the lawyer addressed himself first to Mrs. Apjohn; though she expected the next minute to hear her crime denounced.

But Prudence was averse to transacting business in the presence of her neighbor. "I am in no petic'lar hurry," she said. "I can wait, while you attend to that other person."

So the bland-faced lawyer turned to the " other person."

"I prefer to take my turn," Faustina managed to say. "Mrs. Apjohn was here first."

"I'll wait for her," said Prudence, obstinately. "Never mind who come first. The first shall be last, and the last shall be first, we are told," with a significant scoff at the handsome and once haughty Faustina.

The lawyer looked bothered, and he once more applied to his younger visitor.

"I — really — cannot come in before her; it wouldn't be fair," Faustina stammered.

"Wal," exclaimed Prudence, sharply, "I hope I ain't so silly as to stand upon ceremony and all that nonsense! My business is ruther private; but if Mis' Dane wants to stay and hear it, I've no petic'lar objection."

"I'll go," — and Faustina made a flutter toward leaving.

"No, you needn't, — you may as well stay. I jest as lives you would. Come to think on't, I'd a leetle druther you would."

For Mrs. Apjohn, who had hitherto, for reasons of her own, kept her financial concerns a secret from her neighbors, determined of a sudden to manifest her independence and command the respect of the worldlings, by letting her wealth be known. She drew near the desk.

"I have come, Mr. Parker, to see about that fifty dollars."

It needed not the surly, exultant glance she flung at Faustina to carry consternation to that trembling woman's soul. It was time to speak. She began,—

"As for that fifty dollars, Mrs. Apjohn, you can have it almost any time. I suppose,"—

She hesitated, quite out of breath.

"I can,—can I?" said the astonished Prudence, while the lawyer lifted his mild eyes with a puzzled expression.

"Yes—I—I have just a word to say."

"You have,—have you? I should like to know!"

Faustina's face was scarlet, and she spoke in a wild and hurried whisper,—

"I hope—I assure you—your money won't be lost. If you will have the patience to wait "—

Prudence regarded her with grisly scorn.

"Wait? Didn't I offer to wait? I gave you a chance to speak, and you wouldn't take it. Now I'll thank you jest to hold your tongue," she added, with overpowering arrogance, "and let me do my business with Mr. Parker in peace. I've no idee of my money bein' lost! Trust Mr. Parker for that! 'Tisn't as though I was goin' to look to *you* for it!"

This cool cup of impudence dashed the color from Faustina's cheeks. She stood up, white and quivering with excitement, — defiant and desperate now that the worst, as she believed, had come.

"Threaten, — do you? Very well! what do I care? I laugh at you! Get your money if you can! I fancy you'll get it about the time I get the tomatoes stolen out of our garden. Come, my lady" (with frightful irony), "you see two can play at your game. Finish your business with Mr. Parker; then I'll propose mine. You can guess by this time what it is!"

Passion had concentrated the rash young woman's scattered wits, and she had come to the quick determination to enter a complaint against Prudence for a theft of vegetables, if the latter persisted in taking legal measures to recover the stolen money. Perhaps Mrs. Apjohn understood something of the malign intent. Certain it is that her contumeliousness was very suddenly suppressed.

"Mr. Parker, I leave it to you if I've said or done anything to merit sech treatment as this!"

"Indeed," said Mr. Parker, "I am utterly at a loss to understand this unfortunate misunderstanding."

"I offered to explain," cried Faustina. "I'm not ashamed to have Mr. Parker know all, if you are not. Begin now, — tell your story; then I'll give my side," and she sat down with flashing eyes.

"I come here," said Prudence, "on a quiet matter of business. I shall go on with it. I — am sorry — if I have offended you," she humbled herself to say, the words sticking in her throat. "Now, Mr. Parker, le's see ! About that fifty-three dollars" —

"Fifty !" spoke up the excited Faustina. "It was only fifty ! Don't try to make it more than it is."

The simmering wrath of Prudence came near boiling over again at this interference.

"I said fifty at first," — she spoke patiently as she could, — "but with interest it's fifty-three and a trifle over."

"Interest ? interest since yesterday ! — but go on; go on !" said Faustina, "see what you'll make of it."

Mrs. Apjohn could hardly restrain her fury.

"Will you stop, and wait till I am through ? I guess me and Mr. Parker knows what we're about. Interest since yesterday !" she repeated. "Think I'm a fool ? It's interest for the past year, as Mr. Parker knows."

Mr. Parker smiled assent, and inquired if she had the note.

"Yes, I brought it with me," said she; "for it's on demand, and you spoke as if you'd like to pay it, and we're making up a little sum for the first of October, which'll be here next week; and if it's jest as convenient to-day, why, you can pay it to-day ; if not, some other time; though we should like it by the first, anyway."

It seemed to rain riddles around Faustina, who heard, and stared, and rubbed her forehead, as if to awaken some benumbed sense which would enable her to see through the bewildering drizzle.

12

" I'm very glad to pay you now," said Mr. Parker.

A little time was consumed in computing the interest to Mrs. Apjohn's satisfaction; which gave Faustina an opportunity to recover herself, and see upon what a brink of folly she had rushed once more, hurried thither by her own accusing conscience.

" What a simpleton I am ! " she said to herself, trembling at her narrow escape. " Fool to think I had been found out, or would be ! "

And she resolved she would not open her lips again to speak of the transgression which she now firmly believed would never be discovered.

She was still hardening her heart with this determination, when Mrs. Apjohn exclaimed, —

" Why, Mr. Parker, where did you git that bill ? "

" The fifty ? " said the lawyer.

" Yes ! I declare, it's jest like one I've got to hum, — on the Manville bank, — my mark on't, too ! " with increasing trepidation.

" I had that bill not over an hour ago, of neighbor Hodge," replied Mr. Parker.

" Do ye know where he got it ? " demanded Mrs. Apjohn, her russet face actually pale with fright.

" No, I don't; but I've no doubt he can tell you."

" If he didn't have it of my husband, then I've been robbed ! And John Apjohn wouldn't dare — no — I — is Mr. Hodge to his store now ? " And Prudence hastily rising, lifted along with her the chair into which her ample proportions were compressed, upsetting it with a noise that went to Faustina's quaking soul like a crash of thunder.

The next moment she was gone. And Mrs. Dane, rousing from her stupor, ran to the window to see which way she went.

Prudence, issuing from the office stairway, started first towards Hodge & Company's store. Then she changed her mind, determining to rush home and know for a certainty if her till had been robbed. Then she changed her mind again, and concluded that she had better see Mr. Hodge. While she was hesitating thus, something fell at her feet. She gave it a glance: 'twas a ripe and well-mellowed tomato. She did not see Tasso tittering in the alley; but, casting a lurid look upwards, caught sight of Faustina's sleeve, disappearing from the window.

Faustina was moved by another gust of impulse to give chase to Mrs. Apjohn. But how was she to run the blockade of that craft of the law, — the man-of-warrants, — standing off and on to ascertain what had brought her into those straits ?

" Excuse me if I have acted rudely this morning," she said. " Circumstances have made me irritable. I am in great haste. I "—

She was trying to beat out of the channel betwixt the table and the wall; but he intercepted her, and, tack which way she would, she found herself running under his bows.

" What can I do for you, this morning, madam ? "

This round shot brought her to.

"I wish — to — raise a little money. I thought perhaps you might" —

"Might aid you. Likely enough; but you will have to enlighten me in regard to your plans. Sit down."

"Thank you — I must go — unless" — a new idea. "I have some jewels here which I should like to borrow fifty dollars on."

Mr. Parker smiled curiously, as he glanced at the trinkets, and returned them to her.

"This is a kind of business I never do," he politely informed her.

Her heart sank; but she drew herself up coldly and proudly, as she put the dross back into her bag, begged his pardon for calling upon him, and quickly took leave.

In the street, Prudence was nowhere in sight. Faustina, in an agony of shame, apprehension, and uncertainty, was hesitating which way to go, when she saw Mrs. Apjohn issue from Hodge & Company's store and run — actually run — up the opposite sidewalk. She crossed over to accost her; this time with the full determination to tell her everything.

"Mrs. Apjohn!"

"Don't you stand in my way!" screamed the furious woman. "Git out, you thing! No more of your insults to me, or I'll" —

Faustina stood aside as the broad red face blazed past her.

"You better!—Throw any more tomatuses at me, if you da's't!—I've been robbed, or I'd 'tend to your case now, you stuck-up silly upstart!" And Prudence, with a glare of rage, turned her capacious back, and set off at an elephantine trot; while Tasso walked softly out of the alley, and joined Faustina.

"Wish she'd tread on that tomato, and slip up; wouldn't she make a spread?" observed that genteel youth.

"I won't try again! That's twice I've tried to tell her; and you saw how she treated me!" said the incensed Faustina. "Let her find out if she can!"

Tasso regarded her admiringly. "By George, you look splendid, now—perfic'ly superb! 'S wuth while to see you mad once, if's only to get one flash of them splendid eyes!—What's the scrape?"

"You got me into it, Tasso!—not that I blame you. We mustn't stand talking here. Come along with me, and I'll tell you all about it."

12 *

XV.

TRAGICAL.

WE left the cooper noosed. And we must beg his pardon for neglecting him so long in that ticklish situation. It was necessary to bring forward the array of events to the moment when he heard the noise which precipitated the leap. That done, the reader is prepared to learn the nature of that noise; and he will, we hope, be gratified to know that it is the bustle of Prudence returning. She flings open the door, and is plunging straight into the house, bent on the examination of her coffers, when the lamentable spectacle meets her eyes.

The chair overthrown, face to the floor and heels up, as if cowering in fright and horror; the kitchen pole sagging and shaking with its unusual burden; the red silk tied to the pole; and John Apjohn tied to the red silk: this was the tragical picture. As when some foggy morning Phœbus, belated, having overslept himself, or lingered too long over the Olympian beef-steaks and coffee, looks at his watch, cries " Bless me ! is it so late ? " claps on his hat, mounts his omnibus, and whips in hot haste out of the stables of night into the broadway of the zodiac: like that original red-faced stage-driver, Prudence, all in a fume, blown as was never fat woman before, glows in the entrance of the misty and dismal kitchen; her eyes so inflamed with heat and sweat that she can hardly discern at first the character of the ghostly object strung between the zenith and nadir of that little universe.

Then the truth, or at least a fragment of it, bursts in upon her preoccupied mind. John has discovered the robbery and hung himself! The hanging was obvious; though Prudence, who would have deemed the finding of superfluous vegetables on the door-latch a very poor excuse for the deed, and the loss of a large sum of money the very best excuse, fell naturally into an erroneous conjecture of the cause.

John's attitude was extraordinary for that of a hanged man. He did not kick. Was he then past kicking? No; he had not indulged at all in that little conventionality of the gallows. He had other work for his legs to do. They were straightened and stretched to their utmost, whilst his feet maintained a painful tiptoe posture, in the effort to avoid the extremely disagreeable exercise of dancing upon nothing; for the sanguinary handkerchief had relented a little, and the remorseful pole had yielded a good deal, so that he could just reach and support himself on the floor, as the sagacious reader has no doubt foreseen, having been all this time, like the cooper, only imperfectly held in suspense.

And there, in the midst of the kitchen, hung, or rather

stood, or partly hung and partly stood, the melancholy
man, considerably dark in the facè, his eyes protruded
and rolling, mouth open, and tongue out, with serious
symptoms of asphyxia, and both hands raised, one above
his head, grasping the red halter for a stay, and the other
struggling in terror and haste with the silken knot under
his ear.

"John ! John Apjohn !" ejaculated Mrs. J. A., "what
you doing ? "

" Ich — ich — yaw ! " said John.   For you have only
to choke a man sufficiently in order to make him talk
like a Dutchman.

" Be ye dead, John ? " cried his spouse.

" Yaw — yaw," gurgled Meinherr.

"O John !" groaned Prudence, clutching the handkerchief, and swaying down the gallows to ease his wind-
pipe.   "Tried to hang yourself ! Why did you, John ?
Oh, dear ! About killed ye, has it ? "

John essayed to speak, but only croaked and clucked.

"Oh, dear ! oh, dear !   Misfortins never come singly !
What *shall* I do, if I lose you and the money too ? " Her
mind flew between those two buffeting disasters like a
distracted shuttlecock.   "Don't die just at this time,
John ! don't.   Can't ye git it off now ? "   And she pulled
the red silk like a bell-rope, in her endeavor to unhang
him.

" C-c-u-t i-it ! " cackled John.

" Wal now, you've said it ! " exclaimed Prudence.
" Guess you'll git along !   Cut a good new han'kerchief

like this 'ere! Why didn't ye take somethin' else, some old thing, if you was detarmined to hang yourself? Your Sunday silk! Jest like you, John Apjohn, for all the world!"

"Knife — in my p-p-pocket!" strangled the cooper.

"Come!" cried Prudy, losing patience. "I wouldn't try to talk if I couldn't talk sense. Can't you untie a knot? Take your teeth!" Query: how was he to apply his incisors to a knot under his own chin? But Prudy did not consider that little difficulty. "Bite it!"

"C-c-a-n-t!" quacked John.

"Can't! let me then! Why, it's a slip-noose! Why don't ye slip it? Oh!" moaned Prudence, "if I was half as sure of gittin' back my money as I be of gittin' you out of this trap! How did we git robbed, John?"

"Robbed?" said John, in a more human accent.

"Why! didn't you know it? Ain't that what you went and hung yourself for?"

"No!"

"And — haven't you been to the till?"

"No!" said John, getting his eyes back into his head again. But the relief was only temporary.

"Haven't you? Then — maybe — wait a minute!" and in her agitation she let up the pole, which carried with it the handkerchief, which once more tightened around John's gullet.

"Oh! what you 'b-b-bout?" he bubbled.

"Hold on!" cried Prudence, "you can stan' it a minute! I'm dyin' to know!"

"Yiz — iz — ich !" choked the cooper, up again on his toes.

Prudence, eager as she was to get to the till, stopped to right the chair and help him up on to it, where he stood, like a reprieved culprit, with the noose about his neck; while she snatched the key from the clock, flew to the chest, unlocked it, and unlocked the till with another key from beneath it.

Her great fear was that all her money had been stolen; for the possibility of a burglar taking the trouble to extract fifty dollars and leave the rest had not entered her mind. Equally great now was her joy when she saw the pocket-book in its place and money in the pocket-book. Her fright, then, had been causeless. There were two bills on the Manville Bank precisely similar; and somebody had put a private mark, exactly like her own, on the extraordinary duplicate. Such were her reflections as she came out of the bedroom, with delight on her countenance, and her treasure in her grasp.

John had in the mean time slid the ends of the pole out of its supports, taken down his gallows, and seated himself, with it across his lap, on his scaffold. And there he was, bent double, patiently loosening the tie of his red choker, when Prudy threw herself on the wood-box, exclaiming, —

"We hain't been robbed arter all, John ! Here's the wallet and all the money, I s'pose, — though it's the greatest mystery about that fifty-dollar bill ! And oh ! it's well for Abel Dane that he hain't been meddlin' with our cash. I've bore enough from them Danes. To think that stuck-up Faustiny had the impudence to fling one of her nasty tomatuses at me in the street, the trollop!"

John uttered a lugubrious whine, and dropped his hands from the noose as if he had half a mind to leave it where it was, get up, and finish the hanging.

"So I KNOW now 'twas one of the Danes that tied 'em onto our door! And only think! she had the meanness to twit me of 'em 'fore Mr. Parker! Oh! only give me a chance, and I'll make her and Abel smart! I'd be willin' to lose a little money, if I could prove Abel Dane had stole it. Come, John! don't have that mopin' face on. You look blue as a whetstun. And don't you go to hangin' yourself ag'in, if you expect *me* to help you down, for I shan't." Here Prudence, who, in her excitement on the subject of her neighbors and their insulting ways, had held the pocket-book open, commenced a more careful examination of its contents. "Gracious!" she screamed.

"Was't a spider?" inquired the cooper, in a weak voice. For Prudence, with all her strength of character and robustness of frame, had a horror of spiders, and he was used to hearing her shriek at them.

"That bill, it's gone! We *have* been robbed!" Again she turned over the money. "Sure's the world, John! 'thout you have took it. Have you, sir?"

John, who had succeeded in removing his uncomfortable cravat, was resting the pole on his knee, and

meekly rubbing his throttle, with a most piteous expression. " No, Prudy; I hain't," he answered, taking
no interest.

"Then, oh ! " Vengeance gleamed in Mrs. Apjohn's
eyes. " The bill ain't lost; for we can both swear to't,
and recover it as stolen property. I left it in Parker's
hands; he must look to Hodge, and Hodge must look to
Abel; and Abel, — let him be prepared to give a pretty
strict account of how he come by that bill, or it'll go
hard with him ! He'll have trouble, or I'll miss my
guess ! A man that would serve us sech a trick with the
tomatuses would hook our money. O Faustiny ! Faustiny ! you'll come down from your high-heeled shoes !
you'll haul in your horns ! "

And Prudence, still reeking from her recent exertions,
set off again at full speed for Mr. Parker's office, — the
cooper rolling his eyes after her with feeble astonishment, foreboding fresh woes, but scarcely comprehending the seriousness of her charges and threats against
the Danes.

XVI.

THE ARREST.

ABEL, flattering himself that his pecuniary difficulties were ended, sat down that evening to enjoy himself.

"Thank Providence, I've weathered this storm. Though I thought I was going to have another little squall this afternoon. I had a lawyer's letter, — from Mr. Parker, — and what do you think he wanted?"

Fancy Faustina's alarm at hearing that name, and seeing Abel's honest eyes look over the tea-table at her, as he put the question.

"You needn't be so frightened," he laughed. "I was a little bit startled myself, though, till I ran up to Parker's office and found out what the trouble was. It seems Mrs. Apjohn is determined to be revenged on me for an offence I never dreamed of committing. She won't believe it possible that anybody else could see what was done in our garden last Sunday, and contrive a sorry joke to remind her of it; but *I* must have done it! And how do you suppose she has gone to work to pay me?"

"I can't imagine!" said Faustina.

"I laughed in Parker's face when he told me. She

13

accuses me of a robbery. At least she claims that a bill
I gave Hodge last night was stolen from her !"

"Who ever heard of such a thing ?" said Faustina.

" Ridiculous, isn't it ? I told Parker I wasn't going to
submit to any annoyance from that source. I referred
him to Deacon Cole, from whom I had all the large bills
that I paid to Hodge. But what is curious," added
Abel, "I can't remember receiving that particular bill,
though I noticed it when I was settling with Hodge last
night. Here ! hello ! you're making my cup run over !"

" What was I thinking of ?"   And the trembling woman, to make matters worse, instead of pouring the
superfluous liquid into the bowl, turned it into the
cream-pitcher.

" I should think *you* had been accused of stealing, and
might be guilty," Abel jestingly said. Then, as he
watched her, a grave suspicion crossed his mind, — that,
notwithstanding her positive denial of the fact in the
morning, it might be through some complicity or indiscretion on her part that the affront for which vengeance
was now threatened had been put upon the Apjohns,
and that her agitation arose from the consciousness of
having thus brought him into danger.

"Faustina," said he, with deep seriousness and kind-
liness, "if we are aware of having committed any fault
by which our neighbors are aggrieved, we ought to
acknowledge it, and, if possible, make reparation for it.
The honestest course is the wisest. A word of frank
avowal now may save a world of vexation and vain

regret hereafter. At least, do not keep anything from me; but, I beg of you, if you have anything on your mind that I ought to know, speak it now."

It seemed that Faustina could not resist this earnest appeal. She felt that her husband was, after all, her best, her only friend; and she longed to confess to him, and throw herself upon his generosity and mercy. But she remembered her last interview with Tasso, who had counselled her by no means to avow her misdeed to her husband or to any one, but persistently to deny it, whatever happened.

" That's the only way when you've once got into a scrape," said Tasso. "It's bad; but you must lie it out."

These words she recalled, and again the dread of Abel's condemnation dismayed her, and Tasso's prediction, that the Apjohns, though they should try, could prove nothing, comforted her; and the false wife, in an evil moment, looked up at her deceived husband with feigned wonder, and replied, —

" I can't think of anything I've done, Abel. Why do you ask ? "

" Well, then, never mind," said Abel. " I'm not suspicious; but I feel extreme anxiety to be entirely free from offence toward my neighbors, and I put as strict questions to my own heart as I put to you. Consciousness of being in the wrong makes me a perfect coward; but let me be assured of the righteousness of my course, and I can face any misfortune. The longer

I live, the better I know what a precious refuge truth is, and what a den of serpents is falsehood."

"Oh, yes ! I know it ! " assented Faustina, with the accent and the aspect of a saint, and with her soul in that den, amidst the writhing and the hissing, at the moment.

Abel was convinced; for that creature could assume a seeming that might have deceived even the elect; and, shoving back his chair with satisfaction, he called to Melissa, who showed her face at the door with Ebby in her arms.

" Come to your supper. Give me the young gentleman. Did you leave mother comfortable ? Hó, you Goliath of babies ! " — tossing the delighted Ebby. " Ha, you fat pig ! " — tickling him. " Ebby has no cares yet to work down his flesh. Care is a jack-plane, that takes thick shavings from the breast and ribs. You little sultan ! " — standing him up on his knees in a royal attitude; for he was a proud and splendid child. " Wonder if my little fairy will ever be a man, and have whiskers, and a little boy to pull 'em, — a real, plump, loving little boy, to make him forget all his troubles when he comes home at night ? " And, with a sense of his own blessedness, and with a gush of affection, he clasped the happy boy to his heart. " Come, now let's go and see grandma."

" Poor thick ga'ma ! " said Ebby, with his chubby fingers in the paternal hair.

" Yes, poor sick grandma; and we'll go and make her well."

Abel had risen, and was carrying Ebby gayly on his arm, when, as they passed the door, there came a rap upon it. Faustina, at the sound, grew pale, — more apprehensive, now, of fateful visitors, than Cooper John himself. But Abel, joyous of countenance, and free of soul, feeling, like Romeo, "his bosom's lord sit lightly in his throne," — ignorant that the gleam, which illumined that moment in his life, was not sunshine, but a flash out of the gathering thunder-cloud, — the young father, holding up his boy with one hand, threw open the door with the other, and met the sheriff face to face.

The sheriff was a kind-hearted man, and, at sight of the happy domestic scene, which it was his thankless office to disturb, no doubt his feelings were touched. He shook hands with Abel, — for they were well acquainted, — and gave a hard finger to the fat little hand which, at the paternal instigation, Ebby bashfully stuck out to him.

"Come in, won't you?" cried Abel, thinking of him only as friend Wilkins, and not once connecting him with his commission.

"Perhaps you'd better step out a minute," answered Wilkins. "I've a disagreeable errand to do."

"Here, mamma! take baby!" cried Abel. But baby did not want to go to mamma. And mamma had no word or look for baby, in the consternation of thinking the sheriff was there to arrest some one, — it might be Abel, — it might be herself! "Well, then, where's his little shawl? and papa's hat? We'll go out and see the man. Hurrah!"

13 *

" Co-ah ! " crowed Ebby, throwing up his arms with delight. He liked papa best of anybody at all times; and now he and papa were going to have an adventure.

Sheriff Wilkins was sorry to see the boy come riding out in triumph on his father's arm. He felt it would be easier to do his errand out of sight of wife and child. "He has such a pretty wife ! and such a beautiful child ! " thought sheriff Wilkins.

It was a moonlight evening; and there, in the quiet and white shine, with the shadows of the pear-tree mottling the ground at their feet, spotting old Turk's shaggy back, as he snuffed suspiciously at the officer's shins, and flinging an impalpable shadow-crown upon King Ebby's head, — in low voices, friendly and business-like, the two men talked, and the errand was done; Faustina, meanwhile, peering eagerly from the kitchen-window, and those other witnesses, the stars, looking placidly down through the misty skylight of heaven.

Then Abel, bearing the babe, returned into the house; and Faustina, like the guilty creature she was, started back from the window, and stood, white and still as the moonlight without, waiting to hear the worst.

Abel came up to her, with a curious expression of amusement and disgust, — a smile married to a scowl.

" It grows interesting ! " he said.

" How ? what ? " whispered Faustina.

" I am arrested ! " growled Abel.

" Arrested ! " Faustina tried to echo; but her voice refused to articulate.

"Don't be alarmed,—*I* am not!" added Abel, with mocking levity. "It's such a neat revenge! Mrs. Apjohn is welcome to all she can make out of it. Wonder how it will seem to go to jail? How would you like to go with me?"

For an instant, Faustina thought she was arrested too, and that this was his mild way of breaking it to her.

"Fudge, child!" he laughed; "don't take it so seriously. I thought it would be a good joke for you to insist on keeping me company, and to take Ebby along with us. I guess we could enjoy ourselves as well in jail as the Apjohns out of it."

"Ebby go!" cooed the enterprising infant, thinking some pleasant journey was contemplated.

"No, Ebby can't go; he must stay at home with mamma, to take good care of grandma. She may as well not know it," continued Abel, the smile dying, and leaving the scowl a grim widower. "It would disturb her too much. I almost wish Turk had finished Mrs. Apjohn when he was about it. I shall get off, or, at all events, get bail in the morning; but to-night I may have to sleep in jail."

"In jail! O Abel!" said Faustina, relieved to learn that it was he, and not herself, who must go, yet terrified at the consequences of her folly.

"There! don't be childish!"

Abel put his right arm about her tenderly, still holding Ebby with the other.

"I don't care a cent on my own account. I'd just as

lief go to jail as not. You and I are not to blame, and
why should we be disturbed ? Mrs. Apjohn, or whoever
is to blame, will get the worst of it. Or perhaps you
think we shall be disgraced ? Villain of a husband, to
put his innocent young wife to such a trial ! You forgive me ? "

"Oh, yes ! "— Very magnanimous in Faustina.—
" But what — what proof is there ? "

" Proof ! " exclaimed Abel. " Do you think there is any
proof ? Do you — heavens and earth, Faustina ! — do
you imagine I am a scoundrel ? "

"No, Abel ! But if you had — taken money," she
gasped out, — "I could forgive you."

"I should despise you if you could ! " he answered,
haughtily. " I could never forgive myself."

"But — you forgave Mrs. Apjohn," she reminded him,
almost pleadingly.

"That's another thing. A few tomatoes. But
money ! — I could no more take my neighbor's cash
than I could take his life; and I don't suppose anybody
really thinks I could. Deacon Cole has no recollection
of paying me the bill Mrs. Apjohn says was stolen from
her; and they have got up an absurd story about finding
the envelope of one of my letters in their house, — proof
positive that I got in and lost it there when I stole the
money ! That's the *proof*, as you call it. Come, be
yourself, Faustina, and let me see a hopeful smile on
your face when I go. What's a clear conscience good
for, if it can't sustain us at such times ? "

"Oh, I *am* sustained!" Faustina tried the hopeful smile, but it was a failure. "I know my dear, noble husband is innocent!" And she put her lovely arms about his neck and kissed him.

"Good-by," he said, more convinced than ever of late that she loved him. "I am on parole, and Wilkins is waiting for me. Tell mother I have business, and put her to bed. And, Faustina, whatever occurs, let us be true to each other and to our own consciences, and all will be well."

"We will! we will!" she murmured, kissing him again with lips as chill as dew.

"Now, mamma, take Ebby," said Abel, with moist eyes.

"No! no! Ebby go! Ebby go!"

"Oh, Ebby can't go with papa to-night. Mamma take him."

"No! no! no!" remonstrated the child, stoutly. And he flirted his ungrateful hands, and kicked his unfilial feet, when she reached to receive him; and lamented, and screamed "Ebby go! Ebby go!" with ungovernable persistence.

"What shall I do?" said Abel, with strong parental emotion. "It would almost seem that his wise little spirit foresees some greater wrong than we suspect. The instincts even of babes are so wonderful. See! he won't let me go without him!"

And Abel looked proud and gratified, though perplexed, when the subtle-sensed child, shunning the guilty parent with all his might, put his arms about the neck of the innocent, and hugged him with all his heart and strength.

"He knows !" cried Abel, with laughter and tears, little guessing how much more there was in the divine instincts of the infant than even his words had expressed. "There now, Ebby, be papa's good boy. Melissa, take him."

Then Ebby loosed his hold, stayed only to kiss the father he loved, one long kiss over his whiskers, put out his hands to Melissa, and, without a murmur, only the corners of the little serious mouth drawn down, went to her unresistingly, though he still refused the hospitality of the maternal bosom.

Faustina was cut to the heart. For, though she had never loved her beautiful boy too well, she was jealous of his affection; and to feel, at this time, when she was conscious of having forfeited her husband's esteem, that neither had she any part in her child's love, made her seem to herself worse than a widow and childless.

"'By-'by, Ebby ! — Keep good heart, Faustina !" These were Abel's parting words; and, rejoining the sheriff, he walked off gayly with him to the magistrate's. But Faustina, with an indescribable sense of heaviness, loneliness, and guilt, — wishing herself dead, wishing herself where she might never see husband, or child, or any face she ever knew, again, — shrank back into the house, with the long night of remorse and dread before her.

XVII.

FAUSTINA CONSOLES HERSELF.

THE long, dreary night! how could she endure it? Never a woman of courage, or of resources within herself against ennui, no wonder that the coming lonesome hours were awful as phantoms to her. She gazed out of the windows; the moonlight and the stillness were chill and forbidding. She could not content herself a moment with the old lady; Ebby was no comfort; and Melissa, who knew her secret, she was beginning to hate and fear. She went to her chamber; its solitariness was intolerable; a gust from the door, as she closed it, extinguished her light, and the moonshine came between the curtains like the face of a ghost.

Pitiful for one who at all times loved company so well, and was never willingly alone an hour in her life! What would she not resort to for relief from her own fears and imaginings? She would have swallowed laudanum, if she had had any. She thought of a bottle of brandy in the kitchen closet. That would do. She would stupefy herself.

Melissa was in the kitchen, suffering great distress of mind at the occurrences of the evening.

"O Mis' Dane!" she exclaimed, "ain't it too bad he has to go to jail! And we know he didn't take the money!"

"Hold your tongue!" said Faustina. "Of course he didn't; and they can't do anything with him."

"Can't they?" cried Melissa, eagerly; for she had felt the remorse of an accomplice in sharing Faustina's secret. "Oh, I'm glad!"

"You stupid girl!" — Faustina seized her arm. "Melissa! Melissa!" in a menacing whisper, "hear what I say! As you value your oath, as you value your life, never breathe a syllable of what you know!"

"La, ma'am!" — with open-mouthed astonishment, — "what will happen to me if I do?"

"You will die! You will die a most sudden and dreadful death!"

"La, ma'am! will I though? Oh dear!" And Melissa began to whimper with fright, thinking her mistress must surely be in league with supernatural avengers.

"There! stop crying! They shan't hurt you, if you mind me." There was something awfully suggestive in the indefinite, mysterious plural *they.* "Only keep your oath, Melissa! An oath's a shocking thing to break. Nobody is safe afterwards."

"Why, what happens to 'em?"

"Some are sent to prison, — lucky if they ever get out again. Some are struck by lightning. Some are murdered in broad daylight, nobody ever knows how. Some are found dead in their beds, though as well the night before as you are this minute. A great many disappear, and are never heard of again; — it's supposed the goblins catch them."

"Oh, la, ma'am ! how you scare me ! "

"You needn't be scared, only keep your oath. Remember ! Now go and put Ebby to bed, and see to the old woman. *I* can't, — I'm sick. Where's that brandy ? "

The brandy was got. Melissa was gone. And Faustina in her madness began to drink. She placed the bottle on the table, with water and sugar, and sat down, deliberately and systematically to lay siege to the castle of oblivion, of which drunkenness opens the gates.

"Hillo ! by George, I cotched ye at it this time ! "

Faustina started up with trepidation; but when she saw what visitor had entered so softly as to stand beside her before she was aware, she was pacified, and sat down again.

"I've an excruciating toothache, Tasso ! I was putting a little brandy into it."

"I've an excruciating toothache, too," said Tasso. "I'd like to put a little brandy into mine."

The liquor had begun to do its office. Faustina was delighted to have company. She was social; she was ardent; she wrung Tasso's hand confidentially, and brought him a glass from the closet.

"Seein' Abel's off, thought I'd drop in. Hi, hi ! 'tain't a bad joke after all ! Got *him* up 'fore the justice ! Couldn't help laughing ! " And Tasso illustrated with a giggle, which he quenched with a dash of sweet-

14

ened brandy and water. "That's good liquor, I swow!"
He smacked, and filled again, confirming his verdict, —
being no doubt a discriminating judge of strong waters;
for he had tended bar in Boston till he was suspected of
pilfering from the drawer, when he retired at his em-
ployer's urgent request, seconded by a boot which
accelerated his progress down the stairs. He had lost
his situation, but retained his taste.

"It's dreadful, Tasso!" said Faustina. "He won't
come home to-night, I suppose. Oh, I'm so glad you've
come; it's so horrible lonesome here! Let's go into
the sitting-room; for Melissa'll be back in a minute.
Bring the sugar."

"Toothache hain't a chance in this house," observed
Tasso, smilingly holding up the bottle to the light.

"Come! I've so many things to tell you!" And
Faustina led the way, carrying the pitcher of water
and the candle.

XVIII.

"HE ENTERED IN HIS HOUSE, HIS HOME NO MORE."

LATER in the night, when the village streets were
silent, and the village lights mostly extinguished, a man
appeared briskly walking across the common, in the
moonlight.

It was Abel Dane. He was softly whistling a lively
air, to which his feet kept time. He had not yet seen
the inside of the big stone jug, as the jail was called,
and didn't think now that he ever would. He had had
the good fortune to gain a hearing before the magistrate that night, and to get admitted to bail. Deacon
Cole himself had volunteered to be his surety. Everybody was inclined to take a jocular view of the charge
against him. And Abel was happy; congratulating
himself that Mrs. Apjohn's malice was baffled, and enjoy-
ing, in pleasant anticipation, Faustina's surprise and
delight at his unexpected return.

For Abel, poor fellow, was so eager to snatch at every
bubble of circumstance in which his hope or fancy saw
glimmer some floating, unsubstantial image of domestic
happiness! He was rushing to grasp a very large and
extremely flattering bubble of this description now. His

wife's distress, on seeing him torn from her embrace
and dragged away to jail, — so to speak, — had moved
him greatly. "After all," he thought, "she loves me. A
change is taking place in her character, I sincerely hope.
She never manifested so much concern for my welfare before. And she said she could forgive me, even if I had
taken money! Such charity, such affection, I did not
expect to find in her. Who knows but the faults of her
spoiled girlhood and false education may be cured, and
she may prove a true wife and mother after all? God
grant it!" he murmured aloud, his eyes upturned mistily
to the moonbeams, his features glowing and surcharged
with the emotion of his prayer.

He hurried on. He saw a light in his own house.
"Poor girl! she is too anxious to sleep! She could
not go to bed and rest while I was supposed to be
locked up in stone walls. Foolish child! But I am
glad she is wakeful; I wouldn't have her make light of
my arrest, though I do. I can imagine how lonesome
she is, sitting up, thinking of me. I'll go softly to the
door, and surprise her. Now I shall know, — I'll take
her behavior as a sign, — whether she really loves me."

He drew near. He heard — what? Laughter! That
did not please him so well.

"Who has she got there?" He listened. "Tasso
Smith!"

He went to the kitchen door; it was unfastened. He
entered, and closed it after him. The moon lighted his
steps, and he advanced, stepping noiselessly, to the

sitting-room door. His purpose to afford Faustina a surprise had become a dark and deadly purpose, and the blackness of darkness clothed his soul. He waited; for, in that first terrible revulsion, he felt that Tasso could not fall into his hands without danger, and he feared the violence of his own rage in confronting Faustina. He was determined to be calm; yet it was not easy to get his wrath under control, with the intolerable tittering from within irritating it like sputters of vitriol.

When his hand was quite steady, he found the doorknob, touched it warily, turned it charily, opened it with silence and caution, and laid bare the scene within.

Do you think this dishonorable in Abel? No matter. In his place you would very likely have acted dishonorably too.

The scene: A table, with the tools of intoxication upon it; beside it two chairs, unsuitably near together. In that nearest the door you saw the nice youth, Tasso Smith, — one hand encircling a glass which rested on the edge of the table, the other resting familiarly on the back of the chair beyond, — his countenance, like silly cream, wrinkled up with the last inanity of tipsy merriment.

In that other chair sat Faustina, her eyes swimming with an unmistakable tendency to double-vision, and her lovely head so tipsy that she could hardly resist its proclivity to rest on Tasso's shoulder. A pretty picture for a husband!

14 *

One minute, — two minutes, the petite comedy went on; two unconscious actors playing their parts with perfect naturalness and abandonment, such as you seldom see on the stage, before an intensely interested audience of one.

Then you might have heard a fall. Mr. Smith heard it as soon as anybody. Indeed, something had happened to that individual. He had tumbled, in a most astonishingly sudden and mysterious manner, under the table. Over him stood Abel, and in Abel's hand was the chair which had been jerked from beneath him. And there was danger in the atmosphere, as the sagacious youth sniffed readily when once he put out his head carefully from under the table and carefully drew it back again. He had done curing the toothache, and done tittering, too, for that night.

But Faustina laughed on, not perceiving the spectre of wrath that had stalked in behind her, and now stood holding her companion's tilted chair. She looked down by the table, and was presently aware of a pair of perpendicular legs, not Tasso's. Or was Mr. Smith double, and had he four legs ? He appeared to be rapidly crawling off with a horizontal pair, and, at the same time, to be standing firmly on the two at her side.

She looked up, and was shocked into something like sobriety by the apparition of her husband.

"Abel ! — why — where — I thought you — is it morning ?" And she winked to see if it was day, thinking he had passed the night in jail and come home and caught her carousing.

Abel stood motionless and white, still clinching the chair, as if diabolically tempted to break it over the head of Tasso, rising from behind the table and retreating, with the grimace of a scared monkey, to the door. But with extraordinary self-control, he neither spoke nor stirred until Mr. Smith had slunk out; then he kicked his hat after him, — for that young gentleman had quite forgotten that he was bareheaded, — broke the cane that stood in the corner, and threw the splinters into the retiring face. Then, having closed and locked the door, he turned and confronted Faustina.

XIX.

HUSBAND AND WIFE.

" Why — Abel — what's the matter ? " gasped the wretched woman, trying to gild her guilty fright with smiles.

" *My wife ! — disgraced forever !* "

These words, uttered incoherently, with suppressed fury, carried to the heart of the half-sobered Faustina the stunning conviction that all had been discovered. She slipped down upon her knees before him.

"Mercy ! mercy ! Don't cast me off, Abel, — don't ! I will tell you everything ! "

"Where did you get these trinkets ? " For the jewels had been brought out, and now lay on the table.

" I bought them, Abel."

" You bought them ! With whose money ? "

" With — with yours. I took it from the drawer. Yesterday Tasso came and showed them to me, and made me buy them."

" Faustina, don't dare to tell me anything but the truth now ! " he muttered, wringing her wrist.

" I won't. I'll tell you everything. But, oh, don't cast me off ! Don't shame me before the world ! I've been a bad and selfish wife to you, I know; but I'll be better. Oh, I'll be so true always, always, Abel! if you won't expose me now."

"Speak!" said Abel,—hoarse, bewildered, chills of a strange new terror creeping over him. "What have you done?"

"I was so frightened afterward,—I thought you would kill me when you missed the money!"—

"How much was it?"

"Fifty dollars."

Abel dropped her arm and staggered back. He knew all. No need for her to tell him more. But she talked on, eager in self-excuse.

"I went to borrow it of Mrs. Apjohn. But she wasn't there when I took it; and I didn't dare to go and tell her of it,—and you had paid the money to Mr. Hodge,—and,—O Abel! I have been so wretched! If you only knew, you would have mercy! Don't expose me now, and cast me off!—don't let me go to jail! don't! don't! don't!"

In the most abject servility, with passionate terror and entreaty, she pleaded, kneeling and wringing her hands. Abel had sat down. Under the calamity that had smitten him, he could not stand. He felt weak and shattered and lost.

"Oh, do pity me!" she prayed, creeping toward him. "You pity others! You forgave Mrs. Apjohn the tomatoes. She is nothing to you, and I am your wife;

and such a wife I will be to you, O Abel! if you will
only be merciful to me now!"

She cut her knee on something sharp. It was Tasso's
glass, which had been thrown down and broken when he
fell. It reminded her of the carousal which had been
interrupted. Sobered more and more, she felt now how
unpardonable that scene must have appeared in Abel's
eyes.

"I didn't know what to do. I was so wretched, I felt
such remorse when you were gone. I thought I couldn't
live through the night. I was wild, frantic, and I got
the brandy. I never did such a thing before, — you
know I never did. I meant to kill myself. I hoped I
should. I wish I had! Then Tasso came in. There
was never anything more between us than you saw to-
night, — nor half so much. I swear it! I'll swear it on
the Bible, and call Heaven to witness! It was the brandy, it was the brandy, Abel! Oh, don't look so stony
and cruel at me; for I see my fate in your eyes! They
are like dead men's eyes, — there's no compassion in
them. Don't, don't look at me so, Abel!" And she
grovelled at his feet.

Still he made no motion, but sat as he had fallen, with
a blind and frozen look, which well might awe Faustina.

"Abel! dear Abel! my husband! remember how
you have loved me!"

Her voice, which had been wild and strong in its eloquence of fear, now grew tremulous and fond. She
kissed his feet. She wept and laughed. "Oh, you will

love me again ! You do love me ! Think how happy
we have been ! And we will be happier now. For I
shall never care for anybody or anything but you after
this. If you only forgive me,— and I know you will ! "—
looking up in his face with pleading sweetness and tears.
" You are so good, Abel ! " And she flung herself upon
his bosom, kissing and clinging with the witchery she
knew so well how to use.

But Abel was inexorable. Her caresses — he loathed
them.

" Get off ! " said he. She turned from him with such
semblance of despair that he could not but relent a
little. " Go to bed. You are not yourself to-night ;
and I am sick ! In the morning I will tell you what I
will do."

" I can't go till you forgive me ! " she answered,
fawning upon him, and covering his hand with kisses.
" Why do you say, ' *Go to bed ?* ' It was always, ' *Come
to bed,*' till now. — Oh, I see by your face, so cold, so
cold, that I am not to be your wife any more ! "

She fell upon the floor. There she lay motionless and
unnoticed for many minutes. Then he stooped, sternly
commanding her, and lifted her up.

" Come with me ! "

" Oh, you hurt me, Abel ! Your hand is iron ! "

" There is iron in my soul ! " said Abel.

" Pity me, pity me, Abel ! " she implored, " when I
suffer so ! "

"You suffer! And I? Who will pity me? Alone; and the ruins fall upon me!"

"Dear Abel, *I* pity you. Don't look so terrible! You are not alone, — I am with you."

For a minute he stood in a sort of trance, his visage pallid and awful, his eyes fixed on vacancy. She watched him, in dread and distress, waiting for him to look at her and speak.

"Faustina," he said, with deep and strange calmness — but there was something sepulchral in his voice, — "do you know that I am under bonds to answer for your crime?"

"My crime!" she gasped.

"Crime!" he repeated. "It is worse than simple larceny, — it is house-breaking. I thought it an idle accusation till now. Now I see what it means. It means dishonor. It means endless disgrace. It means trial, conviction, sentence, — for one of us. Years in prison, — for one of us. Does any one know of your guilt?"

"No one, — no one but you. And you will spare me, Abel! dear Abel! won't you?" Thus she lied, and pleaded.

"And suffer in your place!"

"No, no, Abel. You are innocent. They cannot punish you for what you have not done. And you are a man!"

He smiled; but his smile was even more frightful to her than his frown.

"Punishment has no terrors for me now. I think I

shall soon be glad to hide my head even in prison. If it wasn't for Ebby — my boy !"—

"What do you mean ?" she cried. "Don't frighten me so, Abel ! They can't imprison *you*, — how can they ?"

"You have made your act appear as my act. You did the robbery, and I received and used the money. People know how I was distressed for money at the time ;— that is evidence against me. The Apjohns identify the stolen bill; they can produce proof to show how they came by it, which I cannot do. Then there is one of my letter-envelopes, — how came it in their house ? They found it rolled up in the kitchen."

"I don't know, — I don't know !" said Faustina.

"*I* know !" answered Abel. "If others only knew !" A powerful emotion shook him, as he looked upon her, so young and beautiful and proud, and thought of her ruin and disgrace. "'Twas one of your curl-papers. You lost it when you took the money. And you stopped the clock, when you took the key of the chest out of it. Did you leave any other trace of your guilt ?"

Then Faustina's strength went from her, and hope went with it, and despair possessed her.

"I will certainly kill myself, Abel !" she said.

"Would one of us had died already !" he answered. "But killing ourselves now will not mend matters. I am sick enough of the world, to leave it very willingly. But I shall bide my time. Come !"

She followed him, walking in a sullen stupor. He

15

conducted her to her chamber, — their chamber heretofore, — where Ebby lay sweetly slumbering. He led her to the bedside; and there they both stood for some moments gazing upon the lovely little sleeper, each with what different thoughts !

"Go to bed," then said Abel.

She obeyed him without word or resistance. He waited till she had lain down. Then he put his arms gently about the unconscious babe, and took him from her side. At that she roused.

"Oh ! are you going to leave me ? "

" Yes, Faustina."

" Go, then ! Be kind and forgiving to every one but me. But leave me my child, — *our* child, Abel, — won't you?"

" No, Faustina."

Then she turned upon her face, burying it in the pillow, which she clutched and bit convulsively.

And bearing the dewy-cheeked infant in his arms, Abel went out, closed the door behind him gently and firmly, and entered another room.

It was the room that had been Eliza's. In the bed that had been Eliza's he laid down his precious burden, and threw himself heavily down beside him.

"Papa ! papa !" said Ebby, waking, and glad to find the whiskers he loved on his face. And stretching up his little arms, he hugged the dear good head of his father to his sweet moist bosom.

Abel sobbed. And there he lay, thinking of his desolation and remembering his sins. Who could help

him ? God can help us, but not always within ourselves. He uses instruments and mediators. Abel
longed for human sympathy and aid. And he thought
of one whom he had wronged.

"How I wronged her !" he said, and gnashed his
teeth. "Idiot that I was ! and she so wise and good !
Nobody but her ! nobody but her !" he repeated, thinking of those who, out of all the world, might be of
service to him then. "And I grieved her away ! O my
baby ! — my mother ! — my good name among men !
— if only Eliza was here !"

A soothing influence stole over him, as he thought of
her. Something of her spirit seemed still to pervade
the room; and he found rest in it. Then what if she
herself were there ? His longing for her, the cry of
his inmost soul became irresistible. He arose, and
penned the brief letter which called her home; then
returned to bed, drew Ebby to his heart, and slept the
sleep of the innocent.

XX.

THE RETURN OF ELIZA.

THE letter went the next day to its destination. The day after was Saturday. Would Eliza be here before the Sabbath? Would she come at all?

It is another moonshiny night; — the chill mists rising, the village dogs barking, the elm-trees drooping in the dew, with now and then a liquid rustle, and a young woman hurrying across the common through shadow and gloom.

It is a plain, earnest face you see under the brown bonnet, — pale, in the moonlight, and full of anxious thought, — gazing toward Abel's house. Why does her bosom swell so, and her heart beat so fast?

Oh, the realization that she is going home, — that here she is again in sight of the house, which stands with its white gable to the moon, waiting as in the well-remembered bygone sheeny nights! No, it is not a dream, Eliza; you are fully awake.

The feeling of the old, frequented paths under her feet; the familiar scent of the soil and trees; Abel's shop, Cooper John's shop, and Cooper John's squatty house, which always to her mind bore such a ludicrous likeness to good Mrs. Apjohn; again, the night-fog stealing up from the hollow, mingled with which comes an indefinable, tantalizing sense of change in the native atmosphere of the town; something, after all, foreign and forbidding in the features of the landscape lying dim in the moonlight; — all this makes her strangely afraid and strangely glad.

Her hands are encumbered with travelling-gear; yet she walks swiftly. And now she is near the gate; and now she pauses and shrinks. What is this that rushes upon her? All the past in a flood, — the old, warm current of love; the cutting ice of disappointment; the wrecks of happiness; faces of dead friendships; pleasures and hopes and pains; all which she sees, like a drowning person, in one wild, stifling instant of time.

Then comes a sudden dash through the yard. Old Turk, who has been for the last hour assiduously serenading the moon, — his big, bluff barytone, distinguishable afar off amid the chorus of village curs, — leaves that thankless occupation, gives a bounce at the gate, which flies open, and, with yelps of furious delight and frenzied wags of tail, madly leaping and licking, gives her a devouring welcome. Eliza drops bag and bandbox, and hugs the dear old monster in her arms, crying for very joy.

"Old Turk! dear Turk! There, stop, you saucy boy! Can't you be glad without tearing me to pieces? You dear fellow! Down!"

To be thus remembered and greeted by her dumb

15 *

friend is a great comfort. She accepts it as a good omen, and her heart grows light, — only to grow heavy again, however, a moment later.

Her hand is on the latch. Shall she open, as in old times, — the good old times, forever past, when she was as the mistress of that house ? She remembers that another woman is mistress there now, and, awkward and unnatural as it seems, she knocks like any wayfarer. What tremor, what suspense, — waiting there on that door-step for some one to open unto her ! Who will come ? Will Abel's face be the first to meet her, or the beautiful Faustina's, which she somehow dreads, or dear old Mrs. Dane's, benevolent and beloved ? Oh, to think she is now to see these faces once more, — that the moment, which she thought would never come, has at last arrived ! If only the door would open ! But it doesn't.

She knocks again, less timidly, — louder even than her heart is knocking all this time. And now there is a stir within. She is aware of some one peeping out at her from the window. Then the door is cautiously opened, and the edge of a face appears, — a face unknown to Eliza.

" Is Abel — Mr. Dane — at home ? "

Alas, Eliza ! that ever you should come to that door with such a formal question, and stand coldly outside till a stranger's tongue has answered it !

" No; gone away," says the face through the crack — the door yielding only about a hand's breadth.

In her disappointment, Eliza is half a mind to go away too, and come again no more. Indeed, what business has she there? The letter which brought her — she must have merely dreamed of such a letter. Or, even were it a reality, why was she so foolishly eager to answer the summons? Abel did not expect she would be, it is evident. Since he had been so long reticent and cold, ought she not to be ashamed of her ready and ardent zeal?

"I would like to see old Mrs. Dane," she falters.

"She's wus; don't see nobody," replies the face through the crack.

What shall she do? Is this then coming home? Is this the hour she looked forward to with such palpitating hope during her long journey? She turns half round. She sees the moon shining on the trees and fields as she has seen it a hundred times before. Its cold beams are more hospitable than the glimpse of light in the forbidden house. The wide, roofless night is not so solitary as this half-shut guarded door. "Abel! Abel!" says her heart, "if you sent for me, why are you not here to welcome me?"

"But this is morbid," says her better sense.

"Is young Mrs. Dane at home?" she forces herself to inquire.

"Yes'm; but she's sick a-bed too. Don't see nobody."

This, then, is Abel's trouble, Eliza thinks. His wife is ill, — perhaps dying, — and she has been sent for to save for him that precious life. Well, she will do her duty.

" Will Abel be home soon ? "

" Don't know. Guess bimeby. Didn't say, when he went out."

" I will come in and wait," says Eliza. Still the door does not open; and the face at the crack looks out suspiciously at her, with a foolish, doubting smile.

" Do you know if they were expecting any one to-night ? "

" Guess not; hain't heerd 'em say."

" This used to be my home. Did you ever hear them speak of Eliza ? "

At which word, Turk, grown impatient of delay, brushes past her, forcing the door.

" La, ma'am ! is this Eliza ? " cries the flustered housemaid, recovering from Turk and the surprise. " I've heerd old Mrs. Dane talk of you ever so many times ! My name's Melissy, — Melissy Jones, ye know ; though mabby ye never heerd of me afore, seein' as how my folks only jest moved into the place a little more'n a year ago. Old Mrs. Dane 'll be dreadful tickled to see ye, I know ! La, I thought 'twas a straggler ! and I'm kind o' skeery, folks bein' sick so, and Abel away from home. Take a seat and set down, won't ye ? "

Eliza is gazing vacantly about the room, and beginning to take off her things. What object is it which suddenly fixes her sight ?

"That's baby, — that's Ebby," Melissa explains. "I was lonesome, so I kep' him up for comp'ny; but, la! he dropt right off to sleep, jest as he *never will* evenings when we want him to."

In the rocking-chair, sunken in pillows, dimpled cheek on dimpled arm, with the smile of some happy dream just stirring the sweet mouth, the chubby cherub sleeps. Eliza bends over him, kneeling. Her face, bowed low, is hidden from Melissa. Long she gazes, silent. O fortunate Abel, parent of that darling boy! O proud Faustina, to be the mother, and the father's cherished wife! Eliza touches, with quivering lips, the lily-white, dewy skin, the warm, aromatic, rosy mouth. Then she says, calmly, —

"He looks like Abel, I think."

"Yes'm," assents Melissa, "he dooes. Most folks thinks he favors his pa the most."

"How long has his mother been sick?"

"Only sence yist'day."

"Is she very sick?" asks Eliza, surprised.

"Don't know. Perty considerable, — though not very, I guess," Melissa confusedly answers.

"Does she see the doctor?"

"No, ma'am; she don't see nobody. Better take a seat and set down."

Melissa would like to change the subject. Eliza, seating herself, persists in questioning her.

"But she must see somebody. Who takes her food to her?"

"I do; but she won't eat, and she sca'cely looks at me, but keeps her head kivered up under the bedclo'es. Oh, dear!" sighs Melissa, remembering the secret, which she dreads to keep, yet fears to betray.

"But she sees her husband!" says the astonished Eliza.

"Ruther guess not; for he sleeps in t'other room now, 'long 'ith Ebby."

"How long has he done so?"

"Only last night and the night afore, ma'am."

"She can't be very sick, then, — or else he would go to her."

"Wal, I do'no; she don't git up. I guess it's trouble more'n anything."

"What trouble? Tell me! I am come to help them, and I must know."

"Don't ax me! it's too bad! Oh, dear!" And up goes Melissa's apron, and down goes her face into it, with a sob.

Eliza, with her quick sense of the comical, smiles, but faintly. There is no laughter in her heart to-night.

"Melissa," — she assumes authority, — "put down your apron!"

The girl only clutches it more closely to her weeping face.

"Will crying mend matters? Don't keep me in suspense! Tell me at once!"

"O ma'am," — Melissa uncovers her interesting lineaments, but holds the apron under them with both hands, like a basin, to catch the sacred drops of grief, — "it's all sence day before yist'day. She was well enough then. But that night — that night," — another explosion is coming; she has the extinguisher ready, — "he — he — was took up for stealing!"

This time she flings the apron completely over her head, and rocks and wrings herself in it tempestuously. Eliza is calm, you would say. But how very white! It is a minute before she can get herself heard. She takes hold of Melissa's hands as she would a child's, and endeavors to remove the muffler. At length the weeper permits her frizzled head and one corner of the corrugated countenance to be uncovered, peeps out with one streaming red eye over the saturated calico, and whimpers forth the story. It is given in bursts and snatches, incoherently enough; and, of course, one very important portion of it is suppressed, in terror of her mistress and her oath.

Eliza listens, sick at her very soul.

"And Abel is in jail to-night! Why didn't you tell me?"

"Oh, he ain't! He's innocent, ye know. And they can't keep him in jail, can they? Say!" Both eyes come out of their retreat, and appeal earnestly to Eliza, — "Do you s'pose they can?"

"How do you know he is innocent?"

"Oh, I don't know — only — his wife says he is!" so much she dares confess.

"If she says so, and thinks so, why does she give up

to the shame and misery of the thing, and keep her bed, instead of rising, like a woman, to cheer and help him ? " demands Eliza, her heart growing great within her. " I am *sure* he is innocent! My Abel! steal ? — Come, come, Melissa! We have something else to do besides lying in bed or hiding our heads in our aprons. Go and tell mother I have come. It will comfort her to see me, I know. Has she heard about Abel ? "

"I guess he told her yesterday," answered Melissa, finding a dry edge of her apron to wipe up with. " They was alone together for ever so long; and I could see something had a'most killed her afterwards. Oh, I'm so glad you've come ! " — looking up with hope and confidence at Eliza. " The house seems so dreadful lonesome ! Le'me pump you some water, if you want to wash. La, now, there's Ebby waking up jest at the wrong time ! "

" I'll take care of him. Go and prepare mother for seeing me," said Eliza.

XXI.

HOME ONCE MORE.

Now, with slow footsteps and a leaden heart, Abel Dane came home to his dishonored house. For some moments he stood gloomily outside, without the courage to enter. His wife sullen and mad with he knew not what remorse or shame, his child worse than motherless, his own mother broken-hearted by the disgrace of his arrest, though she knew not all; — what was then left to him? And Eliza had not come, as he believed, and would not come, he feared.

He opened the door. Turk bounced upon him, heralding the good news. And there, demurely sitting, with Ebby awake and happy in her arms — who? Could he believe his eyes?

"Eliza!" He ran to embrace her. "Bless you for this, Eliza!" And he bowed himself.

She did not rise. "My brother," she whispered. And with one arm holding his infant boy, and the other gathering his head to her bosom as he knelt, she felt that she was blessed.

"How came you here?" he asked, holding her hand, and looking at her in a kind of rapture. "I have been

16

to meet you. I was never so disappointed as when the stage came without you. I thought I should have to wait till next week, and that maybe you wouldn't come at all."

"If I had only known you would meet me!" said Eliza. "It would have saved me so much. But the stage was coming by the common; so I got out, and ran across. And here I am, though we missed each other."

"And glad to be home again?" he tenderly inquired.

"I am glad now,—now that you have come; for I see you are glad."

"Glad? Eliza,"—and he stroked her hand, still gazing at her with joy and tears. "I can bear anything now. You have heard?"

"Melissa has told me."

"And you believe in me?"

"Implicitly, Abel."

"I knew you would! And you have forgiven me?"

"Forgiven you?"

"Yes; for I was very harsh, very unjust to you, sister."

"But you did not mean to be," she answered, with melting gentleness.

"No, I did not; I was so wise and virtuous in my own conceit. But, Eliza, you were so much wiser and better than I, that I am amazed, I am incensed at myself when I think how we parted. I feel like the prodigal son. I have been wandering, Eliza, wandering! Now I am once more at home. But I am selfish," he

continued, saddening; "I have no such home to offer
you as you left; and, if you stay, it will be to sacrifice
your better interests, and share my broken hopes."

"I never had any interests that were not yours," answered Eliza. "And as for your broken hopes, I will
mend them!"—her pale face beaming so with love
and truth that it warmed his inmost heart.

And now he saw how time and absence had changed
her. She had grown older; but years and affliction had
not curdled the current of her life. Deep and clear and
bright it shone out upon him from the blue of her pure
eyes; and the tones of her voice betrayed how musical
and how full were the waters of that inward stream.

For Eliza, in those years, had not lain supinely on
the bed of disappointment, as many do, while brooding
sorrow sucks their blood; but, by a generous activity
of hands and head and heart, she had driven away that
vampire; and her soul, hungering in the wilderness for
human sympathy, had been fed by manna from God;
and, on the rough brier of trial, for her had blossomed
the white rose of peace.

Who has not suffered? Bereavement comes some
time to all, and it depends upon ourselves whether it
shall be unto us a blessing or a curse. Like the dwarfed
little old woman of the story-book, when ill-received by
a grumbling and grudging housewife, it proves an evil
guest, and goes not without leaving behind some bitter
token of resentment. Yet, when the same dark and
unlovely disguise enters the abode of a cheerful and,

though poor, benevolent host, and is kindly entertained, a wondrous charm enters with it, — the larder is replenished, the fire never goes out, the household work is done by unseen hands, floors are miraculously swept over night, and all troublesome and venomous insects are banished; till, by-and-by, the visitor, departing, lets fall the tattered mantle and brown hood; the fairy stands an instant revealed, then leaps, with a laugh, upon a yellow-tailed sunbeam, and vanishes, leaving the house filled with her beautiful gifts.

Unto Eliza had come such a fairy in that humble, still abode, her breast; and the cupboard of its charities had been kept well supplied, and the fire of the heart had not failed, and those busy fingers, the faculties, were sped magically in their tasks; and lo, when the night was gone, and the morning of consolation come, the world's dust was found swept clean from the chambers! and, though the fairy had flown, her charm and her blessing remained; all because Eliza had used gentle behavior towards her unwelcome guest, and had not shut her door against the messenger of God.

"Mamma!" said Ebby, exploring with his pleased fingers the new, kind face, with which he already felt himself at home. And he looked at his father, and again pointed at Eliza, and repeated, with a little crow of delight, "mamma!" — curiously feeling the eyes and mouth and chin, which he evidently found beautiful, whatever others might think.

Abel was strangely affected.

"Yes, precious!" said Eliza, smiling with suffused eyes, "I will be his mamma if ever he needs one. But I am his auntie now."

"Mamma!" insisted Ebby, trying to put his thumb into her nose. "Dood mamma!"

Abel trembled, and clinched his teeth hard, and tried to fix his features, which worked and quivered in spite of him. Eliza did not speak, but bent over the boy, whom she held close to her heart, gazing upon him with absorbing tenderness; bathing him, so to speak, in softest dews of blessing from the heaven of her soul.

Oh, had his mother such a soul, and such a heart of love! the father thought. But what now was the use, he added bitterly within himself, of vain wishes or regrets?

"I was sorry afterwards that I had written you such a letter," he said. "What did you think?"

"I knew you were having a good deal of trouble about money."

"You knew!" interrupted Abel. "How?"

"By letters. I have two or three correspondents. I heard you were likely to fail; so I thought — I hoped — your distress was nothing worse than that."

"Eliza!" — a new revelation had suddenly broken in upon Abel, — "one mystery is explained! Fool, that I didn't think of you before!"

"Of me?" said Eliza.

"Look in my eyes! 'Twas you that sent me that draft for a hundred dollars! You had it mailed from

16 *

Boston, that I might not suspect you. And that after all my unkind treatment of you!" And Abel bent his face upon her hand, which he wrung and kissed with mingled gratitude and self-reproach.

It is not probable that Eliza was sorry now to have her benevolent action known. And somehow the emotion he betrayed thrilled a nerve of joy in her breast.

"I told you," she murmured, "that I have no interests apart from yours. I never had. It seemed that an eternity of silence could not make me forget that I was still your sister, — that I owed more to you than I could ever repay."

"O 'Liza, 'Liza!" said Abel, "don't heap such coals on my head!"

"And now I have come to share all your troubles," she went on, cheerfully. "And, in the first place, tell me all about them."

Abel's forehead gloomed. He thought of the guilty woman, cowering in the bedclothes in the chamber, waiting to hear her doom from him. He remembered her anguish and her prayers, and knew that he held her destiny in his hands. It was hard to abandon her to the shame her folly had earned. It was easier to bear himself the obloquy, and, if needful, suffer punishment in her stead; for she was still his wife, — the mother of his boy. He could not forget that; and what would life be worth to him after giving her up to ignomini ? Here was Eliza. She might more than recompense him for the loss of a selfish, shallow-hearted wife. But he chased instantly the unworthy thought from his mind.

"Sister," he said solemnly, lifting his head, after a moment's heavy thought,—and there was an ague in his voice as he spoke,—"I shall tell you all I can honorably tell you, be sure; for I must have your sympathy and trust. But some things may be left long untold, and you must not question me concerning them. In due time, now or hereafter, you shall know all. I am innocent, of course; though Mrs. Apjohn's malice has a better foundation than I at first thought."

"Enough," said Eliza; "I trust you wholly, and I ought to be above idle curiosity. But here is Melissa. What did mother say?"

"She couldn't believe me when I fust told her you'd come," replied Miss Jones. "Then she chirked right up as pleased! I had to stop and put clean piller-cases on the bed, though, 'fore she'd let me bring you in to see her; for she says you're dreadful petic'lar, and I guess she don't want you to know things ain't kep' lookin' quite so scrumptious around as they used to be. But you'll find it out fast enough," added the simple-minded girl; "and you'll find 'tain't all my fault, neither."

While she was speaking, Eliza delivered Ebby to Abel, and prepared to accompany her. Melissa went as far as the old lady's door; saw her rise up in bed to meet the long-lost daughter of her adoption; heard the stifled sobs and kisses as they fell into each other's arms; then drew back from the closed door, rubbing her red eyes redder still with sympathy.

Like her let us also retire, and leave these two, re-united, to their sacred privacy. The evening is now advanced. Eliza makes up a bed in her mother's room, resolved to lie there that night and the nights thereafter, so long as her faithful attendance can be of comfort to the invalid. And there, when the deep, still hours come, blissful rest steals upon her, and she sleeps when she would watch. And the invalid becomes herself the watcher, too happy in the wanderer's return to close her eyes that night. And the night passes over them and over all, — aged watcher, youthful dreamer; Abel in the chamber apart, at peace, with Ebby at his side; and Faustina, moaning in her sleep with evil dreams, or starting awake by fits, to find herself alone, and bite her pillow with convulsive teeth until she sleeps again.

XXII.

ANOTHER SUNDAY.

ANOTHER Sunday morning, — how pure and tranquil after the fever of the week ! The farm-wagon is housed, and the unyoked oxen graze in the autumn pastures. The mill is silent; the cool, damp cavern under it echoing only to the plash of the water dripping over the great wheel. The carpenter's chest is locked, the shop closed and solitary; only mice in the shavings rustling, and flies buzzing in the dust and cobwebs of the sunny windows. Even the active young jackplane, resting on the work-bench, has a serious, composed look, — as it were, an air of keeping the Sabbath.

And the cooper's tools lie idle. And the freshly-shaped staves, standing in the corners, seem to be looking at each other, and wondering at the vicissitudes of life; feeling, no doubt, that they have been dreadfully shaved. While the rows of sober, adult barrels and little juvenile firkins, all in their new, clean dresses, are holding a solemn Quaker-meeting, so very life-like, you would say yonder pretty matron in hoops is just going to open her head and say something.

Judging from the aspect of the cooper this fine morning, you would furthermore infer that the said solemnity will never be interrupted by him, that it will be always Sunday henceforth in his shop, and Quaker-meeting among the casks. He himself, he thinks, is through with church-going, and listening to psalms and sermons forever. No more shall he sit piously in his pew, while the words from the pulpit fall and feed him, or the singing of the sweet-voiced choir breaks silvery over his soul. Never again shall he hold up his head, unshamed in the congregation. Even the ringing of the church-bells, in the holy calm, is intolerable to him; their swelling, sonorous roar, their dying moan and murmur, awakening in his breast such vibrant memories, vague terrors, and sick regrets.

Astride his chair he sits, his head bowed upon the back of it, a pitiable object. Not even Mrs. Apjohn's robust bosom can resist a thrill of pity as she looks at him. Or does the ringing of the church-bells disturb her also? She has resolutely put on her black silk, declaring that *she* is going to meeting, anyway; that *she* can hold up her head in church or out of church. But, the hour arrived, her heart succumbs. Can she bear the ordeal of jeers and significant glances? What if she should find a tomato in her pew? Will there not be some text read at her from the Scriptures, or some application to her trespass made in the sermon? She has put on her bonnet with indecision; her fingers hesitate with the ribbons.

" Sick, John ? " she says, turning partly round, as she stands before the glass.

"I ain't well, Prudy; I ain't well; not over'n above," answers melancholy John, under his elbow.

Now, Prudence flatters herself that she is not afraid to face the nation. But John is poorly; John is down-hearted; maybe John will resort again to his sanguinary handkerchief. Ought she, as a faithful wife, to leave him alone ? she asks herself, glancing from his submissive neck to the kitchen pole.

"I declare, John," she says, out of one corner of her mouth, — pins in the other corner, — "I won't go to meetin', after all ! You're sick; and I'll stay to hum and nu's' ye."

"Never mind me; never mind me," says Cooper John. "Go if ye can, and take the good on't. To be sure, to be sure."

These were the only words he spoke, until Prudence had taken off her black silk, put on her every-day gown again, and sat down in the rocking-chair, with the Bible on her lap.

"Come, John ! le's be sociable, and have a sort of comf'table Sunday to hum. What ye thinkin' about ?" asks Prudence.

"What a week can bring forth ! — the difference 'twixt this Sunday and last, Prudy !" And remember-ing how then, in his sleek Sunday clothes, he walked to church, a respected cooper, and the honest husband of an honest wife; no neighbors incensed against them, no finger of scorn pointed at them; the sight of a blush-ing tomato no more to him than the aspect of your chaste

cucumber or innocent pippin; everybody friendly to him,
the deacons recognizing him, the selectmen often deign-
ing to shake hands with him, even the minister saying,
kindly, " Good-morning, Mr. Apjohn ! " or, " I hope
you are well this blessed morning, brother Apjohn ! "
— remembering such things were one brief week ago,
and can never be again, he takes his little bald head in
his two hands, and wrings it, as if he would force tears
of blood out of that juiceless turnip.

" Highty-tighty, John ! " says Prudence; " don't be so
foolish ! "

" It won't be *Mr. Apjohn* any more ! " laments the
cooper. " But it'll be *Old Apjohn;* or *Tomato Apjohn.*"

" Never mind, John ! " says Prudence the inexorable.
" We'll spite 'em to our heart's content ! Le's think
o' that, and take comfort."

" Spite 'em ? — Comfort ? " repeats the cooper. " No,
no, no ! " And the tolling bell says " No — no — no ! "
with slow and mournful roar.   And the angels whisper
in their hearts, " No, no, no ! " But though the sorrowful tongue of her husband, and the iron tongue of the
bell, and angels' sweetly persuasive lips, should all unite
to warn or to entreat, they could not turn Prudence
from her revenge.

" I can't see a sign of their gittin' out to meetin'," she
observes, looking out of the window towards Abel's
house. " No wonder *they* don't go ! They're deeper'n
the mud'n we be'n the mire, enough sight; we've got
that to console us ! Why, John, what's a few tomatuses

'twixt neighbors? only think on't! But breaking into a house, and into a chist, and stealin' fifty dollars in money, — that's a State's-prison job, John! Oh, we'll give folks somethin' to talk about, that'll make 'em forgit the tomatuses, John!" And with a gleam of malicious joy, she sits down again, with the Bible on her lap.

"Read a chapter, Prudy," says the cooper.

And she reads, —

"But why dost thou judge thy brother? or why dost thou set at naught thy brother? for we shall all stand before the judgment-seat of Christ."

"That's it! to be sure!" comments the humble listener. "Prudy, how can we be unforgivin' to others, when we stand so much in need of mercy ourselves? '*Before the judgment-seat of Christ*,' Prudy! remember that!"

Prudence turns to read in another place: "Woe unto you, when all men shall speak well of you!" and thinks that here is solace, — that here is something that will suit her better. But the very next paragraph commences that sublime and beautiful injunction, "Love your enemies, do good to them that hate you, bless them that curse you."

And she closes the book impatiently. The Bible does not please her to-day.

In the meanwhile very different scenes are passing in Abel's house. Faustina still keeps her bed. But Eliza, active, helpful, effusing an atmosphere of cheerfulness

17

around her wherever she moves, more than fills the
place of the sullen, absent wife. She has quickly learned
the ways of the altered household; she has the old lady
once more in her chair, in the cosey kitchen-corner; and
again she is the sunshine of the house, as in old times.
Indeed, it seems as if the old times, and the beautiful,
harmonious order of departed days were now restored.
And, but for Ebby prattling yonder, watching his new
"mamma" with pleased eyes, Abel could almost fancy
his married life a wild dream.

"Oh, this is Sunday!" he thinks. No such day of
rest has he known for months. The light of Eliza's
countenance is joy to him; the sense of her presence is
a balm to all his hurts. He looks at his mother's dear
old face, freshly washed with dews of gladness and
gratitude, and shining in the morning brightness of a
new hope; he sees Melissa inspired with unwonted
activity and cleverness; he observes even the dumb
inmate, Turk, thumping his susceptible tail against
every object he passes, in his restless delight at Eliza's
coming; he almost forgets the guilty, despairing woman
in the chamber, and her crime, which he must answer
for; and still he says in his soul, "Oh, this indeed is
Sunday!"

Again Eliza sat with him and his mother at breakfast; and again she poured the elixir of her own sweet
spirit into the cups she gave them. And the muffins, —
Abel would have known they were of her cooking.
Taste them wherever he might, he could not have been

deceived. They possessed an ingredient which is not mentioned in any receipt-book. They had the real *Eliza flavor.* No such muffins had been eaten in his house since she left it; and as for that unmistakable flavor, how often had he longed for it, sitting down to an ill-furnished table, and turning heart-sick from the uninviting edibles !

Then, sometimes, in the midst of his thankfulness, the recollection of Faustina and of her crime crosses his spirit like an eclipse; and all the future is darkened.

Then, too, the aching thought of what might have been, had Eliza never gone and Faustina never come, pierces him. And the thought of what may be still, if he will but decide to sacrifice his wife, agitates him like a temptation.

For he knows now, with certainty, that all hope of happiness with her is shattered ; that, under the thin veneering of her beauty, there is no true grain of character; that what the deep heart of man forever hungers for, and can find only in the deep heart of woman, — what he has sought so ardently and long in her, and sought always in vain, — can never be his so long as she is his; and that to be her husband now, in aught but the name and outward form, will be a sin against his own divine instinct of marriage.

And, with equal certainty, he knows that, in this woman whom he once called sister, and loved so calmly and purely and habitually, under the illusion of that name, that he never guessed the strength and sacredness of the tie between them, there exists a soul richly furnished with all the grace and goodness and sympathy which he has longed for in a wife, but which he did not find when he set the vanity of his eyes to choose for him.

It avails not for Abel to put away these thoughts. They return: when the small, sprightly, electric form moves before him, or he catches the flash of her sunny glances; when his ears drink the soft music of her conversation or laughter; when once more, as in bygone years, in the mild Sunday afternoon, they read together, aloud, in the consolatory.Gospels, or the mighty poem of Job; when their voices blend in singing again the old beloved tunes, and their spirits blend also in a more subtile and delicious harmony; continually the wishes, the regrets, the passionate yearnings return, with their honey and their stings.

It is too much. Oh that the simple strain of an old tune, flinging out its spiral coil, should have power to lasso the will and master it! that the near rustle of a robe should convulse a strong man's affections! that the mere sight of an industrious little hand setting the supper-table should thrill the heart to tears!

After supper, Abel went out to walk, to calm his emotions, to cool his spirit in the bath of the evening air, — to read the riddle of his life, if possible, in the light of the sunset and the stars. And as he walked, thinking of the two women, — her he loved, and her he loathed, — doubting, hoping, in anguish and humility; he remembered the prayer of Jesus, and a part of it, which had always been dark, suddenly became clear. And he prayed within himself, —

" O Father in Heaven ! hallowed be thy name, which is LOVE !

" O LOVE ! lead us not into temptation ! "

This day it had been revealed to him that, by the deeper law of marriage, he and Eliza belonged to each other, — and that she, with her woman's nature, supreme in matters of the heart, had recognized the truth, long since, and been moved by it when he deemed her conduct so strange and unpardonable. If he had hitherto repented of his unkindness to her, how did he now gnash his teeth at the recollection of his own blindness and madness !

At sunset he stood upon a hill, and overlooked a landscape which had all his life been familiar to him; — the same earth, the same sky, the spectacle of the sundown. But now, for the first time, by some chance, bending his head, he discovered a phenomenon, known to every shrewd lover of nature. His eyes inverted, looking backwards under his shoulder, saw the world upsidedown. The unusual order in which the rays of color impinged the nerve of vision exhibited them with surprising distinctness and delicacy. The green valley, the glimmering stream, the tints of early autumn on hillside and cliff, the light on the village roofs far and near, the blue suffused horizon, the glittering sun beyond, were transfigured with magical loveliness. In the cloudless purity of the sky, which had scarcely attracted his attention before, burned the most exquisitely beautiful belts of color, more splendid than any rainbow. And Abel said, "How blind we are to the glories that are always before our eyes! Eliza was with me every day. I was as ignorant of her dearness and worth as I have always been of the beauty of the world until now. Oh, why have I discovered the charms of the earth and sky just as I am threatened with being shut up from the sight of them in the walls of a prison? And why have I never felt *her* charms until now I look at them through the grated windows of wedlock?"

So saying, or rather thinking, or rather feeling, — for his emotions did not shape themselves in words, — he turned to descend the hill.

"Why should I suffer in that wretched woman's place?" he repeatedly asked himself, in the sweating agony of his heart. "I can force her to write a full confession. That will exculpate me. That may lead to — O my God! let me not sin in this! Let my duty be made plain!"

He walked far. He returned by the common, and stood struggling with himself in sight of his house. It was now moonlight; and the stars twinkled in their eternal spheres. He could see the windows, behind which his wife lay writhing with terror and shame. He could see the door of his house, once more rendered dear to him by her, the very thought of whom could agitate and swell his breast.

"I will talk with Eliza, — I will tell her everything, — and she shall tell me what to do."

XXIII.

ABEL AND ELIZA.

ABEL walked on, strong in his new resolution, and was near his own door, when it opened, and some one came out. It was Eliza with her bonnet on. She was hurrying past him, when he spoke.

" Abel ? " she said, with a start, not glad to meet him then.

" Where are you going ? "

" Not far; a little walk."

" Let me go with you ? "

" Certainly, — if you wish to."

Yet she spoke with a hesitation and reserve which dampened his ardor.

" You are low-spirited ? " she asked, as they walked by the common.

" Do you wonder that I am ? " said Abel.

" No; it is natural; but all will come out right, Abel, I am sure. We must all go through the wilderness some time, if we would see the bright land beyond."

" You have been through ? " asked Abel, falteringly.

" I have," she answered in a low, very tender voice. " Thank Heaven ! "

"And you are happy ? "

"I am happy, Abel."

He was startled. That she could be happy, and at peace, while before him was tempestuous darkness, gave him a pang.

"Your happiness is not my happiness," he said despondingly.

"But I can reach out a hand to help you, dear brother ! " And she pressed the hand that was laid upon hers.

That was meagre comfort. Reach out to him ? Only that ?

"Eliza, I am miserable ! My married life — you may as well be told — is a wretched failure ! "

"I know it; I have known it all along," she answered.

"Yes; and you foresaw it. And you warned me," groaned Abel.

"Did I ? " There was a slight tremor in her sweet, clear voice. "Well, it was better, I suppose, that you should follow your own choice."

"When it was leading me into the pit ! " he exclaimed.

"We are sometimes permitted to go very, very wrong, for the benefit the experience will bring with it, Abel."

"But a life-long experience of disappointment and misery ! "

"There is something that will sanctify and sweeten all that to you," said Eliza.

"What is it, for God's sake ? "

"Duty ! Never swerve aside from that."

"But what is my duty?" demanded Abel, with a bitter outburst. "What is the duty of a man, who wakes from a dream of folly, to find himself bound for all time to a woman who proves unworthy of his trust and repugnant to his whole nature?"

"It is the question of questions!" said Eliza, after a deep pause.

"Which you cannot answer," cried Abel, "any more than I can."

"No; nor as well. What your private relations to her shall be," said Eliza, timidly, "must be left entirely to your own conscience. But you have assumed outward obligations towards her," she added, in a firm, unhesitating, spiritually clear tone of voice; "you have taken her from her father's house, and you have vowed to cherish her through evil report and through good report. You must never forget that; you must remember how we all stand in need of charity and forbearance, and suffer long and be kind. Do not shrink from suffering. In the end it will be gain to you. I know."

She spoke with generous sympathy, yet out of the depths of a spirit whose tranquillity and firm faith seemed to remove her farther and farther from his troubled sphere. For she perceived his fever and weakness; perhaps, also, she knew his temptation; and had fortified herself. To the strength which had been born to her out of trial and endurance, had been added a power beyond herself for this hour and this meeting. So that Abel might well exclaim, —

"You seem nearer to the cold stars up there than to me. You talk like an angel. It is all beautiful and true, what you say; but I'd rather you'd be a woman now. You do not know all, Eliza!"—Emotions crowded his voice. — "I have something terrible to tell you."

They were passing near the post-office.

"Wait a minute," she said; "then I will hear you."

She stepped aside to drop a letter in the box, then rejoined him.

"A letter!" murmured Abel. A jealous fear overshadowed him. He took her hands; he stood looking down at her pale face in the moonlight for a minute, without a word.

"You were going to tell me something," she said.

"*You* are going to tell *me* something! Eliza, who have you been writing to?"

"To a friend. Why do you ask?"

"A dear friend?"

"A very dear friend." And the pale face met his gaze with a frank smile in the moonlight.

"A man, Eliza?"

"A man, Abel. Why not?"

He gave her wrist a convulsive pressure, then dropped it, and, with a tremendous sigh, drew back from her, almost staggering. She was alarmed. She took his hand.

"What is the matter, Abel?"

"It is well; it is well! Come, Eliza; we will go home now."

· She leaned upon his arm, too full of love and pity and regret for the mockery of words.

"I am glad you have found friends in your absence," he said, after a brief silence.

"I have found some very excellent friends," she answered.

"You did not wish me to know you had a letter to mail. I understand now."

"I think it is better you should know, Abel."

This was not the reply he hoped for. Every minute and every word seemed to sharpen the fangs that gnawed his heart. He could not endure suspense.

"When are you to be married?" he demanded, abruptly.

"I don't know. Not while I feel that I am needed here," came the low, unfaltering response.

"I beg of you," said Abel, "don't let your regard for us interfere with your happiness," — with something of his irrepressible despair writhing in his voice.

"Duty first and always, and happiness cannot fail," said Eliza.

"I hope he is worthy of you," he added.

"I wish," she replied, "that I was half as worthy of him."

They passed on in silence; his hot thoughts almost stifling him.

"But you were to tell me something," she reminded him.

"It is this," said Abel. "I thank you from the bot-

tom of my soul for your advice to me. I shall do my
duty."

" I am sure you will, Abel ! "

"Yes, — thanks to you. Whatever happens, I can suffer. God grant your married life may be happier than
mine has been ! "

Eliza's serenity was fast forsaking her. She loved Abel
too well, she sympathized with his sorrow too much, to
answer now with calm words of counsel. Misgivings,
also, it may be, with regard to her own future and duty,
disquieted her.

What right had she, loving this man, to be happy in
another's arms ? Had she sinned, when, lonely and cold
and famished, she accepted the solace of a good man's
affection ? Because one hope had perished, should she
go through God's bright universe refusing to be comforted ? Because Abel was married, should she forever
obstinately shun the high destiny of woman, — wifehood
and motherhood ?

These were no new questions. Long, in anguish and
supplication, she had wrestled with the great problem.
Many a woman and many a man has wrestled with it
the same, — wrestles with it still. Each must solve it for
himself or herself. It is good to live true to one's own
heart ; sacrificing all things else to that ; through absence, and lapse of time, and death of hope. And to
renounce the impossible, accepting cheerfully the best
that is given, is also good. Consider it well ; let the
soul choose ; and who shall condemn ?

Eliza had chosen. Yes, and even now she felt that she had chosen wisely. Excepting only Abel, this other, of all men, stood highest in her regard. She had acquainted him with all the doubts of her heart; nor had she left him to enter this ordeal of danger without his consent and blessing.

And in all things, so noble did he appear to her, so dear had he rendered himself by his generosity and truth, that she knew she could make him a true and happy wife. Yet once more, to-night by Abel's side, stirred by his love and grief, the old perturbations arise. Only solitude and prayer can put them again at rest. She was glad that the gate was near, and that Abel did not offer to go in with her.

"I shall walk a little further," he said. "Comfort mother till I come."

And the gate closed between them with a harsh sound. And both felt that another gate shut also between them; the gate whose hinges are providence, and whose latch is fate.

"Idiot! idiot!" muttered Abel, with angry and bitter scorn of himself. "I merit what I have. I will take with calmness what is still to come. Tongue, hold your peace! Misery, do your worst! Misfortunes, rain, hail, pour!"

He walked in the placid and smiling moonlight. And something of the silence and vastness and chasteness of the night glided into him. His thoughts grew great and solemn and tender. To go to prison for another's

18

sake did not seem much to him then. To die for another's sake did not seem so bitter. He murmured Eliza's name with a prayer for her happiness. He thought of Faustina with gentleness and compassion. He remembered how near his mother's feet were to the still portals of eternity, and smiled. Only when he thought of his child he wept.

For his child's sake he would willingly humble himself; and, seeing a light in the cooper's house, he bethought him to go in, and try if it were possible to conciliate the enemy.

XXIV.

THE NIGHT.

THE Apjohns were just going to bed; and Cooper
John came to the door, with a candle, in his shirt and
trousers. He looked aghast at Abel.

"Come in: to be sure, to be sure!" he said. "Prudy!
Prudy!"

Prudy came out of the bedroom, presently, in her
petticoat, with a shawl over her shoulders, nodding sar-
castically.

"How do you do, Mr. Dane?" she carelessly inquired, arranging a corner of the shawl the better to
cover her portliness. "John Apjohn," — turning to the
shivering cooper, — "go to bed!"

Meekly snuffing, John set the candle on the table, and
withdrew.

"Is it peace?" said Abel, holding out his hand.

"Peace, Abel Dane? I should say peace!" retorted
the grim housewife, scornfully laughing. "I wonder
the word don't blister your mouth! Peace, after sech
treatment as I have had from you and your upstart
wife! I say for't!"

"Prudy," whispered the cooper, putting his head out
of the bedroom.

" What now ? " she demanded, sharply.

" Let it be peace, Prudy; let it be peace," said John.

" Shet up ! " ejaculated Prudence.

And the imploring visage was slowly withdrawn, and the door softly closed again.

" When you were in my garden a week ago," said Abel, " did *I* look at *you* with scorn ? Did I magnify your offence ? Did I set myself up as *your* judge, and make haste to pronounce sentence ? "

" No, no; to be sure ! Remember that, Prudy ! " answered a ghostly voice in the direction of the bedroom.

" No, to be sure ! " repeated Prudence, with a vindictive toss. " He didn't da's to, to my face. But what did he do behind my back ? — the sarpent ! Strung tomatuses on to my door ! And that wasn't enough, but you must come and rob us of our hard-earned money, — thinkin' we wouldn't da's to make a fuss about it, I s'pose. But you'll see, — you'll see, Abel Dane ! Talk of peace ! Ha ! ha ! "

Abel commenced, protesting his innocence of the string of " tomatuses."

" Tut, tut," said Mrs. Apjohn; " I s'pose you'll deny you stole the money next ! "

Once more the meek, bald pate of the cooper was pushed into the room.

" Hear what the man has got to say, Prudy dear, — do ! "

" John Apjohn ! "

" What, Prudy ? "

" I said go to bed."

" Yes, Prudy ! "   (Exit bald head.)

" My worthy woman," then said Abel, seating himself, and speaking candidly and earnestly, " I have come to talk with you as neighbors should talk, and I beg of you to hear me with patience and without prejudice."

" Wal, sir," — Prudence occupied the wood-box for a seat, and pulled her shawl together and looked crank, — " I hear you, sir ! "

" I see it is useless for me to deny the charge of insulting you with tomato-vines, and I have no intention of setting up a claim to the fifty dollars, which, I presume, belongs rightfully to you; but I here solemnly protest that I never meant to rob you, or injure your reputation, or wound your feelings.   I call Heaven to be my witness ! "

Again the bedroom-door opened, and again the cooper's head appeared, this time with a night-cap on.

" Prudy," he said, in an awe-struck voice, " he calls Heaven to witness ! "

" He didn't call *you* / " retorted the Juno of this little Olympus, and the night-capped Jupiter disappeared again.

" Furthermore," said Abel, " I pledge you my honor that whatever reparation can be made for the injuries you complain of, shall be made.   And I tell you I am sincerely sorry for all that has happened; and for whatever I have done amiss I humbly ask your pardon."

18 *

" Wal, sir ? "

" Well, Mrs. Apjohn, I believe it depends upon you whether this charge against me shall be prosecuted. If we can come to an understanding, and you withdraw your complaint, there will not be much difficulty in avoiding an indictment. Question your own conscience before you answer," said Abel, foreboding evil from the grimace and toss with which she prepared to reply; " and consider whether you can afford to be unmerciful; remembering that what mercy we show shall be shown to us."

Prudence pulled her shawl together nervously and compressed her lips, and elevated her chin and said, —

" Wal, Abel Dane, you've had your say; now hear *me.* Nobody can accuse me of havin' an Injin temper; and you can't say't ever in all my life I spoke of you one misbeholden word. You was always as decent a kind of a man till you got married, as ever I knowed; and you would be now, if it wa'n't for that pesky proud wife of your'n, that I'm bound to come up with some way, and I only wish it was her that took the money, and not you ! She's made a fool of ye, and made a proud, desaitful, mean, underhanded scamp of you that was a perty honest and tolerable respectable neighbor afore. I feel bad for you, Abel Dane; and, as I said, I only wish it was her that I could prove took the money; then if she wouldn't smart for't, I miss my guess."

Abel sighed; for now he saw how vain it would be to shift the responsibility of the theft from himself to his wife, in the hope that their enemy would be more merciful to her than to him.

The night-capped head was at the bedroom door again; but it was only moved with a slow and dismal shake, in silence.

"You are a hard-hearted woman," said Abel, sadly smiling, as he rose to go.

"Mabby I be ! I can't help it ! Human natur' is human natur' ! " Prudence grinned, put her hand on her knee for a support, and got up from the wood-box. " I tell ye, I never laid up anything ag'in you, Abel; and if it wa'n't for that stuck-up critter, your wife, we never'd quarrel; though I don't know but you're 'bout as bad as she is now. There ! " — holding her shawl together with one hand, and taking up the candle with the other, — " You've had your say, and I've had my say, and now good-night."

" One word more. Remember I have a mother and a child." The emotion in Abel's voice would have shaken Prudence, if it had been possible to shake her. But she only compressed her lips as before and said, —

"I've thought of them; I've thought it all over; and I've said all I've got to say."

The cooper, at these words, retreated, and crept in between the sheets with a groan.

"Very well," answered Abel, sternly and impressively. " I have done. I leave you to your conscience and your Maker."

" I guess my conscience and my Maker will use me

perty well, sir!" And, with sarcastic courtesy, Mrs. Apjohn lighted him from the door with the candle. "Remember me to your wife," she added; "and tell her, if you please, what I say."

Eliza had retired with the old lady to her room, when Abel returned home. He found the kitchen forsaken, silent, and lighted only by the pale shimmer of the moon. He entered the sitting-room; that, too, was forsaken, silent, and lighted only by the pale shimmer of the moon. There was something in the aspect of his house that struck like desolation to his soul.

Half an hour later, he opened gently the door of Faustina's chamber, and stood at the threshold. There he stood, dark and stern, for a minute or two, and looked in. By the bedside sat Melissa, with Ebby crying in her arms. In the bed, covered completely, even to the crown of her head, round which the bedclothes were twisted in a disordered heap, lay the boy's mother.

"O papa!" said Ebby, stretching up his little arms, in his night-gown.

Melissa started, and gave a frightened look at her master.

"Put that child to bed!" said Abel.

"Oh, I did, sir!" Melissa hastened to explain. "I put him to bed all of an hour'n'a'f ago."

"Then what is he here for?"

"She wanted him; she had me take him up, and bring him to her, jest so's't she could see him, she said; her own baby, so!"

Abel was touched; as no doubt Faustina meant he should be, when he should learn what the yearning, maternal heart of her had prompted.

"Why don't she look at him, then? What was the child crying for?" she heard his deep voice demand.

"O sir! mabby you think she don't keer for her baby; but she dooes!"—This was a part of the lesson Faustina had taught Melissa, and she repeated it very pathetically.—"And when she wanted to have him in bed with her, and he didn't want to go, she was so worked! her own baby so, you know. And she jest kivered up her head, and said, no matter, she would die, and he wouldn't have no mother, not no more; and that's what made him cry."

"Me dot new mamma!" Ebby declared, with a sob of subsiding grief between the words.

"Take him to bed," said Abel.

"Tiss, papa!" implored the beautiful, aggrieved face, through its tears.

The father gave the wished-for kiss; and Melissa took the child away. Then Abel shut the door, and sat down by the bed.

All this time, Faustina had not stirred. Abel gazed at the vortex of bedclothes in which she had coiled herself, and sighed, and clenched his teeth hard, and waited. O memory! was this his marriage-bed?

"Faustina!" No motion; no response. "Have you anything to say to me?" he continued.

"I won't stir. I'll make him think I'm dead!"

thought the wretched being under the clothes. Then she almost wished she was dead, and could stand by and witness his terror and remorse when he should lift the sheet and discover her lifeless form.

But it was a difficult part to play. Madam was smothering; and if she kept covered much longer, she felt that, instead of making believe dead, she would be dead in earnest. That was not so pleasant to think of, notwithstanding the fancied satisfaction of breaking his heart with the sight of her lovely corpse. Vanity and spite was not quite equal to the occasion; and she waited accordingly, with increasing ache and anxiety, for him to make another and more moving appeal, which she resolved beforehand not to resist. Why didn't he speak, and afford her the longed-for excuse for uncovering? He was in no hurry; he took his time; deliberate was Abel, — a good deal more so, she thought, than he would have been, had his own head been under the blanket.

But it was serious business with her, poor thing, despite all her foolish artifice. Dread and despair were with her there under the bedclothes.

"If you have nothing to say to me," Abel resumed, at last, "I have still a few words which I want you to listen to. Will you hear me ?"

At that, the arms were suddenly disengaged, the clothes thrown back, and staring eyes rolled up wildly at Abel, from a tragic face still half concealed by rumpled pillows and tangled hair.

"Is this you, Faustina ?" exclaimed Abel, astonished and heartsick at the sight.

Upon which she glared, and rolled her orbs, and grated her teeth, with superior artistic effect, for a matter of twenty seconds, or thereabouts; then dived again, and twisted herself up in the bed-covering, with writhings and moanings extraordinary. Abel sighed deeply, and waited patiently for her to come up to breathe again, which she was not slow in doing, then said, —

"When you are calm, and in your right mind, I will speak."

In her right mind? That gave her a cue to another fine piece of acting. What if she could convince him she was insane, — overwhelm him with a spectacle of the wreck his hard-heartedness had made of her? She would try it, — the inconsiderate and impulsive creature. And, indeed, she was not altogether in her right mind, but just excited enough with fear and suffering to enter well into the part.

This is what she did:

She sat up in bed, swept her hair from her face with both hands, in a terrific frizzled mass, stared at Abel again frightfully, rolled her eyes hideously, grinned idiotically, chattered her teeth, and burst into a laugh of frenzy.

She laughed to be heard a mile. She laughed with an ease and inspiration for the exercise which astonished herself, and without cessation or interval, except to catch her breath and recommence. She laughed, in short, until she laughed away all self-control, and could not stop, for the life of her; having, as you perceive, like an actor of first-class imagination, slipped swiftly from the counterfeit into the reality, — just as sometimes the elder Booth, from playing Richard, became Richard, and would rant and foam at the mouth, and fight the feigning Richmond in right deadly fashion.

Madam had, in fact, gone off in a genuine fit of hysterics. She laughed till she sobbed, and sobbed till she fell into convulsions, in which she was wrenched and rolled, like a body in the breakers of an Atlantic storm, and which finally heaved her, breathless and quivering, upon the strands of unconsciousness.

And Abel thought her dead. He stood like one stunned, gazing at her with a stony wonder, his lips parted, and his hair lifting with horror. Deep, solemn gladness, an awful hope, mingled with his fear.

He looked across the bed at Eliza, for she was there, — all the women in the house having been summoned by the hysteric shrieks. Their eyes met over the insensible form. Something like lightning flashed between them, — an instant only, — and it passed — forever.

Faustina was not dead, nor would she die yet for a score of years at least. Things do not happen in life as they do in romances. 'Tis pity, for now might we bring our tale joyfully to a close, would she but revive enough to make a free confession, before witnesses, of her sins against the Apjohns, murmur her repentance, ask to see a clergyman, place Eliza's hand in Abel's, declare they are for each other, smile contentedly, and die at a most convenient season. Then Eliza's absent lover should be opportunely tossed by some iron bull of a locomotive, or sent to heaven by an exploding steamboat boiler; leaving, of course, a will in her favor; when nothing would remain but for the surviving hero and heroine to be married, and enter upon the enjoyment of that limpid existence of lymph and honey miscalled happiness, which never was on earth, and never will be anywhere, probably, except in story-books.

But this is no fine fiction; no far away Eden of unimaginable beauty this, but a plain little garden-plat, where a few common flowers grow, with many coarse plants and weeds, rooted in this homely New England soil, and breathing the actual air of the present. And we must plod our way patiently to the end of the prosaic path.

"Rub her hand!" cried Eliza, setting a brisk example, having first dashed water into Faustina's face.

"Stand her on her head and let the blood run back into it ag'in!" gasped Melissa, seeing the utter pallor of her mistress, and-having some dim notion that the head was a vital part, and that when the blood forsook that, then came death.

"Bathe her nostrils with the land of Canaan!" said the old lady, meaning the contents of a camphor-bottle which she brought.

"Brandy!" ejaculated Abel, remembering that a few drops of his little store of spirits had been saved by his timely interruption of a certain convivial entertainment, not many nights ago.

All the proposed remedies were tried, except Melissa's, who could find no one to favor her novel theory of the blood. And the result was that Faustina came duly back to consciousness, without having been stood upon her head; and Abel had — shall we say the satisfaction? — of seeing her breathe and live again.

But by this time all his unworthy thoughts and wicked wishes regarding her had given place to repentance and pity. And as soon as he could dispense with assistance, he sent the rest away, and remained alone to watch by her bedside.

"Don't let me die!" whispered Faustina, in a weak voice of entreaty.

"No, no," said Abel, confidently, "you shall not die."

"I didn't mean to do it," she added, whimperingly, in terror of what had happened.

"I know you didn't," he answered, kindly. "But you must keep perfectly quiet now. I shall stay with you. No harm will come whilst I am here."

She looked up gratefully into his face.

"Oh, you are good, Abel! Kiss me, — won't you?"

And he touched his lips to her cheek.

"Oh, we can be happy yet, — can't we?" she pleaded.

"I hope so," he replied, to quiet her.

"Oh, and you will not" —

He knew what she would say.

"No, I will not," he promised.

"Oh, thank you, thank you!" and she covered his hand with kisses. "But tell me true, — you will save me?"

" I tell you true, I will. At every risk to myself, I will shield you. And I forgive you, too.. There; now rest."

" Oh ! oh ! oh ! " she cried, in an ecstasy of gratitude; " you are such a good Abel ! And we shall be so happy once more ! "

But Abel's brow was dark.

" You must keep quiet, Faustina," he said. " If you have another such fit, you may die in it."

" And you don't want me to die ? " she said, with that childlike simplicity which was one of her girlish arts to please or touch.

" I want you to live," replied Abel, in a low voice, out of a conscience grim as night.

" Come to bed then, — won't you, my Abel ? "

" No; I shall sit up and watch."

" But you won't leave me ? " she implored, with self-ish and clinging fear. " And — tell me again you won't expose me, not even to her, — Eliza."

" Not even to her. The secret is locked here." Abel's hand pressed his bosom. " Now sleep."

And she slept. And he watched by her side all night. And the lamp burned out, and the moon set upon his watching, and the sun rose.

And Abel had not said to her what he entered her room that night to say; but he kept that also locked in his breast.

XXV.

FIAT JUSTITIA.

ELIZA had written to her friend of the condition of affairs in her old home. He promptly and generously replied: —

"Your place seems to be there for the present. . . . I trust all to you; for I know you will do what is right."

So Eliza remained. And more, — she placed what was left of her savings at Abel's disposal.

It was a grief for him to be obliged to accept still further pecuniary assistance from her.

"It is all one," she said. "Even if I did not owe you more for years of kindness to me than I can ever hope to acknowledge, still I am your sister, you know, and all that is mine is yours." And she forced her earnings into his hands.

"I can't!" he exclaimed. "I have no right to your poor little purse, Eliza."

"Don't you go to making fun of it, if it is little," she cheerily replied. "*I* am little, and, I tell you, little things are not to be despised."

"But your marriage," said Abel. "You must not go to your husband penniless.'

"He is well-off, and needs none of my money. He has told me so."

"I — am glad he is well off," faltered Abel, with an indescribable contraction of the heart.

"So am I — for his sake. And for ours, too, Abel," she added, frankly. "For you will need more than I have, to pay your lawyers; he mentions that in his letter, and offers to lend you."

This was rather too much for proud Abel Dane. He choked upon it a minute, and wrung her hand.

"Thank him for me. I am in your power; I am at your mercy, Eliza. Don't be too kind to me!"

So it was settled that Eliza should remain till after Abel's trial. And there was need; for the old lady could not endure even the thought of her going; and Ebby clung to his new mamma; and Faustina continued a prey to depression and nervous caprice; and both the management and cheerfulness of the household depended upon Eliza.

And the weeks went swiftly by, and the time of the trial arrived.

It was now December, — a bleak sky overhead, a barren, paralyzed world beneath, cold winds blowing, streams freezing over, and thin flurries of snow flying here and there in the sullen, disheartened weather.

During two days the trial progressed; two days of dread and uncertainty to the innocent accused, and no less to the guilty unaccused; two days of general excitement in the village, and of sharp forensic fencing,

19 *

harassing legal quibbles, flushed and gaping crowds, and much unwholesome heat and fetor in the court-room.

With the feverish details of those days, — how Abel bore himself in that shameful public position, confronting the abusive attorneys, the grave judges, the silent twelve, and the open-mouthed multitude; what his mother suffered, awaiting the result which was to decide not his fate only, but which would also prove a word of life or death to her; and how Faustina experienced a plentiful lack of amusement during those two days and nights, — it is needless to weary the reader.

It was the wish of Abel's lawyers to have both his wife and mother present in the court-room. The age, infirmities, and tears of the elder lady, and the beauty and affection of the younger, could not fail, they argued, to have a favorable effect on the jury. And Ebby, held up in their arms, would have been an important addition to the group. But old Mrs. Dane was already worn out with anxiety in his behalf, and he knew that it was not possible for her to support the fatigue and agitation of witnessing his arraignment. And Faustina was kept at home by her own miserable terrors and an illness either feigned or real.

With two invalids to care for, Eliza could not easily leave, to go and sit by Abel's side in this hour of doubt and peril. But, on the morning of the third day, she felt irresistibly impelled to the court-house. The case had been given to the jury the night before, and at the opening of the court it was expected they would bring in their verdict. She could not wait for the news to reach her; but she must hasten, and be on the spot.

Accordingly, she left Melissa in charge, and set out on foot for the centre of the town. It was full two miles to the court-house. She walked all the way, through a blinding storm. The snow, which had evidently been trying hard to fall during those two days, was now filling the air, and whirling in the wintry gale. It drove full in Eliza's face, but little she cared for it, hastening on a business the thoughts of which were far more biting and bitter.

The court-room was already crowded on her arrival; and, to her despair, she found herself unable to penetrate the steaming throngs that choked the passages. She did not know the way to the more private entrance, where, as a friend of the accused, she might have gained admission and found a seat near his side. So, after all her trouble, she could not get in; and, being shorter than anybody else, she could see nothing but the elbows and backs between which she was soon tightly wedged, the gray, unsympathizing ceiling when she looked up, and now and then, when she looked down, a glimpse of the little close-shaded puddles of trodden and melting snow under her feet.

The court had not yet come in; and some of the spectators near her filled the interval with conversation and comment.

"They say his wife used to be a great belle," said a red-cheeked maiden.

" Used to ? " retorted an affectedly soft masculine voice.
" Handsomest woman th' is in this county, to-day ! "

" I want to know ! " whistled a toothless woman's
voice. " You know her, then ? "

" Like a book; neighbor o' mine ! such a figger ! and
eyes, — glorious, you better believe ! "

" Is she so very perty, though ? " asked she of the red
cheeks, with a slightly envious intonation.

" Pufficly magnificent, I assure ye ! Unlucky day for
her, though, when she married that sneaking Abel Dane."

Moved by an impulse of angry indignation, Eliza
thrust herself forward, till she could see, over the old
woman's hood, the half-shut, simpering eyes and smirking
mouth of the speaker. She would have been tempted to
strike that lying mouth, had it not been safe beyond her
reach.

" So you set it down he's guilty," whistled the old
woman.

" Guilty ! " echoed the young man. " Nobody doubts
that, that knows him as well as I do."

" Oh, ain't it too bad, aunt ! " said the girl. " They
say his conduct has broke her heart."

. " Yes," corroborated the youth. " She's been sick
a-bed ever since he was took up, — apprehended, ye
know," — hastening to amend his speech with the more
elegant word that occurred to him. " Naturally harrowing to a wife's feelings, y' und'stand."

" What a shame, to disgrace his family that way ! "
said the elderly female.

"He might at least have had some regard for his wife!" chimed in the girl.

"Outrageous!" added the smirking mouth. "Take a beautiful girl away from her home, — creature of exqueezit sensibilities, ye know; genteel folks, fust-rate tip-top 'ristocratic s'ciety, ye know; surrounded by the lap of luxury"—

"I want to know if she was, poor thing!" exclaimed the whistler.

"Better believe!" And a dingy hand, presenting a remarkable contrast of foul nails and showy rings, stroked a languid mustache that shaded the smirking mouth. "Outrageous, I say, — get a wife on false pretences that way, and then go to committing burglary, as if expressly a-puppus to overwhelm her with obliquity!"

"Tasso Smith!" cried a warning tongue in the crowd.

The proprietor of the rings started, and looked all around, with a foolish, apprehensive stare, to see who had spoken. It was apparently a female voice, and it seemed to come from some mysterious depths in the crowd.

"Is't re'ly burglary now!" exclaimed the woman, to whose ear the word had an appalling sound.

"Burglary in th' secon' degree," the youth answered, lowering his voice, and still glancing uneasily around. "'Twould have been burglary in the fust degree, if he'd broke into the house — entered the tenement, ye know," he added, in more classic phrase, — "in the night. Per-

petrating the attempt in the daytime, that makes secon'
degree."

"But I thought they couldn't prove just when he
broke in; that's how I understood it," observed a rough-
looking man, whose shaggy coat concealed Eliza.

"·My friend," — the youth, recovering his equanimity,
spoke with a complacent, patronizing air, as if conscious
of showing off his attainments to an admiring audience,
— " My friend, you understood puffic'ly correct. Nobody
seen him break in, of course. But it's mos' probable he
done it — consummated the atrocity, ye know," he translated himself, — " the afternoon the Apjohns was away;
absent from the dormitory, ye understand."

" Absent from the domicile, you mean! " sneered a lad
of fifteen, regarding him with immense disgust.

" Same thing," — and the ringed and grimy paw was
passed once more across the conceited mouth. " Clock
being stopped at certain hour that afternoon, which was
effected mos' probable, when he took out the key of the
chist or put it back ag'in, — ye know, — seems to indi-
cate the time of the operation. That's no consequence,
though; they'll prove a compound larceny, safe enough,
and that covers the hull ground, y' und'stand."

" His lawyers made a bad job, trying to prove his
whereabouts all that afternoon," observed the rough-
coated stranger.

" Puffic'ly ! Ye see, it couldn't be did. Lucky for
him a wife ain't permitted to testify aginst her husband; if he gets off, — successful acquittal, ye know, —
it 'll be on that account."

" What, sir ! " whizzed the imperfect dental apparatus of the girl's aunt, " ye don't think she know'd of his hookin' the money ? "

A peculiarly knowing smile stirred the young man's mustache. " I — ah — apprehend she knowed as much about it as anybody. Ye see, she might 'a' been convicted, in her own mind, of his turbitude, or else she wouldn't been so puffic'ly succumbed by the dispensation ! " he added, with that characteristic elegance of diction which corresponded well with his jewelry, being, one may say, the pinchbeck of language displayed on the unwashed joints of a vulgar mind.

" Have you seen the poor creetur' lately? " inquired the toothless one.

" No, madam, I hain't, not very recent." The youth drew himself up pompously. " Ye see, after that — ah, despisable affair — I cut her husband's acquaintance. A gentleman don't like to compromise his repetation, y' und'stand, by calling at the house of a thief, if he *has* got a charming woman for a wife."

" Tasso Smith ! " called once more the mysterious, warning voice.

" Hello ! " said Pinchbeck, with a gasp, and a sallow grin. " Who speaks ? Good joke ! ha ! ha ! " — with a forced laugh.

" Somebody's callin' Tasso Smith ! " said the woman. " Be *you* Tasso Smith ? "

" That's my — ah — patternimic," the young man acknowledged.

"Now I wan'to know! Huldy Smith's boy, be ye? Huldy Bobbit that was? Why, me an' her was school-gals together. Didn't ye never hear her tell of Marshy Munson?"

"Can't say I ever did!" and the young man lifted his head superciliously.

"Wal, you tell her how you seen Marshy Munson to the trial. It's *Munson* still, tell her. I'm a livin' now to my brother's, 'Gustus Munson's; this's his darter. Your mother married a Smith, I heerd, and had a son Tasso; though it's years sence I've seen her; but I hope now we shall visit back and forth a little. Dear me!"—the scraggy-toothed spinster interrupted herself, regarding Tasso admiringly,—"is it possible Huldy Bobbit's got a boy that tall! smart and good-lookin' too; I can say that 'thout flatterin'. And to think I should meet you here, and find out who you be, and that you knowed all about the case 'fore ever it come to trial!"

"I—congratulate myself," said Tasso, haughtily, "that I was 'bout as well posted as mos' folks,—generality of individuals, y' und'stand."

"How about the letter he lost in Apjohn's house?" inquired Marshy Munson's niece. "Was that proved against him?"

"It was, miss, supposed to be," smiled Tasso; "and it's one of the mos' overwhelming circumstances in the case."

"And the tomatoes, that was hung onto Apjohn's door—wasn't that mean?"

"Mean? I believe ye!" said Tasso, slightly wincing.

"And of course he done it, you think?"

"Of course? Nobody mean enough to — perpetrate such a thing, without it's Abel Dane; as anybody that knows him"—

"Tasso Smith, you are a liar!"

Tasso turned yellow as his linen, and stopped short as if the little hand, instead of the little tongue, of the concealed speaker, had smitten him. From that moment, he became singularly reserved, not venturing to open again his mendacious mouth. He now turned his eyes steadfastly towards the bar; and the tittering occasioned by his discomfiture had scarcely ceased, when the court came in.

"Hello, my little girl," said the rough-coated stranger to Eliza, "you seem bound to git a look."

"Oh, sir! if I only could?"

"Sho! some friend of your'n, is he? — this Abel Dane?"

"He — is — a dear friend — my adopted brother!" faltered Eliza, from her anxiously throbbing heart.

"Ye don't say! Here, I'll make a place for you. Give way a little there, you square-shouldered fellers; let this young woman pass in; she's the man's sister,— Abel Dane's sister!"

Although ashamed of being thus publicly announced, Eliza was glad of the advantage the kind, rough man obtained for her; and in a minute she had passed, she scarcely knew how, the close barrier of the crowd, and

20

stood in front of it, with garments sadly disordered by the strain and pressure they had sustained.

Before her was a railing as high as her arms, and within that a bewildering scene; — the lawyers and privileged visitors, whispering, writing, arranging papers, or getting their seats, — in the midst of whom her eye singled out the well-known side-head of the man she sought. He was seated, composedly awaiting the arrival of the jury with their verdict. He turned to speak to a friend by his side, and then she saw his features, which were firm, but careworn and haggard. She dared not move beyond the rail; but at sight of that dear, suffering face, she flew to him in spirit, and flung her arms about him, and irrepressible tears ran down her checks. Order was soon secured in the court, and from a distant door an official-looking personage entered, bearing a portentous perpendicular staff, and ushering in a file of twelve men, who silently took their places upon seats reserved for them beyond the bar, at the right-hand of the judicial bench. Eliza almost forgot to breathe, and leaned faintly upon the rail before her, as she thought that the fate of Abel lay in the voice of these twelve men, and that in another instant she might hear his doom pronounced.

There was a brief delay, she knew not for what; then the question was asked, — had the jury agreed upon their verdict.

They had agreed. Low and ominous came the response from the foreman.

Was the accused at the bar guilty or not guilty ?

Eliza's brain reeled. She did not know whether she heard the answer, or only a part of it. She looked dizzily around. She saw the excited faces; she heard the whispered echoes; then all was chaos and darkness about her. But she still clung to the rail, and did not faint.

"Told ye so!" said Tasso, with a look of malicious satisfaction at his new acquaintances. "Yes!" he whispered to the tiptoe listeners behind him; "GUILTY! GUILTY!"

When Eliza recovered the mastery of her senses, she saw, as in a dream, Abel standing up in court, erect and pale; and heard some one inquiring if he had anything to say why sentence should not be passed upon him.

Abel's voice was deep and agitated, as he answered, —

"I have nothing to say, but once more to protest my innocence, and that is idle now. I believe the jury have come honestly to their decision; but, God knows, they have condemned an innocent man."

Silence followed these impressive words, broken only by a single cry of pain, — a sharp moan wrung from Eliza's very soul.

Abel, after hesitating a moment, as if there was more he would have said, passed his hand across his forehead, and sat down. But he was presently required to stand up again, and receive the sentence of the court.

"Oh, his poor old mother! his poor little baby!" sobbed Eliza, audibly.

Abel hid his face with his hand for a minute, struggling with the emotions that had well-nigh mastered him, then stood up, stern and calm.

In the midst of the hushed and crowded court-room, — confronting the jury that had pronounced him guilty, and the judge who was to declare his sentence, — the focus of a thousand eyes which well might burn his cheeks to coals, or whiten them to ashes, — the one absorbing object of pity, or wonder, or gloating satisfaction, to all those packed benches, and thronged windows and doorways, — a spectacle also, no doubt, to bands of angels, weeping over the weakness of human judgments, or tenderly smiling with joy at the divine wisdom which underlies them, and works through them, and changes the bitterness of wrong into the sweetness of mercy at last, — there, on that wild December day, which blinded the windows with snow, and darkened all the air with storm, Abel Dane, the carpenter, stood up to receive the doom of a felon.

In a slow, monotonous, and dogmatic speech, the judge commented on the majesty of the law, which had been offended, and the necessity of dealing justice to the offender. Next, the enormity of Abel's crime against society was duly made clear to him. He was also reminded of the obligation he was under to feel grateful for the enlightened process of law by which he had been convicted, and for the patience and impartiality with which his case had been heard. It now remained to determine the punishment, which should be at once a just retribution for his offence, and serve as a solemn warning to other wrong-doers.

Then, in the same unmoved, formal, droning tone of voice, the court proceeded to discharge its heavy responsibility, by pronouncing judgment.

This was the judgment.:

To serve a term of FIVE YEARS, AT HARD LABOR, IN THE STATE PRISON.

This was the doom of Abel Dane.

It smote the appalled heart of Eliza. FIVE YEARS ! It seemed to her that the heavens had fallen, and justice had *not* been done.

Abel bowed his head, and sat down, and the sentence was irrevocably recorded against his name. He was committed to the charge of the sheriff, to be taken from the court to the jail, and thence to be conveyed to the place of his long, weary, ignominious confinement.

He was marched away by the officers. The distant door opened before him and closed again behind him. It was done. And Eliza, forced into something like calmness by the very intensity of her despair, or stunned by the awfulness of the stroke, or held by a ghastly unbelief, looked about her, — saw the soulless visage of the judge still sitting there; the misty sea of faces around; the windows streaming, as it were, with tears; the vast, dim, empty space under the dome, but nowhere Abel; receiving, in that instant of time, upon the tablet of her brain, a picture of blurred desolation, of sickening unreality, to haunt her days thenceforward, and to wake her by night from harrowing dreams. 20 *

She was roused from that momentary palsy of the soul, by the audience breaking up; — for the show was over, the tragedy ended; the strained chord of excited interest had snapped; and the next case on the docket was too tame to excite the public appetite after such a highly seasoned entertainment as had just been enjoyed.

The jury went out and another came in. And the court coldly turned to the next case. And the lawyers scribbled and quibbled. And the darkening storm whirled and whistled without. And the affairs of the great world went on, and there was joy, and there was laughter, just the same now as when Abel Dane, the convict, was a free and happy man.

XXVI.

THROUGH PRISON-BARS.

BUT now the heavy doors of the jail were clanging behind him, and the keys turning in the locks. He was no longer of the world.

Henceforth solitude, hopeless toil, years of corroding misery, which seemed a lifetime to look forward to, and years of reflected infamy afterwards, if he was so unfortunate as to live to be old,—a despised and broken-spirited old age; such was the dismal vista of the future.

There was no escape now. The cold walls of the jail, the suppressed, sad voice and compassionating look of the sheriff, as he took leave of him, the portentous click and jingle of the retiring keys, the grated windows, and the wild, white-maned storm plunging by outside, as if to mock him with the terrors and beauty of its magnificent freedom,—all conspired to assure him that, marvellous and past belief as such a fate appeared to him, it was no dream, but a stern, stony reality.

An hour ago there was hope; but now there was no hope. Then it seemed not impossible but the bitter cup might pass from him; and the thought of returning to

his humble occupation, to his mother and his child, to his
old home, and the old life of care and trial, which did
not seem so bad a life after all, would thrill his heart
most tenderly.   But that is denied him — inexorably !
The lot of a felon is his.

To go with inglorious cropped hair; to work at his
trade under a task-master, in a silent company of con-
victs; to be dressed like them in the shameful prison
uniform; to be marshalled in degrading mechanical order to the workshops in the morning, and driven back
in a dull tramping row at night, — himself one of that
jeering, grotesque, melancholy file, stamping with bi-
colored legs, in sullen time with the rest; crowding close
at the prison-doors, with some reckless horse-thief before him, and some muttering murderer treading close
behind; turning his head now over his red shoulder, and
now over his blue one, for a breath of untainted air; to
take his turn at the kitchen slide, receiving his morsel of
black bread and tin plate of mush, and carrying them to
his allotted cell in the row of cells; his lonely supper; no
wife, no child, to comfort him, no friend dropping in of
an evening, no plans for to-morrow, or for next week,
or for next year; no human face to cheer him ever, —
only the dreary face of the chaplain, the unsympathizing
countenances of his keepers, and the morose, brutal vis-
ages of his fellow-convicts; a spectacle to curious visitors, who come to stare and make careless remarks while
he marches in or out, or feeds, or cringes at his work,
forbidden to look up ; and this life day after day, and

week after week, and month after month, and year after year; — O merciful God ! must it be ?

Did the judge, who enunciated the sentence with business-like precision, or the listeners, who heard it with keen relish of the tragical, measure the depth and breadth of its fearful significance; or weigh well one little grain of the load of grief and shame those few easily-spoken words heaped irretrievably on the convict's head ?

And Abel was innocent; but what if he had been guilty ? It seems, when we think of it, a very special act of divine favor that any man is innocent of crime. The coil of circumstance has such subtile entanglements; and the glue of evil, wherever we move, is so plentiful and adhesive, and the way to the pit is so often in appearance the very path of necessity, and to advance step by step is so easy, while to return is so difficult; and ever the illusions of sin are so seductive, and the human heart so weak, — how is it any one escapes ?

Guilty ! innocent ! — are these mere words ? Who is there that never did a wrong act, or felt a sinful desire ? And what is the mighty difference, in God's sight, between wicked wishing and wicked doing ? or between the great and daring transgressor, and the small, weak, timid one ? or between him who is powerfully tempted, and sins accordingly, and him who is tempted not at all, and so never, as we say, sinned ? Man provides punishment for a few; but how about the rest, who may be equally deserving? Are there no murderers, loose in society, whom the law cannot touch, whose victims died, not by bludgeon and drug, perhaps, yet by the poison of secret wrong, and the strokes which make broken hearts? How many robbers, think you, walk abroad with high heads, respectable, and defiant of grand and petit jury; who have committed no literal larceny, indeed, nor positive act of pocket-picking; but, by more cautious practices in craft, have possessed themselves of their neighbors' goods, rendering no equivalent? On the other hand, how many comparatively honest men, like Abel Dane, have been subjected to punishment and life-long dishonor more by the iniquity of others than their own? And, to pry closely into the roots of things, what precious right have you, sir, or you, madam, to condemn your brother or your sister? Have you thought of it, ye proud, who esteem yourselves better than the rest? And you, O virtuous judge! have you considered it, sitting there on your cushioned bench, and uttering judgment, while your less fortunate brother stands trembling in the dock to be doomed?

If these be riddles to the wise, well may they puzzle the poor wits of honest Abel Dane. Social order must be had. The time has not come when the prison-house can be safely demolished. The world is not yet wise and good enough to put into practice the sublime and sweet doctrine of love, which knows neither gallows nor chain. In the mean while appearances and the rule of force have their day. The outward semblance of good-citizenship shall pass for good-citizenship. The gross transgressor, who maintains but one virtue to a thousand crimes, if that one virtue be a hen-like prudence hiding ᷑the evil brood under its wings, shall be, perhaps, one of the guardians of society. And the man of many unknown virtues, and one poor little crime that betrays him, shall be delivered over to the judgment. What else? Peace, loud-mouthed reformer! Patience, ye seething brains, that have begun to think, or to think you think! Charity, all! charity not for the criminal only, but for those, also, who hate the criminal; and, if they did not help to make him what he is, at least help to keep him so. God lives; and his infinite providence enfolds alike the noble and the ignoble, the accuser and the accused; and the proud have their reward, and the meanest are not forgotten; and perfect justice is perfect mercy; and that shall comfort us.

But was Abel Dane so comforted? The hour of anguish is not just the time to compute carefully the compensations of suffering. No doubt truth shall triumph in the long run; and the gloss of appearances shall not always avail; and every wrong shall be made right at last. *At last!* — but is that a salve to quiet the grief of a present wound?

Staggering and heavy within him was the soul of Abel, as he stood and looked around him in the jail, and tried to understand, to feel, to be assured of himself. A convict! a jail-bird! one of the despised and outcast of the earth ! How was it ? He had endeavored to prepare himself for this emergency, but somehow it found him altogether unprepared. He had anticipated, even if condemned, a light sentence, — not more than a year, at the most; and he had believed he could endure so much. But FIVE YEARS ! — the thought bewildered him. He remembered how lately he had said in his heart that it would be easy to go to prison for another's sake; but now that seemed an idle conceit, a flower of sentimentalism that could not stand the withering heat of this terrible day; and the memory of it sickened him.

He could not help feeling that there was some mistake about the sentence. In his shaken state, he even had a dim hope that it had been pronounced only to try his manhood; or that the judge would think better of it, and order him to be released. Yes ! there were the rattling keys again, — the sheriff was coming to set him free.

Abel indulged in these miserable fancies, as sometimes men, in the most utter hopelessness, will play with the phantoms of hope, — as the child at its mother's funeral will gaze on the pallid face; and though it knows what death is, and that this is death, thinks it impossible but that the closed eyes shall open again and the cold lips smile once more.

But the sound of the keys and of opening locks was no delusion. And what was this that flew like a bird, yet with a human cry and sob, to the grated door, and looked in upon him, clinging to the iron bars ?

"Abel! O Abel!"

He had sat down, without knowing it, upon a wooden bench. His face was buried in his hands. But at the call, he lifted his head, and then got up, moving slowly to the door.

"Eliza!" he said, in a hollow voice, trying to smile.

He reached her his hand. She seized it and kissed it through the bars.

"Why, Eliza—Eliza,"—he spoke in the same hollow, broken voice, but tenderly and soothingly, much as in old times,—"don't cry, child! there, there! don't cry."

"O Abel! I never thought it would be so!"

"Neither did I, my girl. But so it is. I try to believe there is a God!" he said, and paused,—the blackness of atheism rising like a cloud in his soul, shedding a sullen gloom, and darting defiant lightnings. He stood, with clenched teeth, grim and dark.

"O brother! don't!" sobbed Eliza. "There *is* a God!"

"I say, I try to believe it," returned Abel; "and I suppose this is all right, if we could only see it so. But there is a black devil in my heart. He says to me what Job's wife said to Job,—'Curse God, and die!'"

Eliza could only wring his hand and weep.

"Why did you come to me?" he asked. "Haven't you begun to think of me as the world will think? I am going into a living tomb; to be buried five years; to rot in the memories of men, and be eaten by worms.

21

There are worms that eat the body, and there are worms that consume heart and hope and good name. In a little time my friends will think of me with loathing, — that is the worst to bear."

"Never! never!" Eliza interrupted. "You must not imagine such a thing. I would die for you now, Abel! And do you think I will ever forget you, or distrust you, or anything but love you?"

"You are a good girl. I know you are sincere, and mean all you say. But I see!" — And the prisoner sighed with unutterable sadness, and shook his head. "In a little while you will be a wife, and happy, and full of interest for your husband and household and little ones. And you will have new acquaintances, and a bright world all open to you, and occupation, and diversion; and what will I be to you then?"

"What no one else will ever be!" she answered, with strange energy. "No one can ever fill your place, — not even my husband. Abel, you never knew how I loved you, — I never told you, — but I will tell you now; and, oh, if my love could only give you strength and comfort! If I could give up all my happiness, which you speak of, and save you, how gladly I would do it!"

"What! your husband, your future, your friends, — all, Eliza?"

"All! I would give all to you, and feel that I was more blessed by the sacrifice. Then don't say I will ever forget you. Don't think I will in spirit forsake you one moment in all those dark coming years. Never

imagine, though all should neglect you, that I shall for
an instant neglect you in my wishes and in my prayers."

"Eliza ! angel !·" murmured the prisoner, thrilling
from head to foot, and regarding her with a look all
love and tears; "if we had only known each other,
I should not now be here, — I should not now be the
son of a worse than childless mother or the father of a
worse than fatherless child, or the husband of — of anybody but you, darling Eliza !" he said, with ineffable
tenderness, folding her hand between both his, as if it
were the most precious thing to him in all the world.

"We do not know," said Eliza with a strange abstrac-
tion, her face full of pain and vague yearning, her eyes
full of sorrow and tears, looking, not at him, but, tremu-
lously, far away. She seemed neither to be offended nor
much surprised by what he said; but to accept it as simple truth that might be spoken and heard without shame,
now that prison-bars and the gulf of years were between them. "God only knows," she added. "And
his ways are best, Abel. Oh, believe that ! Oh, let us
never doubt that, whatever comes !"

"Pray for me !" said the prisoner, his whole manhood shaken. "I am afraid I have lost the power to
pray for myself. I tried to, as I sat on the bench there,
but couldn't. My thoughts were like lead. Frozen
clods weighed me down. And I said, 'I will pray no
more, for God will not hear.' But you awaken something
in me that I thought was dead. For your sake, for
your love's sake, Eliza, I would not be lost. For your

sake, for your love's sake, I would live through the
dreary years before me, and keep my faith in God, and
in man, and in justice. Pray; and save me from that
scepticism that is ten times worse than death ! "

Eliza did not answer. She was weeping softly and
unrestrainedly now, holding his hand pressed close
against her cheek. Her head was bowed against the
iron bars, through which, reaching, he laid his other
hand soothingly upon it.

" Don't cry ! " he said again, with wondrous depth
and sweetness of love in his tones; " I am better now
and stronger. You have given me strength. Bless
you, sister, — dearer than any sister ! Go to your husband. Be happy, dearest. I want you to be very happy.
It will lighten my heavy loneliness, thinking of you and
your happiness. From this day I am but as a dead
man. But you are still in the world, and you do right
to enjoy it."

" How can I ever ? " burst forth the heart-broken
girl. " O Abel, how can you say so ? "

" I am not speaking bitterly, but in all soberness and
truth. It *will* solace my solitude to remember you, and
know you are happy. And, though I am dead, I shall
hope for the resurrection, in this world or the next,
when we shall meet again. Go now, darling. I want
you to carry the news to my mother — and my wife.
My horse is at the tavern; you can drive him home.
Make haste; for I don't want mother to hear the news
from anybody but you. You will know how to be

gentle and tender with her. Heaven comfort her poor old heart!"

"How can I tell her? Abel, it will kill her; she loves you so, and you are all she has!"

"Not all,—she has *you* now. Stay a little while with her, Eliza, if you can. It will not be long that she will need you."

"I will never leave her while she lives,—be sure of that!" said Eliza.

"Then I am content. I have settled up my affairs, so that I think the little remnant of my property will last out her days. As for my wife,—she has friends she can go to, if necessary. But Ebby,—my boy,— what will become of him?"

"If his own mother cannot provide for him, I will take him, and be thankful for the privilege. I will be his mother; and I will love him for your sake, Abel."

"Will you? Then my mind is at rest. He may call you mother; but, darling, do not forget, nor let him forget, that I am his father. I could not bear to have him learn to call any one else father,—even so good a man as your husband. And, Eliza, you will bring him up to think of me with affection, and without shame for the name he bears. Forgive me for saying it; I know you will be true to us both. There, wipe your tears, child. You must go."

"Go! and not see you again? Oh, I can't," she sobbed, "I can't say good-by!"

"I am told I shall not be removed till to-morrow,"

said Abel; "so any one that wishes to visit me, can do so this afternoon. If Faustina wants to come, maybe you will come with her. And bring Ebby. I would like to kiss him for the last time, and have one last look to remember him by; he will be changed, he will be another child, five years from now. You must bring him to me in prison, at least once a year, Eliza. I can't bear the thought of his growing beyond my remembrance."

With incoherent words, Eliza promised. And now, consoled by the thought of returning to him again in the afternoon, she found strength to take leave.

"I hope mother will not think of coming with you," said Abel. "She couldn't stand it, and it would be too much for me. By all means, persuade her to stay at home. Yet" — a spasm twitched the muscle of his mouth — "perhaps I shall never see her again. But it will be better, — yes, it will be better for her not to come. The storm is dreadful." And he looked up at the gusts of snow driving by the jail-windows.

"Kiss me, brother," whispered Eliza.

Between the bars of the grated door their lips met. Their hands clung together in a last embrace. Neither spoke. Then Eliza, hiding her face in her veil, disappeared in the dark passage. At the end of it was another door, which had been locked behind her as she entered. She gave the necessary signal; it was soon opened again, and closed again; and Abel was alone and she was gone.

XXVII.

THE CONVICT'S BEAUTIFUL WIFE.

MEANWHILE Faustina waited, in torments of anxiety, to learn the result of the trial, — Abel's fate and her own. Now she tossed and groaned upon the bed. Now she went to the window, and looked out upon the tempestuous snow-storm, straining her eyes to see, through the white, driving cloud, Abel or Eliza, or at least some friendly neighbor coming with the news. But no Abel appeared; and nevermore would she behold, in storm or shine, that goodly form of manhood returning home to her as she had seen it countless times and cared not, in the by-gone, wasted years.

Sigh, wretched wife ! Wring your passionate, white hands, O woman fair to see ! Weep; blind your eyes with hot, impatient tears, as you gaze ! He is nowhere in the storm. He is not just beyond the corner of the common, where you could see him but for the dim vortex of snow, as you sometimes fancy. He will never come to you again, he will never smile kindly upon you again, at noon or evening, coming from his work, in all this weary world. Toss then upon your bed, and groan, thinking of what has been lost, and fearing what is to come.

For she was tortured also with fears. Up to the last she could not believe that Abel would really sacrifice himself for her. If conviction became certain, then surely he would save himself by giving her up. It was for his interest to preserve her good name, if possible to do so and at the same time avoid suffering the penalty of the law in her place. But more magnanimous conduct she could not understand. Each day of the trial, therefore, and now on this third day especially, she trembled with dread of exposure. And when she looked for her husband, she more than half-expected to be frightened with the sight of an officer sent to summon her before the awful court.

But nobody came. She could not have even the miserable satisfaction of knowing the worst. And there was no one to sympathize with her, and listen to her conjectures and complaints, and help her waste the lonely hours of waiting, except Melissa. She made the most of Melissa, which indeed was not much. Now she called her to her bedside, and clung to her desperately, and confessed to her, and questioned her; promised extravagant favors if she remained true to her, and threatened all the pains of death and hell if ever she betrayed her secret. Then she would send her to the windows to look, or to the outer door to listen, to know if anybody was coming, — or at least to form some opinion whether anybody would come or not.

" What do you think ? " she asked once when the girl had been absent some minutes from the room, and returned to it — as appeared to Faustina — with the same slow discouraging step as usual. "Is he coming? Has he got clear? Oh, dear! dear! Melissa, why don't you speak?"

But it was not Melissa who mournfully drew near the head of the bed, and stood there, unseen by Faustina, regarding her with speechless grief.

"Oh, I shall die! I shall have another dreadful fit, I know I shall. Melissa, if you would save my life, why don't you tell me again you think he is acquitted, and will be here soon? I want you to keep saying it. That's all the consolation I have. And he *wouldn't* betray me, *would* he? Do you think he would?"

No answer from the figure at the bed-head. But now wonder began to mingle with the heavy sorrow of the eyes that watched the writhing woman.

"He promised me so faithfully! But if he should *not* get clear! Oh, what shall I do? What would you do in my case, Melissa? I wish I had run away a month ago! What a fool I was! I'd have done it if it hadn't been for Tasso. He told me not to be afraid, but to stay, and never care what happened to my husband, — as if a body could! — as if I hadn't before my eyes every minute what may happen to myself. Oh, dear!"

And Faustina, restless, rose up in bed, and pushed back her hair, moaning as she twisted it away and threw it over her shoulder, and looked with burning languor and despair around her, as if in search of some object of hope on which to cast her weary heart; but saw instead, with a start of alarm, the silent figure behind her pillow.

"Eliza !" she scarcely articulated, staring pallidly. "Where — where is Melissa ?"

"She is gone to put the horse in the barn," replied Eliza.

"The horse ! What horse ?" Faustina hardly knew what she was saying, so great was her trepidation, thinking of what she had already said, and Eliza — not Melissa — had heard. "How did you come? I — I — what did I say ?"

Eliza advanced to the side of the bed, and sat down upon it. The two looked at each other, — one with a countenance full of anguish and pity, the other with guilty, affrighted eyes.

"You know best what you were saying, and what you meant by it," Eliza answered. "I was thinking of what I have come to say, and what you must prepare yourself to hear."

"Abel ?" Faustina whispered, "did he — has he come ?"

"Mrs. Dane," Eliza said, with indescribable repugnance in her heart, when she felt that she ought to show all sympathy and pity to the distressed creature before her, "your husband cannot come now; if you wish to see him you must go where he is."

Faustina did not speak; but, putting both hands to her head, slid them into her hair, and clenched them thus entangled over her neck, with an aspect of abject fear.

"I have come for you, if you wish to visit him. You must get ready, while I go and break the news to mother."

"Where is he?"

"In jail. To-morrow he will be taken to prison."

"To prison? O heavens! You are dreaming, trying to frighten me!"

"It is only too true," said Eliza. "I heard his sentence,"— clasping her hand on her heart at the remembrance.

Faustina was not so full of astonishment and grief for her husband, as not to reflect, with a secret, selfish hope, that her own guilt had probably remained concealed. She remembered also, in the midst of her consternation, that she had a part to play.

"To prison, did you say? What prison?" she asked. "For how long?"

"To the State prison. For five years," replied Eliza.

"State prison!—my husband!—Five years!"— And the miserable woman wrung her hair, and thrust it into her mouth, biting it. How much of this seeming, too, was real and unaffected, and how much disguised or assumed, it would be hard to say. And whether it was chiefly grief for Abel, or remorse for her own misconduct, or only a selfish sorrow and alarm, who shall judge? But that fear and dismay were upon her, there could be no doubt.

And why did not Eliza endeavor to soothe and encourage her? She believed it her duty, and accounted it

a privilege, to give aid and counsel wherever they were
needed.   But, when she would have spoken sympathizing words to this unhappy being, her heart contracted
and her tongue refused to utter.   It was not her own
affliction, it was not jealousy, or vindictive hatred, because of the irremediable wrong she knew this woman
had done to her and to Abel, which made her shrink
away and close her lips; but rather a sense of falsehood,
and of a deeper wrong concealed, which her sensitive
nature scented like a corruption in the very air Faustina
breathed.   She arose from the bed.

"Will you be ready ?" she asked, going.   "We are
to take Ebby with us."

"Oh, I can't !" cried Faustina.   "Such a storm !—
Besides, I am sick.   How can I go ?"   She threw herself upon her face.   To confront her husband in jail; to
be present, knowing what he suffered, and was doomed
still to suffer, for her,— and she wickedly permitting;
to listen to his reproaches, or, if he uttered none, to witness the uncomplaining trouble his soul was in for her
sake, more cutting than any reproach; to hear his tremulous words of leave-taking, to look into his face, and to
part for so long,— oh, it seemed impossible to go
through all this !   Nevertheless, she reflected that it
would be far the safest policy to visit him; to go, and
show her love; yes, and carry Ebby with her, to touch
his heart; repeat her professions of fidelity, and make
him promise again, and once for all, never to betray her.

" Tell me what to do !" she cried. " It shall be as you say. Did he send for me ? "

She raised her head as she spoke, and looked for Eliza. But Eliza was not there. She was at another bedside now, holding in her arms the almost dying form of the convict's stricken mother; trying in vain to impart to her a little consolation out of her own scanty store.

Then Faustina, left alone, resolved to rise and dress herself whilst she was deciding in her mind what to do. She found a sort of distraction and relief in the occupation. And though she vowed incessantly to herself that she could not go, and that she would not go, she continued to put her apparel on, even to her mantle and furs; so that, when Eliza sent for her, lo, she was ready. And though she now, almost frantically, informed Melissa that she could not and that she would not, nevertheless, as if a spell had been upon her which she was powerless to resist, she went trembling and sighing to the outer door, where the wagon stood, and got into it, and took Ebby with her under the buffalo-skin; and did not faint dead away, as she had determined to do in Eliza's sight, so that she might be left behind, but, irresolutely holding that strategy in reserve until it was too late, rode through the storm of wind and snow, and through the wilder storm of her own thoughts, to the centre of the town, and found herself at last alighting at the jail-door, as weak and helpless as Ebby himself, in Eliza's governing hands.

22

XXVIII.

THE CONVICT'S CHRISTIAN NEIGHBORS.

FROM the window of his shop John Apjohn had seen
Abel Dane's wagon arrive and depart again. For the
cooper did not attend court that morning. The two
previous days, when he was required to be on the spot,
had been enough for him, yea, too much. To swear
the solemn oath; to stand up, in the presence of judge
and jury and spectators, and bear witness against his
neighbor, whose eyes were upon him; to tell, in terror
of perjuring himself, the story of the tomatoes, and to
hear the tittering, had been the most fearful ordeal of
his life. How he was gored by ruthless forensic horns,
and ferociously trampled and tossed as if the truth had
been his life-blood, to be worried out of him in this mad-
bull fashion; how he fainted, and was carried out to be
revived, and then brought back into the arena, to be
whirled again in the air and trodden again in the dust;
and how he was at last pitched carelessly out of
the arena, a used up man, covered with sweat and
flushes, while Prudence took the stand, and made sport
for the Philistines, — all this he remembered sufficiently

well to be made sick ever after by the sight of a court-house.

But John's was no merely selfish woe. He had been in a measure diverted from his own shame by his conscientious concern for Abel. With the vindictive feelings, which animated his worthy wife, he had no sympathy; and this third morning, he waited and watched from his shop-window, afflicted with pangs of conscience, and unable to work until he should learn that his neighbor had been acquitted. After seeing the wagon come and go, his restlessness grew intense. Remain in his shop he could not. A bold resolution inspired him, and putting on his coat, and turning up the collar about his ears, he issued forth. Mrs. Apjohn called to him as he passed the house; but the said collar, and the storm that whistled about it, prevented her being heard.

"Where on airth can he be goin'? Why, he's stoppin' into Abel Dane's gate, sure's the world. The man's crazy!" said Prudence.

When the cooper returned, after a short absence, she flew to the door to meet him.

"Wal sad, John Apjohn! What have you done?" she cried, grasping him as if he had been a little boy, and dragging him into the house. "Give an account of yourself, sir!"

"What *have* we done?" iterated the cooper; "what *have* we been and done, Prudy? To be sure, to be sure!"

"*We?* what do you mean by *we?*" She helped him

shake the snow from his coat, not very gently. " What have *we* done, say ! "

" I've seen Abel's mother. She's a sight to make any man sick of life, — most of all, one that's been helpin' to heap her troubles on to her. For Abel, Prudy, Abel — he's sent to State's prison for five year' ! for five year', Prudy ! And it's all our doin's; it's all our doin's from the very fust ! " And as he uttered this speech, the agitated and remorseful John, having previously un-buttoned his coat, began to button it up again excited-ly, with the collar about his ears.

The moment of triumph had arrived for good Mrs. Apjohn. But, alas ! where was the satisfaction ? She looked somehow as if smitten by ill tidings. She had achieved a signal victory over her supposed enemy, and she was not glad. All the imps that had been goading her on, and whispering in her soul night and day how good the revenge would taste, seemed suddenly to have deserted and left her to bite barren ashes. She sat down on the wood-box; and it was some seconds before she spoke.

" Wal, I don't know as it's my fault now. I'm as sorry for ol' Mis' Dane as anybody, and for her little gran'child, — he's a re'l pooty little boy, and I pity him. And nobody can say't ever I hated Fustiny bad enough to want her husband sent for five year' — that seems mos' *too* bad, I allow ! " Prudy's voice quavered, and her countenance betrayed trouble. " And I'd no idee of his gittin' so long a sentence ! had you, John ? "

John had been busy tying his red silk in a broad fold, over his upturned coat-collar, around his nose and ears, so that he now stood muffled to the eyes; and the voice of him seemed to issue from a tomb.

" I'm a goin' for to see him, Prudy."

" To see — who ? "

"Abel. I'm a goin' with ol' Mis' Dane. 'Lizy and Faustiny and the boy had gone off; and she was in a dreffle state, sayin' they'd insisted on her stayin' to hum; but she know'd she never'd see Abel agi'n in the world, if she didn't see him to-day, and she didn't keer for the storm, nor for sickness, nor for nothin'; but go she must and would; and if I'd harness up and carry her over, she'd be obliged. And I'm a goin', Prudy ! " With which announcement, he closed up the aperture which he had opened between his handkerchief and his nose to make a passage for the words, and, putting on his hat, tightened the muffler about his ears as if determined neither to say nor hear more on the subject.

" Now, John ! " began Prudence disconcerted, " I don't know 'bout your goin' off on any sech wild-goose chase ! Why didn't you ask my advice ? Old Mis' Dane ain't fit to stir out of the house, in the best weather, 'cordin' to all accounts; and to start off in sech a storm " —

" I'm a goin', Prudy," said the voice from the tomb. And John's hand was on the door-latch.

" No you ain't goin', neither ! " exclaimed Prudence, astonished by this act of rebellion. " Jest stop a minute, can't you, and hear to reason ? You do beat all

22 *

the obstinate, headstrong critters ! Come ! " She put her hand quickly on her knee, and got upon her feet with all possible dispatch, and launched herself towards the door, with arm extended to seize him. But too late. Obstinate or not, John Apjohn meant to have his own way this time. Headstrong or not, for once in his life he determined to defy her conjugal authority, and take the risks. If she was the more muscular of the two, he was the more nimble. She was ponderous; but he was fleet. Prudence saw that she had no chance; and to stand in the door, and shout, against the indriving tempest, for him to return, she soon perceived to be idle. So she retired into the house, baffled, and inspired with a certain respect for .her husband which she never felt before.

He was going to take Mrs. Dane over to the jail, — that was settled. What should she do in the mean time ? Suffer it to be said that she was less neighborly than her husband ? And leave him alone to be wrought upon by the scenes he was to witness ? She seemed boiling with trouble for a minute; then she, too, formed a novel resolve. Off went her old frock, and on went her second-best gown, in a twinkling. The hooks and eyes flew together with amazing rapidity, considering the capaciousness of the charms enclosed. And so great was her industry, that, by the time John had obtained a pony at a stable near by, and harnessed him, Prudence had locked the house, and stood ankle-deep in the snow, with her bonnet and cloak on, ready to accompany him.

At sight of her, John was alarmed. But she said kindly, —

"Put in a board, John, for you to set on. Me and Mis' Dane I guess 'll about fill up the seat."

And John, without a word, put in a board.

XXIX.

IN JAIL.   LEAVE-TAKING.

ELIZA warmed her numbed hands in the vestibule of the jail, while Faustina, with Ebby in her arms, followed the keeper.

He opened the first heavy door, and, after ushering her in, clanged it together and locked it again. Then they were ready to advance to the second door. The ring of the iron, the formality and preparation, the dim light in the passage, the sound of the keeper's feet on the echoing stone floor, added to the thought of so soon meeting her husband, filled her limbs with trembling, and her soul with almost superstitious dread.   She could scarcely support the burden of her child upon her fainting heart.   As if to enhance her trouble, Ebby began to cry.   She stood waiting for the jailer to precede her.   White and terrified, she obeyed his summons to follow.   Before her was the grated door, through the bars of which he called Abel to approach; and she heard his slow footsteps coming along the floor of the hollow cell, — tramp, tramp, — while each moment there was danger that the swoon she had

had in contemplation so long, and kept in reserve, would take vengeance for being trifled with, and master her in good earnest.

But the grated door was opened also; and Ebby, as he slipped from his mother's breast, was caught in the arms of his father. And Faustina, bowing her face upon Abel's shoulder, clung and wept there until her limbs fairly failed beneath her, and she sank down helplessly upon the jail-floor.

Half-kneeling and half-sitting, she sank and bent her fair head, from which the bonnet had fallen, and covered her fairer face, — a rather graceful and exceedingly pathetic figure; the sight of whom, together with the prisoner standing by, hugging the child, and saturating his little curls with big, manly tears, did mightily wrench that unofficial part of the jailer's nature, called a heart; for the jailer was the sheriff also. It was excellent Mr. Wilkins, whom we remember; the same who went to arrest Abel, and was sorry to see him come out of the house with Ebby in his arms, that moonlight night in autumn. He was not one of the brutal, relentless turnkeys you read about in romances, but a man. And now, retiring with the keys, having locked the duplicate doors, and wiped the duplicate tears that surprised him, he went and sat down in the vestibule, and talked feelingly to Eliza, and told her how grievous a thing it was for a young wife, so beautiful and affectionate, to see her convict husband in jail, and to take leave of him. And he brushed his misty eyes again, — good, honest gentleman, — and no doubt thought he was informing her of something new; for Eliza did not find occasion to wipe her eyes, but sat in a sort of dreamy stupor, and warmed her benumbed hands, and tried to warm her benumbed heart by the fire.

Abel assisted his wife to arise, and led her, reluctant and sobbing, to a bench. There they sat down, silent both, a long time, — he with Ebby in his arms, Faustina weeping still.

"Papa," said the child, frowning with dislike at the walls, as he glanced furtively around, "go home, papa ! go ! "

Abel heaved a tremendous sigh.

"Home, my poor boy ? Papa can't go home any more," he said, in a convulsed voice.

The baby frown contracted to a scowl of pain and terror.

"Home, papa ! home ! " he entreated. "Ebby 'f'aid."

"Hush, my boy," answered Abel, soothingly, stroking the child's hair, and kissing again and again his beautiful white forehead. "Papa will go home some time, — yes, some time, darling ! Ebby must love mamma, and mamma must take care of Ebby now."

"O Abel," uttered Faustina, with wild and stifling grief, "I can't have it so ! I never believed it could be ! It is too hard ! too unjust ! "

"Hard and unjust, truly," said Abel; "but it must be borne. Be calm, now, Faustina; for I have many things to say to you, and the time is short."

But the distressed one seemed resolved not to be calm.

She threw her face down despairingly upon his lap, uttering moan after moan. At length she lifted her head, and, with wet, flashing eyes, whispered passionately, —

"Abel, I am determined! You shall never go to prison! If either must go, I will! I'll see the judge, and tell him everything. I'd have done it before; but I thought you would be acquitted. You know — you know I can't let you suffer in my place, — for my fault," — looking around to see that no one was listening. And she made a motion towards rising, — thinking, no doubt, that Abel, the devoted, would detain her.

But he didn't. Whether he suspected the sincerity of her declaration, or was indeed willing that she should assume the responsibility and odium of her own act, he sat seemingly content to let her do as she pleased. That was a more effective damper to her resolution than any opposition could have been. She had no more than half-risen when she fell again upon his breast. He regarded her with a dreary smile and head-shake, but said nothing.

"Oh, what *shall* I do?" she inquired, embracing him.

"Ask your conscience, not me," said Abel. "I've as much as I can do to give counsel to my own heart. These are bitter days, Faustina. I shall try to do my duty, and I pray God you may do yours."

"What is my duty? Tell me, and I'll do it, if it is to kill myself!" vowed the fair one.

"It is not to kill yourself, but to live, — if not for yourself nor for me, for our child here," said Abel.

"I will! I will!" Faustina eagerly cried; for truly she had no very lively wish to die; and to promise that she would devote herself to Ebby out of prison, whilst Abel devoted himself to her in it, struck her as an easy and reasonable compromise.

"As for your acknowledging to the world the error for which I suffer, I have no advice to give," he went on. "At first, I should have honored you, had you been so brave and true. Such nobleness would have more than purchased my pardon. But I have given you my pardon without it. And I don't think now that you have any heart to redeem me from infamy and imprisonment by criminating yourself. Well, I am satisfied. I have given you my word not to expose you; and I shall keep my word. In return I ask only one favor, — and that not for my sake, but for your own and our child's. Remember me in prison. Think of the long days and long nights of those terrible and solitary years. And atone, Faustina! before God, atone for the wrong you have done, by becoming a true woman and mother!"

She only wailed in low, disconsolate tones. And he continued : —

"So this awful calamity may be made a blessing to us all. For I shall not regret it, if, five years from now, I see you the woman you may be, Faustina! Oh, put away falsehood and frivolity now! Conquer that restlessness, that hankering for excitement, which argues a mind uncentred in itself, and unblessed by duty. Let your tender care of our child occupy you now. It will be occupation enough; it will be amusement enough. For what other amusement can you have while I am serving out my sentence? Oh, deepen your heart; deepen your heart!" he entreated her. "It is shallow, Faustina; even here, and now, it is shallow and vain and full of pretence. I say it not unkindly, but pityingly and in sorrow."

He laid his hand upon her head; and for the moment something of his own overmastering earnestness seemed to pass into her.

"Oh, yes! pity me!" she said. "Be sorry for me! I can't help being as I am,—I would help it if I could. But I will be better; I will try, oh, so hard!"

"I think you will try," said Abel.

"Every day, every night, I will remember you; and I will not be vain any more. I will not be idle and proud any more. How *can* I be proud now?"

"Poor child! poor child!" said Abel, very heavy-hearted, but full of the tenderness of mercy. "God help you! Pray to HIM. Oh, be faithful and sincere! Again, I entreat you! don't forget me; and love, oh, love and cherish this our darling boy!"

Ebby cried again, shrinking from his mother, and nestling in Abel's bosom.

Vehemently, then, Faustina pledged herself to do all he required of her. She would avoid unprofitable associates. She would do everything he could wish. A crop of fair promises, profuse and instantaneous as fungi,—

23

and alas, equally unsubstantial, — whitened over the rottenness of her heart. And once more Abel almost believed in her, and almost hoped.

"And Abel!" she said so softly and sadly and fondly, that it was impossible for the strong, tender man not to be touched,— "I want you to say one thing. Only one thing, dearest! I can't be strong, I can't hope, I can't even live without it!"

"Speak, and I will say all I can," replied Abel.

"You know," murmured the sorrowful one, — resuming more and more of her old winsome ways, which became marvellously her depressed and tearful state, — "you know, Abel, you haven't been to me what you were before" — (with a shudder). "You have forgiven me; and you have been kind, — too kind. But the dreadful separation! Oh, if I have nothing better to look forward to, I had better die now. If I am never to have your confidence and affection again, if you are not to be my husband again, but only as a friend, a father, so distant, so cold, — oh! what have I to live for?"

Abel kept silent a moment, mightily shaken by this appeal. He thought of Eliza, — a wife. He recalled his first hopeful and fresh passion for this erring daughter of Eve, —

> "His life and sole delight
> Now at his feet, submissive, in distress."

And the wreck of himself thrown back upon the world, broken, despised, after five years of shame and insult to his manhood, he well enough foresaw. Who would love him, who would comfort him then? She kissed his hand; she pleaded. Oh, would he not give her one word of hope?

"I will! I will!" said Abel, with quivering lips. "Faustina, be assured. In the sight of Heaven, now, we will plight our vows, — not idly, as when we plighted them for our first, false marriage; but this second marriage shall be solemn and true. It is a long engagement, — five gloomy, gloomy years; but the probation will be blessed to us, if we are equal to it. And, hear me now, — if, when I come again into the light and air of liberty, I find you faithful to your promises, a true woman and mother, then I will be indeed your husband, and give you more love and confidence than you ever had or asked."

With a cry of joy and gratitude Faustina clasped him, and entered into this strange second engagement with plenteous vows.

Then Abel spoke to her of his worldly affairs, and finally came to the subject which he had reserved for the last, because what he had to say on that he wished especially to be remembered and esteemed sacred, — her duty to his mother.

But hardly had he commenced his earnest charges when, greatly to his amazement and alarm, Mr. Sheriff Wilkins reappeared, jingling keys and opening doors, followed by Eliza and excellent Mrs. Apjohn, who supported between them the feeble, tottering form of old

Mrs. Dane. Hat in hand and awe-stricken, the bald little cooper walked humbly in the rear.

Abel, at sight of his mother, set Ebby hastily down and rose to his feet. He extended his arms, and, with a cry, she fell forward upon his neck. Eliza supported her still, and helped to place her gently on the bench; whilst Prudence found her handkerchief and wiped her red nose, and the honest man, her husband, hid his face behind his hat.

"Come, John !" said Prudence, turning away; "this ain't no place for us. We've done our duty, and showed our good will; and now le's leave."

But, lo ! the door was locked, and soft-hearted Sheriff Wilkins had retired. And John, strangling behind his hat, gave no heed to his good wife's suggestion. And now Abel, emerging, as it were, from the sea and tempest of his grief, lifted his head, and addressed the Apjohn pair.

"No, don't go ! I have something to say to you. Neighbor Apjohn, I have to thank you for your kindness. *You* have not persecuted me. *You* have not willingly borne witness against me. And you have done a neighborly act in bringing my mother here to see me; though, Heaven knows, I hoped she would not come. Still, I thank you; I thank you for your good will from the bottom of my heart."

But the cooper did not seem to hear. He stood where he had stood from the first, stifling behind his hat. Prudence changed from purple-red to sallow-pale, and looked with an embarrassed, restless expression about her, and coughed, and blew her nose, not knowing what else to do.

Abel sat with his arms about his mother, endeavoring to solace and soothe her. But she, heart-broken, could do nothing but weep helplessly, and choke with her own tears, — a piteous spectacle, — she was so old and feeble, and loved her son with such entire and dependent affection, and had always been so proud of him, and was left so desolate now.

"If you had died, my son!" she broke forth incoherently, "it would not have been so hard. I shall die soon, and we might hope to meet again. But this!— Oh, I can't be reconciled to it! Heaven forgive me, but I can't!"

It was singular that sorrow seemed to have swept away the old obstruction in her speech, and that her words flowed now with her tears.

Eliza could not endure the scene; but, turning to the iron-grated door, she put her face between the bars, and sobbed alone. And she was guiltless of any wrong towards Abel: what, then, must have been her pangs had she felt upon her conscience the burden which Mrs. Apjohn was trying to carry off so stoutly, or that which Faustina was laboring to conceal? As for the latter, she occupied the time in crying, and so played her part; whilst Prudence pinched her lips together, and used her handkerchief, and tossed her chin, and so played hers.

23 *

XXX.

THE OLD LADY TAKES FINAL LEAVE.

EAR mother," said Abel, "it is not so bad as it might be. Though convicted and sentenced, still I am innocent; and that ought to comfort us. Whatever others may believe, we have that knowledge, and that comfort."

"Poor comfort!" replied his mother, convulsively. " The innocent suffer, and the wicked go unpunished. The wrong is too great to endure. I have no malice," — she went on, after a paroxysm of silent anguish, — "I never cursed anybody in my life; but I do pray that them that's done this deed, and made you the scapegoat of their sin and spite, I pray they may feel the evil they have done recoil upon their own heads. I may not live to see it; but I humbly pray it may be so."

This was uttered with an energy which the mild and benevolent old lady rarely manifested; then she relapsed again into unconstrained grief. Faustina still kept masked; but Mrs. Apjohn winced.

"Wal, Mis' Dane," she began, "I 'spose you mean that for a hit at me and my husband here" —

"Not your husband ! not John ! " — the old lady interrupted her, — "I believe he's as harmless as this child here."

At which allusion to himself, Master Ebby, who had long been looking on, in wonder and terror and pity, to see the grief of them all, and especially the grief of his good old grandmother, in that strange, ugly place, set up a scream. Eliza came and took him. John Apjohn, meanwhile, touched by Mrs. Dane's testimony in his favor, might have been seen strangling harder than ever behind his hat.

"Come, come, mother," said Abel, smoothing her thin, gray hair with his troubled hands, as he strove to pacify her; "we will blame nobody; we will bear all patiently, and blame nobody."

"Yes, I would, now ! " said Mrs. Apjohn, flushed, her lips violently compressing and relaxing, and her entire frame (which is saying a good deal) trembling with her emotion. "You may blame me; I'm perfectly willin'. And I don't mean to say but what I'm desarvin' of *some* blame, but not all. I jest as much believed Abel hung them tomatuses on to my door, and stole my money, as that my name is Prudence Apjohn; and I hain't seen no good reason yit for changin' my mind. And I consider I had a right to feel hurt, and make a complaint 'fore a justice, under the circumstances. But as for wishin' Abel Dane to go to State's prison for five year', my husband here he knows I never wished any sech thing; and I'm as sorry for't as anybody." So saying

the worthy woman dropped some penitent water from
her eyes, — without appearing to know it, however, for,
instead of using her handkerchief, now there was really
need of it, she bore up like a good ship against·the storm,
carrying her head high.

"Well, well! the Lord knows! the Lord knows!"
murmured old Mrs. Dane. "He knows many a secret
that's hid from our eyes. And the day of reckoning will
come for us all soon. I bear no malice; I bear no malice," she repeated. "You was kind to come over here
with me; though I don't suppose you'd have come,˜if't
hadn't been for John. I had always generally found
you a kind neighbor enough till this quarrel. You got
a terrible quirk into your head then, which I never could
account for; though it was nat'ral enough, I presume.
But that you may know how you have misjudged my
son, let me tell you this, that he never mentioned, even
to me, about your taking the tomatoes from our garden
till after he was arrested."

"As for the tomatoes," spoke up Faustina, seized by
one of her unreasonable impulses, "you have been a
fool, Mrs. Apjohn! It was not my husband who hung
them on to your door. It was" —   .

She had commenced speaking under the influence of a
wild feeling that the misunderstanding about that unhappy retaliatory trick of Tasso's was the origin of all
this trouble, which might even now be remedied by
declaring the truth. But having spoken thus far, a
fear that she was saying something indiscreet caused

her to hesitate. Abel had started with surprise; and the suspicion that alarmed him had entered Mrs. Apjohn's mind also.

"It was you, then! Own up now!" cried Prudence. "You can't deny it! It's too late! you've half-confessed it!"

That decided Faustina to avow the truth.

"It wasn't me, nor my husband. But I'll tell you who it was; it was TASSO SMITH."

Prudence was struck dumb.

"Do you know what you say?" demanded Abel.

"Yes, I do; for he told me."

"And how did he know tomatoes would insult Mrs. Apjohn?"

"I — I suppose I — told him!" confessed Faustina, perceiving now what a rash thing she had done. "But I — I had forgotten it."

Abel breathed thick and hard, restraining himself, as he looked upon her and listened to these words.

"And why on airth," burst forth Prudence, with all her power of astonishment and indignation, "didn't you never tell it was Tasso, and so save all this trouble to all on us?"

Poor Faustina scarcely remembered why she didn't. Ah, yes! it was because she feared Tasso would betray her, if she did! And here she was implicating him, and laying herself open to his revenge! — ever as foolish as she was false. But she would see him and excuse herself to him, she thought. And now a convenient lie suggested itself as an answer to Mrs. Apjohn's reasonable inquiry. "Because," said she, "I never knew it myself; Tasso never told me till — long after. I met him the other day in the street, and he was very sorry, and begged of me not to tell. Abel was indicted then, and I knew nothing could prevent his having a trial."

Abel groaned. "But you should have told me, Faustina! Why didn't you?"

"I didn't want you to know I had seen Tasso. I didn't mean to see him, — it was an accident, — but you dislike him so, I thought you would be offended."

Faustina possessed a decided talent for mendacity; by the exercise of which she was now in a fair way to repair her recent indiscretion. There was such a varnish of *vraisemblance* on these lies, that all were deceived by them.

"O Tasso Smith! Tasso Smith!" muttered Prudence, quivering with rage.

Abel groaned again. "You see, my friends, you had truly no reason to seek revenge against me."

"And some day, Mrs. Apjohn," cried old Mrs. Dane, "some day, you will know that my son was as innocent of stealing your money as of contriving that trick with the tomatoes. I shan't envy you your conscience then! I shan't envy you your conscience then!"

Poor Prudence, confused, convinced, pricked to the heart, knew not which way to turn or what to say. At this juncture, however, there occurred a circumstance

which gave her something to do. Cooper John, de-
fending himself from observation behind his hat, and at
the same time shutting out from his eyes the spectacle
of the convict's interview with his family; strangling
more and more; and leaning latterly against the wall
for faintness, as he listened to the last stunning revelation; the sensitive and conscientious little man, over-
whelmed at length by a cumulative sense of error
and fatality, as by a slowly-gathered tremendous wave,
grew dizzy under it, saw all things color of dim purple
a moment, and was carried off his legs. A cry and a
tumbling fall announced his catastrophe.

"Prudy, P-r-u—" he weakly gasped, and measured
his length along the jail floor.

The swoon, which Faustina had kept by her so long,
had deserted, and gone over to Mr. Apjohn. And a
very mortal-seeming swoon it was. Pallid, breathless,
and apparently pulseless and bloodless, lay the limp,
insensible cooper, — his tuftless crown having struck
the pavement with a concussion of itself almost sufficient
to rive the rind of life round that "distracted globe."

Prudence picked him up, getting down with no little
difficulty to perform that office. But his lifeless hands
fell from him, and his head rolled this way and that, as
she endeavored to set him up and hold him in position
on her knee and arm. Meanwhile, Abel seized his
pitcher (the prisoner's solitary pitcher), and besprinkled
the white face with its contents. All in vain. The last
tick of life's timepiece seemed over in that still breast.

"O John! John! John!" cried Prudence, wildly, "don't die!—Somebody run for a doctor!—Oh, dear! to be locked up in jail at sech a time, and my husband dyin'!" And she screamed for help, not perceiving that Abel was doing all in his power to summon assistance. "That's right, 'Lizy,—rub him! Blow in his face! Does he breathe?"

No; John did not breathe, and there was no lively prospect that he would ever breathe again. Observing which, all the latent affection and regret in Mrs. Apjohn's large, blunt nature was aroused.

"Oh, I've been a wicked woman! and this is to punish me! I never desarved so good a husband; for he was the bestest that ever was! Do you hear me, John? Squeeze my hand, John, if you do!"

But John did not squeeze her hand. However, Eliza now declared that he exhibited signs of returning consciousness.

"Oh, bless him! bless him! if he will only live!" cried Prudence, hoping fondly for a reprieve from what seemed certain widowhood. "I never'll be ha'sh with him agin! I'll listen to his advice always,—which if I'd done it in this affair of Abel's, we wouldn't none of us be here now! Comin' to, ain't you, John? Don't ye know me, John? Oh, the blessedest man! Give me some sign, can't ye?"

The "blessedest man" had been laid upon his back, with Abel's coat for a pillow. And now, anxiously and tenderly, broad-bosomed Prudence bent over him, looking for "some sign."

"If you love me, John, spit in my face!" she entreated him.

John did not grant this expressive token of endearment. But he moved his mouth, uttered a faint groan, and opened his eyes. About this time the jailer appeared; some spirits were quickly brought and administered; and the cooper was soon able to rub his contused scalp, stare about him, and spit in anybody's face that might request that precious favor.

"I've saved him! I've saved my man!" exclaimed Prudence. "And O Mis' Dane!" she continued, in the fulness of her heart, "I'd save your son for you if I could! I've done wrong, and I regret it, and shall regret it the longest day I live. Oh, that Tasso Smith! that Tasso Smith! Whuther you took the money or not, Abel, I don't know, and I don't keer; for we're all on us liable to be tempted,"—as that virtuous woman knew from experience. "Fustiny hain't used me well, and she knows it; but I'm sorry I've had a spite agin her. And as for you, Abel Dane, I've always sot by you from a boy, and my husband here, he knows"—

What the sad, gaping, half-stupefied cooper knew did not appear, for the good wife's speech was lost in inward convulsion; the snow-mountains of her breast (to compare great things with things which can hardly be called small) had melted, and avalanche and torrent were plunging.　24

When she recovered, and her man had altogether come to, they witnessed an alarming movement. Attention had too long been directed to them. The excitement which had so far sustained old Mrs. Dane, and the emotion which agitated her, had passed away, and taken her life-force with them. Abel and Eliza had simultaneously observed her sinking. They caught her, they bore her to the prisoner's narrow bed. No shriek, no violent outcry for help; but silent celerity, a murmur of grief, and all-absorbing sadness and tenderness, gave token of the entrance within those walls of the unseen messenger, — the same who enters alike the abode of the fortunate and the dwelling of the wretched, and waits not for doors to be opened, and stops not for prison-bolts and bars.

"Abel — children," — faintly fell the voice of the dying, — "where am I?" She revived a little, and saw the beloved faces bending over her surcharged with love and sorrow. "I remember!" And the smile of the dying was sweet. "My son! I shall be with you!"

The assistant-jailer entered, and, failing to perceive the solemn mystery that was enacting, announced that the visitors' time was up.

"True," whispered the scarce audible voice, "my time — is up. I am going. Eliza! do not mourn! Our heavenly Father, — he is merciful! He has sent for me!"

Her clear and beautiful countenance became singularly illumined. Something had been said of calling a physician.

"No—tell them," she roused herself to remonstrate. "Let me go—in peace. Only my children around me. Tell Mr. Apjohn—I thank him. And Mrs. Apjohn—I forgive her."

Aghast and pale, like one lately raised from the dead, the cooper stood behind the bed, and saw and heard. Mrs. Apjohn wrung her hands with unavailing remorse.

"It's me that's done it! it's me that's done it!" came bubbling from her lips.

"Where is Ebby?" the dying woman asked. Abel lifted up the boy. "Here," she added, with a feeble motion of her hand upon her breast. Abel placed him softly there. She kissed him with her pallid lips; she caressed him with her pallid hands, and murmured a blessing; and Abel took him gently away. "Faustina, —where is she?"

The guilty girl was crouching, fear-stricken, over the foot of the bed; watching, with I know not what frenzied thoughts, the death of which her own heart told her she was the cause. Eliza led her forward, strangely shrinking.

"My daughter!" Weakly the cold, death-stricken hand took the fevered hand of the living. Starting back instinctively, Faustina snatched away her hand, and Eliza's was taken instead. "Abel—my son!" His hand was taken also; and, now in the blindness of death not seeing what she did (though I think the spirit saw, and knew), the parting mother placed Eliza's hand in Abel's.

"Be a true—loving wife!—My son! love her always!—God bless"—

She drew the united hands to her lips, which closed
upon them. Astounded, plunged in deepest affliction,
Abel could not withdraw his hand; nor could Eliza
hers. Long and lingering was that prophetic, dying
kiss. Nor did the hold and pressure of the thin aged
fingers relax when all was over.

For all was over in very deed. The fingers that clung
still, and the lips that kissed still, were the lips and fingers of the dead. And Abel and Eliza lifted up their
eyes, and looked at each other with emotion unutterable;
while Faustina crouched again at the foot of the bed,
white and shivering, like an outcast.

XXXI.

THE BEGINNING OF THE END.

THE storm whirled and whistled by the window, and the afternoon grew dim, in that solemn cell. The hands of the living had been withdrawn, and the hands of the dead were placed composedly upon the breast now stilled forever. Abel stood and gazed long ; his countenance emerging from its cloud and agitation into a strange, almost smiling tranquillity.

"It is well ! She is happier." — He turned to his wife: "You have now no care but our child; be faithful and remember." — Then, laying his hand upon Eliza's forehead : "You are free now. Go to your husband and be happy."

Dimmer still grew the afternoon ; and the hour came when the corpse must be carried out, and Abel must look his last upon it, and behold Eliza go with it, to return to him no more. Mrs. Apjohn, assiduous and energetic, accompanied; the cooper had glided out before, like a silent ghost. Lastly, Faustina took leave, with Ebby. And Abel was left alone.

Alone; and the night descended, tempestuous, — sifting snow and sleet beating all night upon the pane; howls

24 *

and moans resounding all night about the prisoner's cell. Sitting or walking, he pondered ; or, lying on the hard couch on which his mother had died, he waked, or slept, waiting for the morrow.

The morrow ! what a day was that ! The storm raging still; the corpse lying in the house; neighbors coming in; preparations for the funeral; the hush as of ashes strewn upon the floor; the utter, bewildering vacancy, — the silent ache of the heart, — which one mourner felt, thinking of the empty morrows still to come, and of her fellow-mourner far away.

The next day was the funeral. Where was Abel then ? When the sexton tramped through the drifts with pick and spade to the graveyard; when the customary sermon was preached, and the psalm sung, and the prayer said; when the little procession followed the corpse to the fresh heap of earth thrown up beside the snowy mound beneath which mouldered the ashes of old Abel Dane, the carpenter, — the dog Turk walking seriously through the snow by Eliza's side, leaving the prints of his feet; when Eliza lifted Ebby up to take a last look of what had been his good old grandmamma's face, before the coffin-lid was closed and screwed down; when the coffin was lowered, and the gravel shovelled in upon it, to the sound of the tolling bell; and the mourners and neighbors returned, dazzled by the sudden glitter of sunshine on the pure, new-fallen snow ; and Eliza entered once more the hollow house, and listened to the drip of the eaves, and the blue sky smiled overhead, and neighbors came and went; — where, all this time, was Abel ?

Side by side now, in the white and quiet field, under the pacified December weather, slept all that was mortal of old Abel Dane the carpenter, and of Abigail his wife; while Abel, son of the preceding, was buried, mortal part with the immortal, in a very different tomb.

Would you penetrate that mausoleum of the living, — behold him with shaven crown, in convict's cap and coat, the livery of the doomed, — visit him when he eats, in his whitewashed solitary cell, the crust by the state provided, — stand by when he subdues his spirit to work under an overseer, at the work-bench of condemed horse-thieves and burglars, his predecessors and companions, — witness the sweat of his body and the sweat of his soul, the days and nights of his long death ? —

> For this living is true dying ;
> This is lordly man's down-lying.",

Nay, rather let us leave him there, as we leave his mother where she also lies buried, and keep with those who still walk abroad in the sun.

Faustina walks abroad, — or is at liberty to do so. And Mrs. Apjohn enjoys that precious privilege. And Tasso Smith, this wild December morning, comes forth, basking.

Pleased is Tasso; smiling and airy his port. A note, sent by Melissa's hand, has summoned him to an interview with Faustina. Locks well greased and curled, coat buttoned close, to conceal his unpresentable linen, his showy red-topped boots drawn over his strapped-down pantaloons, he treads daintily through the thawing snow, flourishing his light stick. For the first time since the memorable night of his discomfiture, he stops at Abel's gate, and rings the door-bell with complacent mien; considering that, by consummate diplomacy and strategic skill, he has, without loss to himself, but through the agency of others, routed his enemy, Abel, whose castle now lies at his mercy; never suspecting that he himself, like all the rest, is the agent of a Power above them all.

The garrison of the place, in the person of old Turk, growls at his red-topped boots, in a way the conquering hero does not like. But Melissa makes haste to admit him, and he is ushered into the presence of Faustina.

In the parlor sits the afflicted daughter-in-law, clad in deep mourning. With a dreary sigh she recognizes Tasso, and, half-rising, gives him her sad hand.

"Come to condole with you," says Mr. Smith. "Awful dispensation, old lady's dying so. Mus'n't let it break your heart."

"Don't mock me, Tasso! I'm in a dreadful situation! You've no idea of it!"

"Well, no, I don't see it."

"Oh, I am! Think of my husband! What will become of me, Tasso?"

"Good joke, I say, 'bout your husband, as you call him!" chuckles Tasso. "Good 'nough for him; jealous, grouty, unhospitable feller, like him ! Don't you go to sheddin' no unnecessary tears on his account, — le'me me advise ye."

But Faustina had fears for her own safety and reputation. "Murder will out, folks say; and I believe it," she declared, in allusion to her own guilty secret.

"Fudge, no danger ! Only you walk pertty straight now, and do as I tell ye, — conform'ble to my s'gestions, y' und'stand. If a feller's only shrewd enough, he can do what he's a mind to in this world, and not git found out. There's my little compliment to Ma'am Apjohn, — *tomatuses*, ye know," whispered the highly satisfied Tasso, — " who's found that out ? By George ! they think 'twas Abel, to this day ! "

"O Tasso ! " exclaimed Faustina, "that's one thing I wanted to see you about. Mrs. Apjohn knows, — she has heard, somehow, — the gracious knows how, I don't ! "

"Heard what ! Not that I " — began the startled, incredulous Mr. Smith.

"Yes; in the jail, before Abel, she declared that it was you, as she had certain means of knowing."

"Most 'stonishing thing ! " muttered Tasso, confused to learn that his brag of superior shrewdness had been somewhat premature. " She must have guessed at it."

"So I suppose. But she turned, and accused me so positively of having first told you of her stealing our tomatoes, that I couldn't deny it. How she ever knew that, I can't surmise."

But Tasso thought he could; for it had not been in his nature to refrain from imparting the pith of so excellent a jest to one or two choice companions, whom he now cursed in his heart. Faustina, perceiving that her version — or rather perversion — of the facts was received, assumed the air of a person who had had injuries, and went on, —

"So you see the blame all fell on me, after all. And I thought it was too bad ! I shall hear of somebody's betraying me altogether, next."

Tasso, completely outlied by the fair Faustina, after all his conceited cunning, protested that her suspicion was unfounded, and volunteered some excellent advice and consolation.

"Don't you have no fears whatever, — indulg'n' in unfounded apprehensions, y' und'stand. No use; all right you are; and you can jest go and take your pick of another husband soon as ye please, — handsome woman like you. Ye can git a divorce now, j'e know it ? "

"A divorce ? " Faustina looked up with interest. "From Abel ? "

"Of course ! didn't you know ? Five years in state's-prison, — that's a sufficient ground for a divorce, in this State. And, by George, Faustina ! — charming woman like you, — of course you aint so soft as to keep tied to a state's-prison culprit, in for five years, when you've only got to say the word, to swap him off for somethin' more attractive, more suitable to your refined tastes;" and Mr. Smith smoothed the curve of his mustache with a significant, seductive smile.

Much more sage counsel of the kind the disinterested visitor gave freely, without incurring any very severe reprimand from Faustina, who only sighed and raised feeble objections. They then parted, on quite confidential terms. Thus Faustina had made haste to break one of her solemn promises to Abel, — that she would avoid all unprofitable associates; and it could hardly be expected that her other promises would be kept more sacredly.

The remainder of the day, and the night that followed, when she should have remembered Abel, in prison for her sake, and have had no care but for his child, what was she feverishly dreaming ?

The next morning, hurried and fluttering, she appeared before Eliza. For Eliza still remained in the house, from which she could not resolve to depart, although those she loved had gone, and a husband and a home awaited her in another place.

"I have concluded," said Faustina, "that I ought to go and see my relations, and make some arrangements for the future. I suppose I can live with them, and this house can be let until Abel — until we want it again."

"And Ebby ? " said Eliza.

"Oh ! — Ebby, — I was about to say, — I suppose — I'd better not take him with me ; for I don't know yet what I am going to do. If I make such arrangements as I hope to, I will either return for him, or have Melissa bring him to me. You wont object to waiting a few days, until I can decide, will you ? "

"By no means," answered Eliza. "I will remain as long as I can be of service here, and do all I can for you. With regard to Ebby, I have had it in my mind to say to you, that, if you cannot conveniently keep him with you, I shall be only too glad to take him."

"What! you ? " exclaimed Faustina, with real or affected surprise. "Abel would never consent to such a thing ! "

Eliza suppressed some words of bitter truth that rose from her heart almost to her lips; and, after a little pause, replied calmly, —

"I ventured to speak to Abel about it. And he said that in case you should find it too hard to take care of Ebby, he was willing that I should have him."

"I'm not willing, if he is," retorted Faustina, decidedly. "I can never, never be parted from my darling boy ! "

Eliza regarded her with deep, sad eyes. "I know," she said, very quietly, "it would be too cruel to separate you from him."

"No," said Faustina; "I could never suffer it. It would not be kindness to the child. Who can fill a mother's place ? "

"True," said Eliza, with something too solemn for sarcasm, from the depths of her aggrieved spirit; "who can fill the place of a mother ? "

"So that is settled," exclaimed the exemplary mother, very positively.

"Still," replied Eliza, "you may remember my offer."

"I'll remember it; and it is very kind in you, certainly. But if you will have the goodness to remain here a few days, as I said, — not more than a week, at the most, — I'll be infinitely obliged to you; after that, I think I shall not find occasion to trouble you any farther."

That day Faustina departed. At the end of a week Eliza had not heard from her. Another week also passed without bringing any tidings of the absent mother. Accordingly Eliza, finding herself in a perplexing situation, wrote to inquire what were her prospects and intentions. Several days after the letter was sent, there came a tardy, despondent, indefinite reply. Faustina had not been able to accomplish her object as yet. She had been ill, — else she would have written earlier. Some of her relatives were absent, and she could not form any plans until their return, etc.

Eliza could not peer through the mists of distance, and see this passionately devoted mother of the child from whom she could never, never be separated, seeking distraction and solace in the home of her spoiled and petted girlhood. She could not hear the objurgations hurled by her flatterers at the villain husband, the utterly remorseless Abel, who had ruined the hopes and happiness of so beautiful a being. She possessed no

25

means to penetrate that beautiful being's breast, and discover, among the selfish purposes there cherished, the secret determination never to return to the convict's home
again, and never to be troubled with the maintenance
of his child. So Eliza remained in doubt, and did her
duty to Ebby, and wrote to Abel as cheerful and comforting letters as she could, — letters, by the way, which
were not nearly so abundant in protestations of affection
and fidelity as those he was at the same time receiving
from Faustina.

At length Eliza became weary. The house had grown
lonesome and ghostly to her oppressed heart. She wished
to be away. She resolved, therefore, to place no more
reliance upon the mother's promises, but to go, and take
Ebby with her.

XXXII.

MISS JONES 'AND MR. SMITH.

" WE will shut up the house, Melissa. You can keep
the key of it until Mrs. Dane decides what she is going
to do. Those things in the closet ought to be sent to
her, so as to leave as few as possible locked up in the
house."

" Them things is mine, if you please, ma'am," said
Melissa, hanging her head, and casting up timid glances
at Eliza.

" Yours, girl ! Did Mrs. Dane give you those
dresses ? "

Melissa hesitated, corkscrewing a foolish finger into a
corner of her mouth, as if she meant to uncork it.

" Yes, she did, if you please, ma'am."

" Why did you never take them, then ? "

" 'Cause, ma'am " — Melissa was making a spiritless
attempt to introduce her fist after her finger, and talking at the same time, — " I wa'n't sure, ma'am, 's I'd
ought'er take 'em. I don't know hardly now whuther
I'd ought'er take 'em, or whuther I hadn't 'dought'er. I
ruther guess " (down went the timid eyes, very meekly)
" I hadn't 'dought'er take 'em, after all."

"If she gave them to you, they are yours, and you shall certainly have them," said Eliza.

But now a sense of guilt and shrinking fear overcame the conscientious Melissa.

"No, no, ma'am; I wont take 'em, if you please, ma'am; it wouldn't be right."

"Why not, if they were given to you for honest service?"

"Oh, dear! they wa'n't! I'm afraid they wa'n't, ma'am!" whimpered the girl. "Don't ax me no more about it, if you please, ma'am." And the apron was got in readiness for an imminent outburst.

Now Eliza had not lived three months in that house, and observed the external daily life of it, without suspecting that there were things hidden beneath the surface which should be brought to light. Especially since the morning when she returned from Abel in the jail, and entered the room where his wife lay expecting Melissa, had she been conscious of extraordinary confidences between mistress and maid, in which, perhaps, Abel's honor was concerned. Still she had avoided hitherto any attempt to pry into these secrets; and, but for the girl's singular conduct on this occasion, what followed might never have occurred.

Miss Jones threw her apron over her head to defend herself, begging for mercy.

"Mercy, child?" said Eliza. "Why do you talk and act in this way? What harm will happen to you, if you tell the truth about the dresses, and, if they are yours, take them?"

"I don't want 'em!" sobbed Melissa in her apron. "Please, ma'am, don't make me take 'em; and don't make me tell the truth about 'em, for Mrs. Dane told me never to tell the truth, so long as I live. Oh! Oh! Oh!"

"Hush! hush! She told you never to tell the truth? Nonsense!"

"Oh, yes, she did, ma'am! She give me the things to hire me never to tell; and I wa'n't never to tell why she give 'em to me; and now, oh, dear, dear, dear, I've been and gone and told!"

Eliza, now fully roused, endeavored to pacify her, then said, firmly, —

"I certainly do not wish you to tell anything which you ought not to. But, do you know, Melissa, it may be very wrong for you not to tell?"

"Oh, yes, ma'am; I've thought so myself many and many a time, and told Mrs. Dane so; and then she'd give me something else, and make me promise ag'in, and tell me buggers would ketch me if ever I lisped a word on't! And, oh, dear, dear, what shall I do?"

"Think it over," said Eliza, "then do just what you think is right. If what you know has any connection with Abel's being in prison, where we are so sure he ought not to be, then, as you fear God more than you do Mrs. Dane, speak!"

"Oh, I will! I will!" exclaimed Melissa, throwing

off her apron, and all concealment with it. And as her face emerged red and wet from that covering, so the truth came out glowing, and saturated with tears of repentance, from the cloud of deception which had been so long laid over it. A tragic interest held Eliza, as she listened.

"Who else knows of this but you? anybody?" she asked.

"Nobody, not as I know on, 'thout 'tis Tasso Smith, — she's told him some things, I don't know how much."

Eliza left the girl wiping her face; and, throwing on her bonnet and shawl, set out to call on Mr. Smith.

As she was passing Mr. Apjohn's house, Mrs. Apjohn threw open a front window, showed her animated russet face, and, putting out an arm of the biggest, beckoned violently.

"Come in here! come in here!" she cried. "Come right straight in, 'Lizy; without a word!"

Not knowing what momentous question was at issue or what lives were at stake, Eliza felt impelled to go in and see. She ran to the door, which the excited Prudence opened for her, and, entering, beheld with surprise the pale, pimpled, simpering face of a worried youth, whom Mrs. Apjohn indignantly pointed out to her.

It was Mr. Tasso Smith, — entrapped, it seemed, expressly for her. Behind Tasso stood Mr. Cooper Apjohn, submissive, sighing and winking, and meekly endeavoring to deprecate his wife's wrath.

"Look at him!" said Prudence. "I want ye to look

at him well, 'Lizy! See if ye can't make him blush, —
for I can't! the miserable, lyin', pompous, silly, con-
saited jackanapes!"

"Prudy! Prudy! don't be rash! don't be rash,
Prudy!" interposed the cooper.

"Oh, let her speak her mind," said Tasso, with a
ghastly grimace. "Like to have folks speak their
minds, — express their honest sentiments, y' und'-
stand;" and he pulled his mustache nervously.

"You needn't be the leastest mite consarned but
what I'll speak mine," Mrs. Apjohn informed him.
"I've been waiting to git holt of ye ever sence the
trial. An' you've kep' out of my way perty well, —
as if you knowed what was good for yourself, you
sneakin', desaitful, underhand, silly, grinnin'," —

"Prudy! Prudy!" interrupted the cooper.

"I was jest walking by, like any quiet gentleman,"
Tasso explained to Eliza, "when she reshed out, by
George! and actchilly collared me, by George! J'ever
hear of such a thing? By George, I thought she meant
to serve me as she did Dane's tomatoes, — steal me and
cook me and eat me for dinner! by George!"

At that Prudence collared him again, and choked and
shook the pale joker till his teeth chattered.

"See here! better take care! my clo'es!" observed
Tasso, startled by the cracking of stitches.

"I don't care for your clo'es!" said Prudence, furiously. "Insult me to my face, will ye? You dirty,
mean, impudent, dastardly, squash-faced, measly," —

" Prudy ! Prudy ! " whispered the cooper.

Eliza now thought it time to interfere. Her calm, decisive manner exerted a Christianizing influence over the energetic Prudence.

" Wal, then ! " said the latter, " to come to the p'int, what I wanted of you is this : I've charged this scoundrel here with hangin' them tomatuses on to my door, and he denies it."

" Certainly I do," corroborated Tasso, — who, it may as well be told, having conferred with his cronies, who he feared had betrayed his secret, and become convinced that they had not, was now prepared to maintain his innocence by stoutest lies. " And I defy her to prove it."

" And I," added Prudence, " of course, told him what Faustina said that day in jail. But he declares she never said no sech thing, but I said it, and tried to git her to own up to it ! Now, what I want of you is, to tell jest what was said that day, and who said it." And Mrs. Apjohn folded her immense arms.

Thereupon, in few words, Eliza related the simple, direct truth. That dashed the spirits of young Smith more than all Mrs. Apjohn's hard names and shaking had done.

" By George ! 'd she say that ? What else 'd she say ? by George ! " — glaring maliciously.

Eliza perceived that the moment was ripe for her purpose. Her eyes held him, as she spoke, by the power of their earnestness and truth.

"She did not say all she might have said. She was more ready to accuse others than to take any blame to herself. It is your turn now, Tasso Smith, to speak the truth concerning Faustina Dane."

Tasso smirked and glared, hesitating between resentment against Faustina and an unforgotten grudge against Eliza.

"Shouldn't think you'd expect much truth from me, after the ruther hard joke you tried onto me that day in the court-house; callin' me a liar, right 'fore all the people, by George!"

Sturdy little Eliza, unabashed by this retort, stood up unflinchingly facing him, her brow beaming with courage and sincerity.

"And did you not deserve that I should call you a liar? Remember what you were saying of Abel at the very time, — and of Faustina, — when you knew every word you said was false. If I had known then, what I know now, I'd have dragged you before the court, and compelled you to testify!"

"Hey? By George! what did I know?" said Tasso.

"That's what you are to confess before ever you quit this house! And don't imagine you can deceive me in any particular. Mrs. Dane had more confidants than one; and everything has been revealed. I was on my way to see you; for it is time you should do something to avert the suspicion of being her accomplice."

"By George! I warn't no accomplice of nobody's: I'll resk that suspicion!"

" Don't be too sure ! " Eliza warned him. " Abel Dane
felt himself safe against a false charge, trusting in his
own innocence. You are in some danger, Tasso ! You
sold Mrs. Dane the jewels; you are aware how she
paid for them, and how she replaced the money with
,which she paid for them. You see the truth is
known."

Tasso saw, and felt sick. It took him not long now to
make up his mind what to do. Since Faustina had set
the example of treachery by betraying him, — and since
her other confidants, of whom, he now thought, she
might have twenty, had also set the example, — he
resolved to waste no time in purging himself of the
aforesaid suspicion.

" Sit down," Eliza directed, with a quick, quiet, domi-
nant, business-like manner. And Tasso sat down.

" Mrs. Apjohn, bring me a pen and ink."

A pen, used in keeping the cooper's accounts, and in
making memoranda in the almanac, was produced, together with some muddy ink.

" Now, sir, tell your story. You are not under oath
yet, but you will be before I am through with you.
Mr. and Mrs. Apjohn, listen."

They listened; and Eliza wrote; while Tasso proceeded to make his astounding revelations, by which
Melissa's statement was fully confirmed.

"O Prudy ! Prudy ! " cried the wonder-stricken
John. "Abel is a innocent man, arter all ! And he is
in for five year' ! and his mother has been killed by it !

and we — we've been — O Prudy ! Prudy ! To be sure,
to be sure ! "

Eliza did not wait to hear the exclamations and
lamentations of the worthy pair; but, fastening herself
to Tasso, informed him that he was to go presently before a magistrate and take oath to the statement she
had received from his lips. They were to stop on their
way for Melissa; and Mrs. Apjohn eagerly volunteered
to "run over and take care of the baby," during the
girl's absence; for that solid and sterling woman was
now enlisted with her whole body and soul in Abel's
cause, showing herself even more anxious for his deliver-
ance than she had ever been for his condemnation.

XXXIII.

ELIZA'S MISSION.

TASSO's elegant signature was soon affixed, under oath and in the presence of witnesses, to the paper Eliza had drawn up. Next, Melissa's affidavit was secured. Then, how to proceed, with these instruments, to effect Abel's liberation, became the important question. For now Eliza could not rest, day or night, until the requisite steps had been taken to restore him to honor, and freedom, and happiness.

She was dismayed when told that the sentence must be set aside by due process of law; and that, to make the necessary appeal, and await the slow course of justice, would require patience and time, — perhaps months, — when every moment was precious. "Besides," she was assured, "any confession Faustina might have made, or might still make, would probably be insufficient to exculpate her husband. They were one, by marriage; for her actions he was in a certain sense accountable; he had shared the fruit of her crime; and her evidence, even if she chose to give it, could hardly be received in court, she being his wife; and there were many other difficulties to be overcome. Individuals might be easily convinced of Abel's inocence; but the law was not an individual. The law had no conscience; it was without sympathy or understanding; it was a machine."

Still she was not disheartened, she would not rely upon the law to right the wrong the law had done. She would rely upon the human heart, and upon the justice of her cause; and nothing should divert her from her purpose, or induce her to waste an hour in idle delay, till Abel was free.

In addition to the affidavits of Tasso and Melissa, she procured those of John and Prudence Apjohn, in which they, as chief witnesses against Abel, now declared their conviction of his innocence, for reasons assigned. She also visited the attorneys who had prosecuted him, the judge who had sentenced him, and each individual of the twelve who had found him guilty. She carried with her a well-worded petition which she had prepared; and such was her eloquence, such her magnetic and persuasive earnestness, that lawyers, judge, and jury, all signed it. To these names she found no difficulty in adding the signatures of a hundred of Abel's townsmen, including three ministers, a congressman, two ex-members of the State legislature, together with several selectmen, deacons, and other prominent citizens.

More than a week was consumed in these preliminary labors, notwithstanding Eliza's utmost endeavors to despatch them in a day or two. From dawn to midnight she was incessantly employed, with a vigor and vigilance and hope that never flagged. At length all was ready. And, armed with her affidavits, her petition, and a formidable legal document which Abel's counsel had furnished, she set out, one memorable morning, on a journey.

The petition was to the governor of the State. Her mission was to him. On the evening of the same day she reached the capital of the State ; and, without stopping even to change her attire, inquired her way hurriedly through the strange streets till she came to the governor's house.

He was at home. How her heart throbbed on being told this by the servant at the door, and being invited in ! And so, tremblingly, yet with a brave and resolute heart, she entered the warmly-lighted hall of the house in which she felt that the question of Abel's destiny was to be finally decided.

XXXIV.

ELIZA AND THE GOVERNOR.

IN a quiet little room she was told to sit down, while the servant communicated her name and the nature of her errand to the governor. She had not long to wait. His Excellency — a kind, affable person — came presently into the apartment, looked at her somewhat curiously, shook hands with her, and sitting down, like any pleasant gentleman, with no frown of the high official about him, listened to her story.

He was a man who loved straightforward dealing and despatch; and the directness, simplicity, and brevity with which she laid her business before him made him smile.

But he was a cautious man withal; and, when she had finished, all he could promise was, that the petition, with the accompanying documents, should be carefully examined, and laid before his council; and that he would endeavor to do impartial justice in the matter. It might be several days, he said, before he would be prepared to grant or refuse the pardon for which the hundred petitioners prayed; but there should be no needless delay; and, if it would be any satisfaction to her impatience, she might call on him again the next evening at his house.

"If I am occupied, and cannot see you, of course," he added, "you will not take it unkindly, nor be discouraged."

She thanked him, with tears, which his gentle and frank speech called forth. Hitherto she had controlled herself well, — concentrating all her emotions to give power to her appeal. But now the grief she had held back, the suffering of nights and days, kept down by constant activity, the hope and fear she felt, and her deep conviction of Abel's innocence, — deeper and stronger than any reason she could give, — found utterance in a few broken but fervent words of thanks and of entreaty. And so she departed; not knowing whether she had spoken well or ill, shedding silent tears, and moving her lips to silent prayers, as she once more threaded the strange streets.

She slept that night — for, after all her toils, she slept well — at a boarding-house to which one of the ex-members of the legislature had recommended her. The next day she felt refreshed and strong. But do you think she spent the hours that intervened till night in viewing the sights of the city? Not she. Having learned, by inquiry, where the state-prison was, she went to learn her way to it; so that, the pardon procured, she could hasten, without an instant's uncertainty, to bear it to her dear prisoner. A half-hour's ride and a few minutes' walk brought her in sight of the formidable pile.

There rose the impassive gray walls, somewhere within which she knew her Abel breathed the air of captivity, that calm winter's morning, while she breathed the air of freedom without. How mournfully and hopefully she walked by them, and far around, viewing them on every side; with what memories and thrills of tenderness she thought of him there immured, hopelessly plodding, never suspecting how near she was to him; with what stifled aspiration and rapture she anticipated their next meeting; and how she lingered, feeling a strange satisfaction in being there, though she could not see him nor make her presence known, — all this may be imagined, but not told.

In the afternoon she returned to her boarding-house, and prepared for the evening. The hope of seeing the governor, and of hearing something favorable to her mission, kept her heart occupied. But the hope was destined to disappointment. His Excellency was absent from home. And the only consolation she received was a notification that he would expect to see her at his office the next day.

The next morning, at the hour assigned, little Eliza was already at the state-house, waiting for the bell to strike the minute. She had taken care to find the doors of the executive department; and punctually, at the appointed hour, she entered the awful precincts, and was ushered into the presence of the governor.

He appeared absorbed in business; but, recognizing

26*

her, and, looking up at the clock, he immediately turned, and motioned her to a seat near him.

"I have not forgotten you," he said, "though I was obliged to disappoint you last night."

He then spoke to a clerk, who brought to him a package of papers, which Eliza perceived to be her petition, affidavits, and so forth.

"I have done something in this unfortunate affair, too," he added; but his manner was not promising. Eliza's eyes were delighted by no pardon, and her hopes began to sink. "But how happens it," he inquired, "that, among all these papers, there is no memorial from the prisoner himself?"

"Sir," said the earnest girl, "I can explain that. He does not know yet that a pardon has been applied for. I thought it best not to inform him; for I would not raise false expectations in his mind. Besides, — for I wish to be entirely frank with you, and rely upon your goodness, — I think it possible that he might not have approved of what his friends were doing."

"And why not?" said the governor, lifting his eyebrows with some surprise.

"I will not conceal anything," replied Eliza. "I think Mr. Dane was aware of his wife's guilt; yet he would not expose her. He preferred to sacrifice himself in her place."

"It would appear, then, that he not only accepted and used the stolen money" —

"O sir! that was without his knowledge, — the affidavits show that, — and I would pledge my life that it is true."

"And yet," said the governor, "according to your own representation, he concealed her crime, and thus became an accessory after the fact."

"Do not, sir ! do not let appearances and technicalities stand in the way of justice !" Eliza conjured him. "If appearances were truths, if the law was infallible, I should not be here. Grant that, in the eyes of the law, he was an accomplice; grant that it was criminal to conceal her crime, — I don't care !" she cried, with flashing spirit. "I know, and you know, sir, that it was nobler in him to conceal than to expose it. It was a holy sacrifice he made of himself, unworthy as she was. His conduct is to be admired, and not blamed. In your heart you must commend it, whatever you may say. If what he did was a sin, I think such a sinner is worthier of heaven than many a precise saint. Such a spirit of self-sacrifice, — it overcomes me now to think of it " — and Eliza dashed the quick tears from her eyes.

"But will this fine sinner thank us for what we are doing ?" asked the governor, with a smile.

"He will at least forgive me for saving him in spite of himself and without his knowledge. And when he learns how his wife has repaid his devotion by deserting his child, he will not regret that justice has come about through her own indiscretion."

"Well," said the governor, smiling again very curiously, "if that does not satisfy him, I have something here that I think will. Have you seen the morning papers?" So saying, he took one from a pile on the desk, and handed it to Eliza, pointing to a paragraph. "That will interest him, I think."

Eliza read, and turned white with astonishment and indignation.

"O sir !" she said in thick, tremulous tones, after a pause of speechless amazement, " after this " —

"After this," interrupted the governor, " I think both he and you will be satisfied with what I have done." With which quiet speech, he opened a drawer, and produced a large unsealed envelope, which he placed in her hand.

Eliza knew well what it contained; and as she drew forth the precious paper, and unfolded it, she could but just see the great shining seal and blurring signature through the tears of joy that blinded her.

XXXV.

DELIVERANCE.

AND now Abel Dane was summoned from the prison workshop. In his bi-colored convict's cap and coat and trousers, — one-half the man from head to heel blue, the other half red; one side the hue of despondency, the other the tint of shame, — forth he came, curious to know what was wanted. Following the warden, he crossed the prison-yard, ascended the steps he had descended on his arrival thither, and entered once more the room he had passed through when he left all hope behind; — so changed, since then, that she who waited for him there did not know him, but took him for some other.

But he knew her in an instant. And at the first sound of his voice, at a look out of those deep, glad eyes, she recognized, in the grotesque wight before her, the transformed manhood of Abel.

How they met; how she revealed to him the cause of her coming, and put with her own hands into his the governor's pardon; and he knew that he was raised from the dead, and that she, his best-beloved was also his deliverer; — I am aware what a moving scene might be made of all this. But enough,—our story draws to a close.

Abel was taken in charge by the warden for the last time. The clothes he put off at his entrance into prison were restored to him; and he left behind his convict's costume, for the benefit of some sad successor. Then he rejoined Eliza; and they quitted the prison together.

But it was all like a dream to him yet. Explanations were needed to relieve his uncertainty and suspense. And as they walked the street together, and he tasted with her the sweet air of liberty, and knew that his brief, terrible nightmare of prison life was indeed shaken off, she told him how his redemption had been achieved.

Abel was troubled. In the midst of his gratitude and joy he was grieved for Faustina. She was his wife still. "And I had hoped,"—he began.

"I know what you hoped," Eliza tenderly replied. "And I know—we all know—you have done everything for her a hero and Christian could do. But in vain. And, Abel, she is no longer your wife."

"True ! true !" said Abel. "By God's law, may-be, she is not. But man's laws,—they are different,—I must abide by them."

He said this with a great sigh; hoping perhaps for some word of comforting assurance from Eliza. She too was agitated. She could hardly control her voice to answer him.

"Yes, Abel. You must — you will be willing to submit, I think. But the law, — human law, — what strange, strange things it is sometimes made to do! Abel, I have brought this to show you." And she gave him the governor's newspaper, putting her finger on the paragraph his Excellency had pointed out to her.

Abel read as they walked the street. It was a notice of divorces granted; among which was one to Faustina Dane, from her husband, Abel Dane. "Cause — state-prison."

Grief and indignation convulsed him a moment.

"The injustice of it, Eliza ! — I in prison for her fault ! — and this after all her promises ! O Faustina ! selfish and impulsive ! foolish and false ! Thank Heaven, it is she that has done this, and not I ! "

So saying, with a deep breath of the pure electric air, a sense of relief, a new sense of freedom, and of something deeply and divinely great and glad, entered into him. Eliza perceived it.

"Yes, Abel; it is better. And oh, is it not wonderful, that God often makes those who would injure us the agents of our good ! Oh, let us trust him, let us trust him always ! "

But even as she spoke, a shadow as of a brooding fatality fell upon them both. Not from the prison of stone alone, but also from the bondage of a false marriage, Abel saw himself, this day, as it were miraculously delivered. And he could see how Tasso's meanness, and Mrs. Apjohn's spite, and Faustina's perfidy, — how all his misfortunes, even that which had seemed the greatest, — had tended steadily, by sure degrees, to this consummation. And here he was, a free man, superior to disaster and disgrace, walking by the side of the woman he loved, and to whom he owed his rescue; and she, — her work was now done, and nothing remained but for her to go and bless the husband who had been so long waiting for her, in the home he had proffered, and which she had promised to accept.

XXXVI.

HOME.

THEY stopped in town to get some presents for Ebby, then took the train, and reached home the same evening.

Alighting at the village, they looked in at the post-office, and found a letter for Eliza. Whence and from whom it came, both knew. Abel was deeply moved; and Eliza, it must be owned, felt heavy misgivings as she pressed it unopened into her pocket.

It was late; the fire was nearly out in the kitchen; the candle burned low in its socket; Melissa had fallen asleep over her knitting; Ebby was dreaming and smiling in the cushioned arm-chair ; and old Turk lay in the corner.

Suddenly the scene changed. Melissa jumped up, rubbed her eyes, and, at the summons of a well-known voice, ran to open the door. Turk bounced from the hearth, and madly welcomed his master. Ebby also awoke, and saw his mamma (as he always persisted in calling Eliza), and his father who had come home with her, and the playthings they had brought him, and was the gladdest boy the round world then contained.

There are kisses, and questions, and supper for the
new-comers; and again the scene changes. Melissa is
sent to put Ebby to bed. Then Abel and Eliza alone,—
the clock telling the minutes of midnight; the long,
earnest, tender, sorrowful talk; — she, yielding to him
one all too sympathetic trembling hand, while with the
other she clasps the still unopened letter in her pocket,
as if that alone could keep her true to the absent one;
there parting at last, in anguish, after all the joy and
triumph of the day, — he lonely and bereft, she faithful
still in purpose to her affianced, despite her most un-
faithful heart; the sound of the door that closed between them, and the utter silence and solitude of the
night that followed; — at which closing scenes of our
drama we can only hint, for were we to relate in detail
all that passed,

> The story would outlast a night in Russia,
> When nights are longest there."

Early the next morning, Abel, " wrapped in dismal thinkings," having vainly endeavored to sleep,
sat alone by the fire, in the home to which he had
been restored, only, as it seemed, to feel its vacancy, —
Faustina lost, his mother gone, Eliza about to go. No
doubt Eliza was fast asleep, and dreaming of her distant lover, to whom she was so soon to return. So
Abel thought, disconsolately enough; reflecting ungrate-
fully that even his saddest night in prison had been

happier than this; when he heard the door softly open, and, looking up, saw Eliza. She smiled faintly.

"Darling!" he cried;—"I knew you could not! I knew you would come back to me!"—though, poor fellow, he certainly knew no such thing, or else, as he sat there, the world would have looked to him somewhat less dreary.

But Eliza, although she smiled, was shivering, and very pale; and he knew not yet whether to hope, or still to keep company with despair.

"There is something here—which I thought you ought to know of"—she said, in a voice shaking with the cold. And the letter of her betrothed, which, after much unhappy delay, she had summoned the resolution to read, she placed in Abel's hand. Ah, different now the times from those long ago, when *he* placed in *her* hand the letter of his love, the beautiful Faustina, and she could not read it for the wrong that was wringing her heart!

Perhaps, by this time, that wrong had been amply avenged; as all wrongs are, soon or late, in this world or the next.

Abel read with interest, which darkened into pain as he proceeded, then kindled into surprise, and brightened at last into a blaze of triumph.

The devoted lover, the generous, disinterested friend, had grown at length impatient. Eliza's letters had not satisfied him; that she cared more for Abel in prison than for him in the home he had offered her, was but too evident; and so, without penning a single reproach (for, indeed, she had dealt truly with him from the first, as he acknowledged), but not without profound regret on his part, he begged leave to release her from her engagement.

"But, Abel!" suddenly exclaimed Eliza, disengaging herself from his arms; and a shadow fell upon her glowing, suffused face.

"What is it?" Abel asked, starting from the dream that their bliss was perfect now.

"I OWE THAT DEAR MAN THREE HUNDRED DOLLARS!"

"Phew!" whistled Abel, pursing up his brows; for he knew this debt had been incurred for his sake, and that she had impoverished herself to fee his lawyers, and could not pay it, and that he had never a cent.

"He must be paid," said Eliza.

"Certainly, he must be paid," Abel muttered, plunged in thought, "but how? All my property is mortgaged. I can't borrow. I've sold even my tool-chest. I can go to work,—and if ever I worked with a will, I shall now,—but that is a debt that should be paid at once. He is a noble man: he certainly deserved you, 'Liza, better than I do, I'm afraid,—I know!" feeling with deep humility how selfishly he had acted towards her from the first.

They sat talking until the morning was well advanced,—Abel's mind still perplexed.

There came a knock at the door, and, Melissa opening it, in walked John Apjohn the cooper, and Prudence

Apjohn his wife; who, having heard of Abel's return, had hastened to be the first to congratulate him.

Prudence was radiant, and John was gay and smiling, all his melancholy having been dissipated by the glad tidings of Abel's release from prison.

"And if ever I heerd a bit o' news that done my soul good," said Prudence, all smiles and tears, "it was when old Mr. Smith come to our house jest now for a firkin, and said you was seen gittin' out o' the stage, you and 'Lizy, up to the square, last night."

"And, I was a goin' for to say," said John, with boyish eagerness, — "knowin' as how you was put to't for money 'fore the trial, — I was a goin' for to say," —

"Fact is," — Prudence snatched the thread of his discourse, — "me and my husband here has got three or four hunderd dollars a comin' in jest about this time, — money we've lent in years past, — an' as we've no 'airthly use for it right away," —

"An' knowin' 't you sold off everything," struck in the cooper, — "an' you must stand in need o' somethin' for to give ye a start," —

"An' if 'twould be any sort o' 'commodation to you," resumed Prudence, "to have the use o' that money, 'thout interest, for a year or so, or as long as ye want, till ye git a little 'forehanded agin, — *'thout interest*," she repeated, emphatically, — "why, you're welcome to it, you're welcome to it, Abel Dane, as much as if you was my own son!"

"To be sure, to be sure," assented the cooper.

"O Abel! how we are provided for!" exclaimed Eliza.

Abel shook his neighbors heartily by the hand, and thanked them with deeper joy and gratitude than he could express, and of course consented to relieve them of their superfluous hundreds; sending them home rejoicing.

The debt was paid, and Abel began life anew.

And so all things came duly round at last: the circle grew complete, — Abel obtaining without long delay a divorce from his already divorced wife, and entering with Eliza the path of blessedness into which the devious ways of difficulty and the sometimes dark ways of duty had led them.

It remains to add only a word. Faustina never saw husband or child again. But while Abel consoled himself, and Ebby found indeed a mother in Eliza, she, the beautiful one, married a second time, and lives, as I learn, a gay life.

And so poetical justice is not done? Very well; divine justice is done, nevertheless. I am not aware that either she or Tasso Smith ever received for their misdeeds what the world calls punishment. But that any one is permitted to live on, unrepentant and unchecked, a life of selfishness, is perhaps, in the sight of a higher Wisdom, the greatest punishment of all.

Popular and Valuable Books,

FOR OLD AND YOUNG,

PUBLISHED BY LEE & SHEPARD,

149 Washington Street, Boston.

Lee and Shepard's Catalogue and Trade List sent by mail, post paid, on application.

OLIVER OPTIC'S BOOKS.

Each Series in a neat box. Sold in sets or separately.

Young America Abroad. Outward Bound; or
Young America Afloat. Tenth edition. Now ready. $1.50.

Army and Navy Stories. A Library for Young
and Old, in six volumes. 16mo. Illustrated. Price $1.50 per vol. The Soldier Boy, or Tom Somers in the Army; The Sailor Boy, or Jack Somers in the Navy; The Young Lieutenant, or The Adventurer of an Army Officer — A Sequel to the Soldier Boy; The Yankee Middy, or The Adventures of a Naval Officer — Sequel to The Sailor Boy; Fighting Joe, or The Fortunes of a Staff Officer — A Sequel to The Young Lieutenant; Brave Old Salt, or Life on the Quarter-Deck — A Sequel to The Yankee Middy. The whole series are admirably illustrated, printed and bound in the best style, and may be obtained in sets in neat boxes, or be had separate.

Woodville Stories. Uniform with Library for
Young People. Six volumes. 16mo. Illustrated. $1.50 per vol. Rich and Humble, or the Mission of Bertha Grant; In School and Out, or the Conquest of Richard Grant; Watch and Wait, or The Young Fugitives; Work and Win, or Noddy Newman on a Cruise; Hope and Have, or Fanny Grant among the Indians; Haste and Waste, or The Young Pilot of Lake Champlain. Each volume handsomely illustrated, and complete in itself, or in sets in neat boxes.

Famous "Boat-Club" Series. Library for Young
People. Handsomely illustrated. Six volumes, in neat box; per volume, $1.25. Comprising: The Boat Club, or The Bunkers of Rippleton; All Aboard, or Life on the Lake; Now or Never, or The Adventures of Bobby Bright; Try Again, or The Trials and Triumphs of Harry West; Poor and Proud, or The Fortunes of Katy Redburn; Little by Little, or The Cruise of the Flyaway.

Riverdale Story-Books. Six volumes, profusely
Illustrated from new designs by Billings. In neat box. Cloth. Per volume, 45c. Comprising: Little Merchant; Young Voyagers; Dolly and I; Proud and Lazy; Careless Kate; Robinson Crusoe, Jr.

Flora Lee Story-Books. Companions to the above.
Six volumes, profusely illustrated from new designs by Billings. In neat box. Cloth. Per volume, 45c. Comprising: Christmas Gift; Uncle Ben; Birthday Party; The Picnic Party; The Gold Thimble; The Do-Somethings.

The above two series are also published in twelve volumes, under the title of Riverdale Stories. They are divided for convenience of both buyer and seller, or can be had, twelve volumes, in a neat box.

The Way of the World. By William T. Adams
(Oliver Optic). 12mo. $2.00.

Oliver Optic's Magazine, "Our Boys and Girls."
Published Weekly. Fully Illustrated. Per number, 6 cents; $2.50 per year.

Arabian Nights. 16mo. Illustrated. $1.50.

The Adventures of a German Toy. A charming story for children. By Miss E. P. Channing. With three illustrations. 75 cts.

Crusoe Library. An attractive series for Young and Old. Six volumes, illustrated. In neat box. Per volume, $1.50. Comprising: Robinson Crusoe; Arabian Nights; Arctic Crusoe; Young Crusoe; Prairie Crusoe; Willis the Pilot.

Robinson Crusoe. 16mo. Illustrated. $1.50.

The Young Crusoe. A book for Boys. 16mo. Illustrated. $1.50.

The Prairie Crusoe; or, Adventures in the Far West. A book for Boys. 16mo. Illustrated. $1.50.

The Arctic Crusoe: A Tale of the Polar Seas. Finely Illustrated. 16mo. $1.50.

Eminent Statesmen. The Young American's Library of Eminent Statesmen. Uniform with the Young American's Library of Famous Generals. Six volumes, handsomely illustrated, in neat box. Per vol., $1.25. Comprising: Life of Benjamin Franklin; Life of Daniel Webster; The Yankee Tea Party; Life of William Penn; Life of Henry Clay; Old Bell of Independence.

Famous Generals. The Young American's Library of Famous Generals. A useful and attractive series of books for Boys. Six volumes, handsomely illustrated, in neat box. Per volume, $1.25. Comprising: Life of General Washington; Life of General Taylor; Life of General Jackson; Life of General Lafayette; Life of General Marion; Life of Napoleon Bonaparte.

Fireside Picture Books. With many comical illustrations. Stiff paper covers, in assorted dozen; per dozen, $1.80. Stiff paper covers, in assorted dozen, colored; per dozen, $3.00. Comprising: Precocious Piggy; Robber Kitten; Nine Lives of a Cat; Picture Alphabet; Little Man and his Little Gun; Fireside Picture Alphabet.

Glen Morris Stories for Boys and Girls. By Frances Forrester. Five volumes, 16mo. Each volume complete in itself, and beautifully illustrated with fine engravings. Per volume, $1.25. Comprising: Guy Carlton; Dick Duncan; Jessie Carlton; Walter Sherwood; Kate Carlton.

Kitty Barton. By Hester Gray. A simple Story for Children. With one illustration. 32mo. 60 cts.

The Little Wrinkled Old Man. A Christmas Extravaganza, and other Trifles. By Mrs. Elizabeth A. Thurston. Illust. 75c.

Minnie and her Pets. By Mrs. Madeline Leslie. Elegantly illustrated. Six volumes. Small 4to. Bound in high-colored cloths, and put up in neat box. Per volume, 75 cts. Comprising: Minnie's Pet Parrot; Minnie's Pet Cat; Minnie's Pet Dog; Minnie's Pet Pony; Minnie's Pet Lamb; Minnie's Pet Monkey.

Little Agnes' Library for Girls. By Mrs. Madeline Leslie. Four volumes, in neat box; each volume elegantly illustrated, and entirely distinct from the rest. Per volume, $1.50. Comprising: Little Agnes; Trying to be Useful; I'll Try; Art and Artlessness.

Play and Study Series for Boys and Girls. By

Mrs. Madeline Leslie. Four volumes. Illustrated. Uniform with Little Agnes' Library for Girls. Neat box. Per volume, $1.50. Comprising: The Motherless Children; Play and Study; Howard and his Teacher; Jack, the Chimney Sweeper. These two popular series are issued in entirely new style, bound in rich fancy cloths, and put up in neat box.

Ned Nevins the Newsboy; or, Street Scenes in

Boston. By Rev. Henry Morgan, P. M. P. 16mo. Illustrated. $1.50.

Old Merry Rhymes for Young Merry Hearts.

Small 4to. Boards. 25 cts.

Little Prudy Stories. By Sophie May. Now

complete. Six volumes. 24mo. Handsomely illustrated. In a neat box. Per volume, 75 cts. Comprising: Little Prudy; Little Prudy's Sister Susie; Little Prudy's Captain Horace; Little Prudy's Cousin Grace; Little Prudy's Story-Book; Little Prudy's Dotty Dimple.

Patriotism at Home; or, The Young Invincibles.

By I. H. Anderson, author of "Fred Freeland." With four illustrations, from original designs by Champney. One volume. 16mo. $1.50.

Rosy Diamond Story-Books. For Girls. A com-

panion set to Vacation Story-Books. Finely illustrated from designs by Billings and others. Six volumes. Bound in high-colored cloths. In neat box. Per volume, 80 cts. Comprising: The Great Rosy Diamond; Daisy, or the Fairy Spectacles; Violet, a Fairy Story; Minnie, or the Little Woman; The Angel Children; Little Blossom's Reward.

Vacation Story-Books. For Boys and Girls.

Finely illustrated from designs by Hoppin and others. Six volumes. Square 16mo. In neat box. Per volume 80 cts. Comprising: Worth, not Wealth; Country Life; The Charm; Karl Keigler; Walter Seyton; Holidays at Chestnut Hill.

Sunnybank Stories. Twelve volumes. Compiled

by Rev. Asa Bullard, editor of the "Well-Spring." Profusely illustrated. 32mo. Bound in high colors, and put up in neat box. Per volume, 25 cts. Comprising: Uncle Henry's Stories; Dog Stories; Stories for Alice; My Teacher's Gem; The Scholar's Welcome; Going to School; Aunt Lizzie's Stories; Mother's Stories; Grandpa's Stories; The Good Scholar; The Lighthouse; Reward of Merit. The same series is also divided into Sunnybank and Shady Dell Stories, of six volumes each. Orders should designate the number of volumes required.

Shady Dell Stories. Six volumes. Compiled by

Rev. Asa Bullard, editor of the "Well-Spring." Profusely illustrated. 32mo. Bound in high colors, and put up in a neat box (to match the Sunnybank Stories). Per volume, 25 cts. Comprising: My Teacher's Gem; The Scholar's Welcome; Going to School; The Good Scholar; The Lighthouse; Reward of Merit.

Sunnybank Stories. Six volumes. Compiled by

Rev. Asa Bullard, editor of the "Well-Spring." Profusely illustrated. 32mo. Bound in high colors and put up in a neat box. Per volume, 25 cts. Comprising: Uncle Henry's Stories; Dog Stories; Stories for Alice; Aunt Lizzie's Stories; Mother's Stories; Grandpa's Stories.

Willis the Pilot; or, Sequel to the Swiss Family

Robinson. With numerous illustrations. 16mo. $1.50.

Arabian Nights' Entertainments. 12mo. Muslin.

With eight full-page illustrations. (The popular edition formerly published by Phillips, Sampson & Co.) $1.75.

Amateur Dramas for Parlor Theatricals, Evening

Entertainments, and School Exhibitions. By Geo. M. Baker. Illus. 16mo. $1.50.

A Trip to the Azores, or Western Islands. By
M. Borges De F. Henriques. 16mo. $1.50.

Bacon's Essays. With Annotations by Archbishop
Whately. In press; new edition. This edition will contain a Preface, Notes, and
Glossarial Index, by F. F. Heard, Esq., of the Boston Bar. It will be printed in
the very best style, by Messrs. J. Wilson & Son, of Cambridge, and will undoubt-
edly be the finest edition ever published in this country.

The Blade and the Ear. Thoughts for a Young
Man. By Rev. A. B. Muzzey. 16mo. Red edges, bvld sides, $1.50; plain, $1.25.

The College, the Market, and the Court; or,
Woman's Relation to Education, Employment, and Citizenship. By Mrs. Caro-
line H. Dall. (In press.)

Darryll Gap; or, Whether it Paid. A novel. By
Miss Virginia F. Townsend. One volume. 12mo. pp. 456. $1.75.

Dearborn's American Text-Book of Letters; with
a Diagram of the Capital Script Alphabet. By N. S. Dearborn. Oblong. $1.50.

Diary, from March 4, 1861, to November 13, 1862.
By Adam Gurowski. $1.75.

Dissertations and Discussions. By John Stuart
Mill. Three volumes. 12mo. Cloth. $6.75.

The Examination of the Philosophy of Sir William
Hamilton. By John Stuart Mill. Two volumes. 12mo. Cloth. Per vol., $2.25.

The Positive Philosophy of Auguste Comte. By
John Stuart Mill. One volume. 12mo. Cloth. $1.25.

Elements of Heraldry; containing an Explanation
of the Principles of the Science, and a Glossary of the Technical Terms employed.
With an Essay upon the use of Coat-Armor in the United States. By William H.
Whitmore. 8vo. Cloth. $6.00.

Essays: Philosophical and Theological. By James
Martineau. Crown octavo. Tinted paper. $2.50.

Facts about Peat as an Article of Fuel. By T. H.
Leavitt. 12mo. $1.75.

First Historical Transformations of Christianity.
By A. Coquerel. Translated by Prof. E. P. Evans, of Michigan University. 12mo.
$1.25.

First Years in Europe. By G. H. Calvert, author
of "Scenes and Thoughts in Europe," "The Gentleman," etc. 1 vol. 12mo. $1.75.

The Gold-Hunter's Adventures; or, Life in Aus-
tralia. By W. H. Thomes, a Returned Australian. Illust. by Champney. $2.00.

The Bushrangers: A Yankee's Adventures during
his second visit to Australia. By W. H. Thomes, author of the "Gold-Hunter's
Adventures; or, Life in Australia." One vol. 12mo. Handsomely illust. $2.00.

God in his Providence. By Rev. W. M. Fernald.
12mo. Cloth. $1.50.

Lee and Shepard's Publications.

Glimpses of History. By George M. Towle.
One volume. 16mo. Bevelled boards. $1.50.

The Heavenly Father: Lectures on Modern Athe-
ism. By Ernest Naville, late Professor of Philosophy in the University of
Geneva. Translated from the French, by Henry Downton, M. A. Published in a
handsome 16mo volume. $1.75.

Home Life: What it Is, and What it Needs. By
Rev. J. F. W. Ware. 16mo. Cloth, red edges, bevelled sides. $1.25.

Herman; or Young Knighthood. By E. Foxton.
Two volumes. 12mo. $3.50.

Historical Sketch of the Old Sixth Regiment of
Massachusetts Volunteers, during its three campaigns in 1861, 1862, 1863, and 1864;
containing the History of the several Companies previous to 1861, and the name
and military record of each man connected with the regiment during the war.
By John W. Hanson, Chaplain. Illustrated by photographs. 12mo. $2.50.

Hospital Life in the Army of the Potomac. By
William Howell Reed. 16mo. $1.25.

The Irish Ninth in Bivouac and Battle. By M. H.
Macnamara, late Captain in the Ninth Massachusetts Regiment. Illustrated.
12mo. Cloth. Sold by subscription. $2.00.

In Trust; or Dr. Bertrand's Household. By Miss
Douglas. One volume. 12mo. $1.50.

Stephen Dane. By Miss Douglas, author of " In
Trust." $1.50.

Some of the Thoughts of Joseph Joubert. With
a Biographical Notice. By G. H. Calvert. 16mo. Tinted paper. Cloth, bvld. $1.50.

Life of Jesus. According to his Original Biog-
raphers. By Edmund Kirke. 16mo. $1.50.

Lincolniana. In one volume, small quarto. pp.
viii. and 344. (Only 250 copies printed.) $6.00.

The Little Helper. A Memoir of Florence Annie
Caswell. By Lavina S. Goodwin. (In press.)

The Life and Works of Gotthold Ephraim Lessing.
Translated from the German of Adolf Starr, by E. P. Evans, Ph. D., Michigan
University. Two volumes, crown octavo. $5.00.

Little Brother, and other Stories. By Fitz Hugh
Ludlow. (In press.)

Manual of the Evidences of Christianity. For
Classes and Private Reading. By Rev. S. G. Bulfinch, D. D. 12mo. $1.25.

Martyria; or, Andersonville Prison. By Lieu-
tenant-Colonel A. C. Hamlin, late Medical Inspector in the Army. Illustrated
with maps and cuts. One volume. 12mo. $2.00.

Memoir of Timothy Gilbert. By Rev. J. D. Ful-
ton, of Tremont Temple, Boston. With Portrait. One volume. 12mo. $1.50.

Neighbors' Wives. By J. T. Trowbridge. 12mo.
Cloth. $1.50.

Twice Taken. A Tale of the Maritime British Provinces. By Charles W. Hall. 12mo. $1.75.

Ten Months in Brazil. By Captain John Codman ("Ringbolt"). In press.

Talks on Women's Topics. By Jennie June. One volume. 12mo. Gilt Tops. $1.75.

A Thousand a Year. By Mrs. E. M. Bruce. One volume. 16mo. $1.25.

Three Years in the Army of the Potomac. By Captain Henry N. Blake, Eleventh Mass. Volunteers. One vol. 12mo. $1.50.

Thomas à Becket. A Tragedy, and other Poems. By G. H. Hollister. 16mo. $1.75.

A View at the Foundations; or, First Causes of Character. By Rev. W. M. Fernald. 12mo. Cloth. $1.00.

The White Mountain Guide-Book. By Samuel C. Eastman. $1.50.

Why Not? A Book for every Woman. By Prof. H. R. Storer, M. D. 16mo. Cloth, $1.00; paper, 50 cts.

Dillaway's Latin Classics. Cicero de Senectute, et de Amicitia; Cicero de Officiis; Cicero de Oratore — two volumes; Cicero Tusculanæ Quæstiones — two volumes; Cicero de Natura de Orum — two volumes; Tacitus Germania et Agricola; Terence; Quintilian; Plautus. Per vol., $1.00.

French Written as Pronounced; a Manual of French Pronunciation, with Extracts from the French Classics, written in Phonetic Characters. By Adrien Feline. Revised, with additions by Wm. Watson, Ph. D. One volume. 16mo. $1.25.

First Lessons in Reading; a New Method of Teaching the Reading of English, by which the ear is trained to discriminate the elementary sounds of words, and the eye to recognize the signs used for these sounds in the established Orthography. By Richard Soule, editor of Worcester's Quarto Dictionary, and William A. Wheeler, editor of Webster's Quarto Dictionary. 16mo. Boards. 35 cts. Sequel to the above. (In preparation).

Charts, designed to accompany the "First Lessons in Reading (on a new method)," and a Sequel to the same. By Richard Soule and William A. Wheeler. Price of the series (six charts), mounted on stiff binders' board, $2.50; any two thus mounted, $1.00; single Charts (not mounted), 30c. These last will be sent by mail to any address, on receipt of the price; they will be found very convenient for posting upon the walls of the school-room.

A Manual of English Pronunciation and Spelling; containing a full Alphabetical Vocabulary of the Language, with a preliminary exposition of the English Orthoepy and Orthography, and designed as a work of reference for general use, and as a Text-Book in schools. By Richard Soule, Jr., A. M., and Wm. A. Wheeler, A. M. A convenient Manual for consultation. $2.00.

Kindergarten Spelling Book. Part First. By Ella Little. 16mo. Boards. 25 cts.

The Phonic Primer and Primary Reader. By Rev. J. C. Zachos. 12mo. Boards. 35 cts.